Killing Time

Books by Suzanne Trauth

SHOW TIME
TIME OUT
RUNNING OUT OF TIME
JUST IN TIME
NO MORE TIME
KILLING TIME

Published by Kensington Publishing Corporation

Killing Time

Suzanne Trauth

LYRICAL UNDERGROUND
Kensington Publishing Corp.
www.kensingtonbooks.com

LYRICAL UNDERGROUND BOOKS are published by

Kensington Publishing Corp.
119 West 40th Street
New York, NY 10018

All Kensington titles, imprints, and distributed lines are available at special quantity discounts for bulk purchases for sales promotion, premiums, fund-raising, educational, or institutional use.

Special book excerpts or customized printings can also be created to fit specific needs. For details, write or phone the office of the Kensington Sales Manager: Kensington Publishing Corp., 119 West 40th Street, New York, NY 10018. Attn. Sales Department. Phone: 1-800-221-2647.

First Electronic Edition: June 2020
ISBN-13: 978-1-5161-0725-4 (ebook)
ISBN-10: 1-5161-0725-X (ebook)

First Print Edition: June 2020
ISBN-13: 978-1-5161-0726-1
ISBN-10: 1-5161-0726-8

Printed in the United States of America

For all of my faithful readers...you kept me on my toes!

1

"Boo!" A horrifying zombie mask popped over my shoulder.

"Arrgh!" I flinched, one hand swiping my coffee cup sideways, spilling liquid down the bar. My other hand flew out toward the grisly Halloween face, blood trickling from its brain to the cavernous mouth full of rotting teeth. I smacked the wearer on the arm. "Benny!"

"Oof," Benny said and whipped the rubber monstrosity off his head. "Sorry! Did I scare you?" The Windjammer restaurant's bartender and my assistant manager grabbed a towel.

"I hope you're not wearing that thing when you take the princess trick-or-treating." The princess was Benny's doted-on six-year-old daughter.

"Nah. My wife had the same reaction as you." He studied the mask. "I kinda like it."

I gawked at him. "You can't wear that in here. The customers will freak out. Probably toss their lunch. Literally."

Benny grinned. "No problem. I got a pirate outfit that's pretty safe. What about you?"

Me? I'm Dodie O'Dell, manager of the Windjammer for the past four years, ever since the devastation of Hurricane Sandy down the Jersey Shore sent me north to Etonville, a stone's throw from New York City. It's my responsibility to keep the patrons happy and ride shotgun on the staff. This year I'd decided to add a little fun to their workday on Halloween by having everyone show up in costume. When I came up with this idea last month, Benny was enthusiastic, sous chef and recent Culinary Institute graduate Enrico consented to be a good sport, though he was rarely in the dining room, and waitress Gillian rolled her eyes, then spent two hours surfing online for a Beyoncé costume. Owner/chef Henry harrumphed and shook his head emphatically. No. Eventually, he came around and agreed to wear a half mask and a chef's hat and apron. Minus the mask, I reminded him that that was his daily costume. He only glared at me.

"Wonder Woman," I said flippantly.

"Hubba-hubba." Benny tossed the bar towel into the sink. "Can't wait to see you strutting around the dining room."

I tried on the getup for Bill last night and watched as my fiancé's eyeballs bugged out of his head—red, sparkly bodice with a dash of cleavage, blue miniskirt, white, knee-high boots. I looked like a tricked-out version of the American flag. As police chief of Etonville, New Jersey, Bill threatened to arrest me for disturbing the peace. I smiled serenely and shimmied my superhero self to the bedroom.

I glanced at the clock on the restaurant wall. We opened for lunch in thirty minutes. Besides the normal midday traffic, I had a lot to oversee today if I was going to be ready for tomorrow's Halloween festivities. The Windjammer was supplying homemade doughnuts and spiced apple cider for the kiddie costume parade down Main Street, and theme food to coincide with the opening of the Etonville Little Theatre's production of—what else?—*Dracula*! Not to mention helping set up the town costume party in the Episcopal Church basement. I had been persuaded to join the planning committee; my civic duty, everyone said, though it felt like collaborating with the enemy. Henry's crosstown nemesis, La Famiglia, was catering the event. To avoid being politically incorrect, I steered clear of any decisions regarding refreshments; I offered to work on entertainment. *Dracula* reminded me that both the theater and I had most likely bitten off more than we could chew. "Ready to open?" I asked.

Benny rinsed his soapy hands in the bar sink. "Let 'er rip."

I unlocked the front door and came face-to-face with Lola Tripper, artistic director of the ELT and my BFF. "Hi! Not running light cues in the theater this morning?"

Lola brushed past me and marched to the back booth near the kitchen door. My unofficial office. Her blond hair in a tangled knot atop her head, her raincoat covered a sweatshirt. "Is it too early for a drink?"

Whoa. Something was up with preparations for tonight's technical rehearsal of *Dracula.* I seated a dozen Etonville citizens, then released their tables to Gillian, who was Instagramming the inside of the Windjammer to her new boyfriend. To impress him. Go figure.

"Trouble in theater paradise?" I plunked onto the bench.

Benny delivered a set-up and a glass of chardonnay for Lola, then slid his eyes my way, raising an eyebrow.

"I'm scared. Really scared this time," Lola said, and took a big gulp of her wine.

I surreptitiously stole a glimpse at my watch. Yep. It was only eleven forty-five. Things must be more chaotic than normal at the Etonville Little Theatre. "So…?"

"Someone fooled with the light board and the cues are all mixed up. Carol said costume pieces are missing." Carol was my other BFF and owner of Snippets salon, Etonville's rumor central. She handled makeup and hair for the ELT. "Penny can't find the stake that Van Helsing stabs into Dracula's heart, and last night JC had trouble with the latch on the coffin." Lola took another swallow. "It's like someone is coming into the theater and messing around with the show." She narrowed her eyes. "Everyone says the theater is haunted. What are we going to do? I don't think I can take much more of this. *Dracula* was a terrible idea!" She wrung her hands.

"Lola, pump the brakes! Haunted? You mean like there's a ghost running loose?" I chuckled.

She sat up straighter. "You can laugh, Dodie, but I'm telling you, something isn't right."

"I know how nerve-racking this time is for you." I had an image of previous productions' tech rehearsals—director Walter tugging on his hair, stage manager Penny blasting her whistle to keep the cast in line, who invariably chatted away in the house when they were not onstage. I sympathized with Lola.

"Ever since Carlos stepped into the theater to audition, I've felt sort of…" Lola twisted a loose strand of her hair. A nervous tic, and not a good sign.

Carlos Villarias played Dracula. "Yeah?" I said encouragingly.

Lola shuddered. "Like an ill wind blew through the house doing no one any good."

She might be overreacting a bit, yet I understood where she was coming from. Though I didn't agree with her, I knew a number of Etonville folks felt the same way. The "ill wind" began about six weeks ago, when Walter, proud as a peacock, announced that the Etonville Little Theatre needed a splashy fall production to continue the momentum from its astonishing first-place award at the New Jersey Community Theater Festival. Lola had argued for a simple, small comedy. However, once the membership of the theater got wind of his verdict, vampire fever hit the town. The auditions spawned a surge of potential actors from the tri-city area—Etonville and its neighbors, Creston and Bernridge—and Walter had a deep acting bench for all roles. Except for Dracula. He wasn't satisfied with his options.

At the same time, a new couple rented the old Hanratty place on the south end of Etonville. It was dilapidated, the previous tenants having done minimal maintenance, and local kids referred to *it* as haunted. Unoccupied for a year when the Villariases toured the house with a rental agent, the newcomers decided to move in. Lola and the welcome wagon paid a social call with assorted gift baskets and proceeded to enlighten the twosome about the regular goings-on in Etonville. The fall pumpkin festival, the Etonville Youth Football games, the Episcopal Church jumble sale.

When Lola introduced the topic of the ELT, and discovered that Carlos had acted in the past, she took a good, hard look at him: tall, suavely handsome, deep-set brown eyes, jet-black hair, and a speech pattern that hinted at something vaguely foreign. When Lola walked into the final day of casting with Carlos in tow, the theater was astonished. Who was he and where did he and his wife Bella come from? He also sported a widow's peak. My great-aunt Maureen said *never trust a man with a widow's peak... Still, he was Dracula!*

"So...you blame Carlos for the problems with the show?"

"I don't blame him. After all, he's doing a super job as Dracula, and he seemed like a fantastic find at the time, but...I don't know. He's a little creepy."

"I admit that they're unusual," I said.

"Renting the Hanratty place..."

"There's nothing wrong with that."

"Where does he work? No one ever sees him during the day. Only at night. At rehearsals," Lola murmured.

"Now you sound like the Banger sisters." Two dotty senior citizens who never met a rumor they didn't like. "Yesterday they told me Mrs. Parker saw a bat flying around the Etonville park." I hooted. "They swore it was a vampire."

Lola was silent.

"What?" I asked.

"Do you believe in vampires?"

"No," I said firmly.

"Did you know Bella is a psychic?" Lola asked.

"Yes. In fact, she's going to read palms at the costume party tomorrow night. The entertainment committee was iffy, but I thought it would be fun."

"Is that wise?" Lola frowned.

"Lola, get a grip. You're confusing life and art. *Dracula* is a play, Carlos is an actor, and vampires don't exist. Of course, if Bella Villarias reads my palm tomorrow and tells me I'm going to win the lottery, it's goodbye Windjammer, hello Paris." I relaxed into my seat.

She wasn't having any of my carefree banter. Lola downed the rest of her wine, refused to consider today's lunch specials—Henry's broccoli cheddar soup and his tasty BLTs—and stood. "I have to get back to the theater."

This was so unlike Lola. She routinely wanted to pull out her hair, or Walter's, during the theater's tech rehearsals, and was known to have tiptoed into happy hour before noon. But this time Lola was downright spooked about the current show. Worry lines creased her forehead. "How about some food to go?"

She waved me off, assuring me that she wasn't hungry. I offered to stop by the theater tonight during the tech rehearsal for some handholding. She headed out the door.

"She's freaked out about *Dracula*," I said to Benny as I drew myself a seltzer.

"*Dracula* or Dracula?" he asked.

"What do you mean?"

Benny muttered, "Half of Etonville's a little twitchy about that actor. Lola's no different."

"I don't get it. I know he certainly looks the part of Dracula—"

"I'll say."

"And his wife is sort of unconventional…" I saw what Benny meant. "They're ordinary people. Trying to fit in," I asserted.

Benny eyed me skeptically as Henry burst out of the kitchen, a skim of sweat on his bald head. "Dodie!" he hissed and startled a customer who sat at a table near the swinging door. She winced and juggled her soup spoon, sending a spray of broccoli cheddar into the air. "I ordered fresh yeast and they delivered active dry yeast. How can I make doughnuts with this?" He brandished a package.

Cheney Brothers, our food delivery service, had blundered again. For the umpteenth time. I wanted to replace them, but Henry was loyal…he hated change. I apologized to the young woman wiping bits of green and yellow off the front of her blouse, motioned to Benny to "take care of her"—which meant a complimentary drink or dessert—and escorted a fuming Henry back into the kitchen.

It was going to be one of those days.

* * * *

At three o'clock I retired to my booth for an afternoon break, a grilled cheese sandwich and a cup of coffee in hand. I settled in with inventory sheets for next week, glad of a short reprieve from the lunch rush.

"Hey, O'Dell."

Penny Ossining, the Etonville Little Theatre's production manager and Walter's loyal sidekick. "Hi, Penny. You here for lunch? We're out of the soup."

"Just coffee. I'm on a diet."

Since when? I wondered.

"Since the end of the summer."

Penny had a habit of worming her way into my head and reading my mind.

"All that shore food packed on the pounds." Penny slapped her rounded midsection, pushing her glasses a notch up her nose. She'd been the production manager for the ELT during the community theater festival down the shore the last week of summer. I'd personally seen her inhale sloppy Joes and Italian hot dogs during the long Labor Day weekend.

"How's it going?" I couldn't see any difference in her five-foot-two, stocky physique.

"You know what they say…"

I could only imagine.

"Nothing ventured, no weight gain." Penny cackled. "I'm on the Mediterranean diet. You know, eat what the Mediterraneans eat."

I decided to play along. "For example?"

"Fruit cocktail, veggie burgers, red wine."

Sheesh.

Penny waved goodbye and headed for the counter to place her order. I followed. "Lola's upset about strange things happening in the theater."

Penny grimaced, suspicious. If something was going on in the theater, it was her job to suss it out. "What kind of things?"

"Costumes missing. Mixed-up light cues. As if the theater was…" Haunted? Did Lola really believe that?

Penny chuckled. "Yep, the theater's haunted. All theaters are haunted. That's why we put a ghost light on stage at the end of the show every night. To keep out the ghosts."

"Also to keep people from running into scenery and tripping over cables. The theater's a pretty dangerous place," I said.

"O'Dell, when are you going to learn there's theater stuff that you can explain and theater stuff you can't explain? Like never whistling backstage, never saying 'good luck,' never saying *Macbeth*—"

Oops!

Penny clasped a hand over her mouth, her eyes bulging. "You're bad luck, O'Dell. I gotta go." She picked up her container of coffee.

"See you at tech rehearsal tonight," I said as she scuttled away.

So Penny thought the theater was haunted too. Penny also thought Mediterraneans ate veggie burgers. Which reminded me of tonight's special: an Italian casserole that featured Italian sausage, pasta, and plenty of oregano and basil. Perfect for a chilly fall night when the restaurant's chef was overcommitted for the next few days. Henry had prepared the dinner last week and now entrees were stacked in the freezer.

I gathered my inventory sheets and mulled over Lola's reaction to Carlos. She was definitely spooked, but every mishap she mentioned could easily be rationalized by the normal bedlam of the community theater. I'd seen worse tech days. I know she'd seen worse…

* * * *

At seven o'clock I left the restaurant and stepped into the evening air. Benny was closing the dining room early tonight—traffic was light, no doubt due to all the Halloween planning occurring throughout Etonville—so that Henry and Enrico could fry doughnuts and prep my theme food meals for the first weekend of the *Dracula* performances. In the past we'd served Italian fare for *Romeo and Juliet*, a seafood buffet for *Dames at Sea*, and 1940s Brooklyn specialties for an *Arsenic and Old Lace* food festival. For *Dracula*? I was taking a chance this time.

It had been a sunny, brisk day, the temperature hovering in the high fifties. A gentle breeze had rustled some fallen leaves from the red oak tree outside the Etonville Little Theatre, sending them into a whorl of activity. I inhaled the scents of autumn—fireplace smoke and crisp air. My second favorite time of year after spring. I walked to the entrance of the theater, next door to the restaurant.

"Hey, wait up!" Bill yelled as I yanked on the door handle.

"Where've you been all day? I texted a few times but no answer," I said and joined him on the sidewalk.

Bill grabbed my hand and tucked it into his, his thumb toying with my engagement ring, and scanned the street. He kissed me quickly. One side of his mouth ticked upward in a recognizable quirky grin. "I'm on duty."

And still skittish about public displays of affection, even though we'd gotten engaged last month. Our love life being the topic of conversation at the Snippets gossip vortex continued to rattle Bill. "Thought you were stopping by for lunch?" Though we'd been a couple for over two years, his former NFL running back physique still caused my heart to flutter.

"Kind of a busy day. Got a call from the NJSACOP."

"The what?"

"New Jersey State Association of Chiefs of Police." He shuffled his feet shyly. "I've been invited to join the New Chiefs Mentoring Program."

I did a double take. "That's wonderful! Congratulations!" I threw my arms around his neck and planted a big one on his lips. Unlike Bill, I didn't care who saw our public displays of affection. "So, does this mean you'll be teaching the new guys how it's done?" I teased.

"Hardly. It will mean meetings around the state and some trips to Trenton this year."

"More responsibility for Suki? She is the deputy chief, after all."

"And a damned good cop," he added.

I knew that was true from personal experience. As a Buddhist, her calm, om-like presence belied the fact that she was a seventh-degree black belt in karate. "We need to celebrate. I was headed to the theater. I could skip it and model my Wonder Woman costume again…" I said suggestively.

He grinned. "I've got some paperwork to do. Let's meet at eight thirty."

"It's a deal." I hugged Bill goodbye.

We parted and I marched into the building, my agenda clear. Watch a little bit of tech rehearsal, demonstrate my support to Lola, encourage her to laugh off the haunted theater thing, then beat a hasty retreat home to Bill.

Inside the theater, I expected the customary chaos to be running rampant: Walter tormenting actors, Lola twisting her hair, JC struggling with the technical side of things, Penny tooting her whistle, the cast chatting, lounging, faces in cell phones. Instead, I was greeted by a wall of silence. Everybody sat in the first row of the darkened house, subdued, as if waiting for something to happen. Lola and Walter stood downstage center staring up into the fly space where light fixtures were attached to parallel rows of battens. JC tinkered with a trick bookcase in the stage left wall of the set, adjusting the hinges and handle, before he moved to a trick chair stage right. Penny fingered her whistle, ready to blast it the moment Walter signaled Go.

"It's as quiet as a church in here," Carol muttered behind me, her salt-and-pepper, curly head bouncing for emphasis.

"I'll say. What's going on?"

Carol whispered conspiratorially, "Carlos."

"What about him?" I scanned the row of actors. "I don't see him with the rest of the cast."

She nudged me gently in the ribs and pointed as Carlos slipped onto the stage by way of the trick bookcase that JC had been adjusting a minute before. The only one in full costume, he wore evening dress and a swirling, black, full-length cape. His dark hair brushed off his forehead, his makeup had an eerie green tinge. The atmosphere in the theater shifted. As if a chill wind *had* swept in with Carlos. Could Lola be right? *Stop*, I told myself. Though I had to admit his appearance was disconcerting.

"Costumes for the tech rehearsal? Usually it's only shoes and hats." I was learning theater practices.

"Not supposed to be. Carlos insisted he needed his costume to 'feel the part.' Even during tech. So Chrystal gave in." Chrystal was the long-suffering costumer of the ELT. Carol shrugged, as if to say, "Actors...what can you do?"

I remembered last spring, when Romeo, who played Conrad Birdie, demanded to wear his gold lamé pants during the tech rehearsals for *Bye, Bye, Birdie*, thrusting crotch and all, to pump up his ego and impress the young girls in the cast. What was Carlos's demand about? I wasn't certain.

Penny's whistle screeched, yanking me out of my musing. Carol patted my arm and headed backstage; the actors came alive and moved into position for the opening of the play. Besides Carlos as Dracula, Romeo played the romantic male lead, Harker; Janice, a high school senior from Creston—and the current girlfriend of my personal tech guru, Pauli—was Lucy, the beautiful young girl swept up by Dracula's bloodthirsty attention; Vernon, a stalwart, ELT regular, played Dr. Seward, Lucy's father. Walter was doing double duty as director and Van Helsing, the vampire hunter. He'd done this before, and though Lola had begged him not to wear two hats during this production, Walter was adamant that there was no one else to play the role. I was skeptical. Lola yielded to his artistic decision and smartly inserted herself as assistant director. Edna, dispatcher for the Etonville Police Department and blooming thespian, was the maid. She wasn't the "attractive young girl" called for in the script, though she was enthusiastic and had mastered the British accent.

Renfield, the bug-eating, maniacal patient at the sanatorium, was new to me and to the Etonville Little Theatre. A slight young man in his twenties, I'd heard he lived in Bernridge and that his name was Gabriel Quincey. He was doing a good job, in my limited theatrical estimation. Wild and physically agile, he hopped and ran and mimed eating flies with passion. Finally, in a bit of nontraditional casting, Walter had given the part of the Attendant, normally played by a young male, to Abby, a middle-aged, female character actor. She'd been in a huff ever since the show was announced when she realized there wasn't a substantial part for her. She'd lobbied Walter to make Van Helsing female. Nope. Or Renfield. No way. Nada. He eventually assigned Abby the role of the Attendant to keep her happy. And off his back. I had to admit it wasn't such a bad choice. Abby was intimidating and bigger than Renfield. I had no trouble believing she might pick him up and toss him out a window.

The tech rehearsal began. Penny shouted "Go" and "Hold," Walter dashed from playing his character to playing director, lights changed from cue to cue, actors moved on- and offstage, sometimes murmuring to one another. Only Carlos stayed silent and aloof. Separated from the rest of the cast and, thanks to his immense cape, literally wrapped up in his own world. I stayed in my seat for twenty minutes until the statute of limitations for a BFF restaurant manager in a tech rehearsal was up. I slipped down a side aisle and scooted into the row of seats behind Lola.

"Looking good. JC did terrific work on the set. Walter's not too crazed." Not *too* crazed.

"True," Lola said softly.

"Carlos looks scary." I regretted the comment the moment the words slipped out of my mouth.

Lola turned to me, eyes wide. "See what I mean? Creepy."

I did see, but there was no way I was going to reinforce Lola's semi hysteria. Too much riding on the production—the ELT banking on the show to bolster the box office and my theme food inspiration. "He'll give a knockout performance. Folks are going to be blown away."

"If they come," Lola whispered nervously. "What if the town is too anxious about the show?"

"You've got to let go of this ghosty-vampiry stuff. Carlos is an actor. Plain and simple."

Lola sighed. "I guess you're right."

"I am." I mentally crossed my fingers that the rest of the rehearsal would run smoothly and Lola would calm down.

Penny yelled "Hold." A crew member rushed onstage to adjust the trick bookcase. Actors fell out of character, Walter motioned to the light booth, and Renfield strode purposefully to Carlos. There was a quick but intense exchange, Renfield pointing in Carlos's face, Carlos slapping the young man's hand away. *Whoa.* I surveyed the rest of the stage to see if anyone else had noticed. Chrystal dashed onto the set to hand out a few accessories. Lola had her head buried in the script.

"Did you see that?" I asked.

"What?"

"Renfield and Dracula. I think they almost got into it."

Lola looked up. "Carlos isn't on stage."

Renfield was now in conversation with Abby. The two of them chatting amiably. Was I seeing things? It was eight fifteen. Perfect. Enough time to sprint home and change for Bill. "I'm heading out." I squeezed Lola's shoulder. "Take it easy, okay? Go home and chill. Drink some chamomile tea." Lola's go-to beverage when theater business was too intense.

"Thanks, Dodie. I appreciate you coming." Lola twisted a strand of blond hair.

Penny tooted her whistle, the blast ricocheting around the theater. It was the actors' cue to get back to work. My cue to cut out. I walked swiftly to the lobby, images filling my head: Wonder Woman's glittery ensemble, some romantic music, Bill's gourmet snacks, an expensive bottle of red wine...

My cell buzzed. A text from Benny: *help! emergency in kitchen! come back.*

I groaned. Best-laid plans.

2

I sprinted next door expecting the worst. I'd only been gone a little over an hour. What could have happened since I left? An explosion in the kitchen? A customer in the throes of the Heimlich maneuver? Henry reading a positive review of the La Famiglia menu?

I burst into the restaurant. "What happened?" I practically shouted. Luckily, the place was empty except for the elderly Banger sisters, tucked into a booth away from the entrance. Their hearing was suspect anyway. They smiled at me and bobbed their identical, curly gray perms, waving their hands to flag me down.

"Hello, Dodie," said one as I walked calmly to the kitchen.

"We're ready for the Halloween party tomorrow night," said the other.

"Good to hear." I eased away from their table.

"We're going as two peas in a pod."

They both beamed.

Despite Benny's traumatic text, I stopped in my tracks. "You are?" I visualized two green beach balls.

One narrowed her eyes and squinted at me. "Unless there's trouble tomorrow and the celebration is canceled."

The other nodded solemnly.

I had to get to the kitchen, but I couldn't resist. "What kind of trouble?"

"We saw a black cat in front of the theater today." The first sister.

"The dogs on our street have been wailing at night." The second sister.

"We're keeping our necks covered." They both tightened the scarves under their chins.

If I wasn't so stressed, I would have erupted in giggles.

"To avoid…"

"Vampire bites?" I asked.

They withdrew garlic necklaces from their purses, holding them up for approval. "Would you like to borrow one?"

"No, thanks." *Geez*. The town's inner daffy was rising to the surface, but their garlic reminded me of the Windjammer menu for the weekend. "You have a good night."

I pushed against the swinging door into the kitchen as Benny, on the other side, attempted to push it in the opposite direction. "Oof!" he said, driven backward.

"Sorry!" I grabbed his arm.

He jerked a thumb over his shoulder. "Check it out."

I'd been prepared for a bloody limb, a body on the ground. I was greeted with Benny shaking his head, Enrico's face and hair covered in a splatter of powdered sugar, pieces of fried doughnuts scattered on the stove and floor, and Henry standing arms akimbo, glowering into the pot of boiling oil.

"What happened in here?" I stared at the mess.

"Dodie," Enrico murmured, "the oil got wet."

How did that happen? What did that even mean? "Henry?"

Slowly, he swiveled, his face dark and threatening. This was all my fault. "I hate Halloween."

'Nuff said.

It took twenty minutes to clean up and to convince Henry that Enrico and I could manage the frying process, minus the moisture that had mistakenly ended up in the oil and caused the doughnuts to explode. Glad I wasn't in the Windjammer to see that... Henry agreed to come in early to prepare the spiced apple cider before the Windjammer opened. We ushered him out of the restaurant, then set to work with the hot oil, monitoring the temperature, vigilantly turning the bobbing circles of dough, letting them drain on paper towels before sprinkling them with powdered sugar. It was a slow and tedious process, but two hours later, Enrico and I had produced and packaged two hundred doughnuts.

Benny had closed the dining room at nine o'clock, wiping down the bar and flicking off the lights. I sent Enrico home at eleven and finished cleaning the stove and swabbing the floor. A manager's work was never done, I thought ruefully, as I swished the mop back and forth. When I'd called Bill to inform him that I had to cancel our date night, he was sympathetic, said he was sorry to eat the gourmet cheese and drink the cabernet alone, amused when he asked how doughnuts could explode. Did we use gunpowder instead of baking powder? Very funny, I told him.

Sheesh.

I was beginning to regret my theme food plan for *Dracula*. I had initially proposed a hearty Eastern European dish that suited the play. "Hungarian goulash!"

"Dracula's from Transylvania, not Hungary," Lola had said.

I was at a loss. Until I spied an article in the *Newark Star-Ledger* about a new restaurant in South Jersey that used garlic in every entrée. In appetizers and desserts too. Every single one. Garlic! Bane of a vampire's existence! I was intrigued and did some research. I came up with a list of recipes Henry could use this week: roasted garlic and anchovies on focaccia bread, garlic roasted baked brie, garlic roasted prime rib, garlic mashed potatoes, shrimp in garlic sauce, garlic chicken, pork chops with sweet garlic relish, even garlic ice cream…the list was endless. Perfect theme food. At least it was, until the town took this whole vampire thing to the next level. Was it a good idea to serve garlic-infused specials during the run of the show?

At eleven thirty I grabbed my jacket and bag, left the restaurant, and locked the front door. The temperature had plummeted during the hours I was in the Windjammer and now there was a nip of frost in the air. Early for fall in New Jersey. A gust of wind sent the streetlight outside the restaurant swinging, casting a yellowish glow on the sidewalk below. A sliver of moon the only light in the sky. A "new moon" my father called this kind of lunar event. I wondered about the weather in Naples, Florida, where my parents now lived after decamping from the Jersey Shore a few years ago. Warmer than here. I strode to my red MINI Cooper, parked in a space beyond the restaurant.

Somewhere down Main Street a dog barked. A shadow flitted in front of the theater, pausing by the red oak. My skin crawled, the little hairs on the back of my neck trembling. It was my radar system, which activated whenever something was amiss. The theater was dark, its occupants having closed up shop after the tech rehearsal. Although I had known Lola and Walter to hang around well into the night when an opening was imminent—

"Good evening," a deep baritone rumbled behind me.

I whirled to my left, my heart leaping into my mouth. I faced a tall shape draped in black. Even in the dim light he was instantly recognizable.

"H–hello, Carlos," I managed to squeak out. "You're working late."

"So are you," he said, bowing his head slightly. An otherworldly gentleman.

"Making doughnuts for the kids' parade tomorrow." I laughed nervously. Why was I nervous? *He's an actor, not a paranormal monster.* "Halloween."

"Ah, yes. Halloween. An ancient pagan festival. The Celtic population believed that the dead could walk among the living at this time."

I shivered.

"Did you know that?" he asked.

"No. I didn't."

Carlos leaned toward me and I shrank back. He reached out and tugged my collar up around my ears. "You look cold."

My teeth chattered. And not because the temperature was dropping. "Yes. Guess so." And then my curiosity got the better of me. "Are you coming to the costume party tomorrow night?"

He smiled widely, his teeth white and shiny in his ghostly face. "I wouldn't miss the festivities."

"You already have the costume. Dracula," I said, a fake laugh bubbling out of me.

"I do." He shrugged. "We'll see."

"Bella is reading palms for entertainment. Should be fun," I added.

He regarded me for a moment in the sinister half-light. "She is very good at predicting the future."

"Everybody will love it. Maybe she can tell if the show will be a hit."

"A hit?" He paused. "Yes, I think *Dracula* will be a hit."

I said good night, hopped into my MC. I swear he glided away and disappeared into the night. My hands trembled as I turned the ignition key.

* * * *

"So you think he's what…a supernatural creature?" Bill asked, buttoning his blue uniform shirt and eyeing me, amused, as I pulled on my Wonder Woman miniskirt. He worked hard to keep a grin out of his voice. Not sure if it was due to our discussion of my encounter with Carlos last night or my efforts to cover most of my body. I was into the Halloween costume thing and WW had appeared to be the perfect choice. Still, I had no intention of scaring little kids or sending Windjammer customers into gales of hysteria. I slipped on my leather jacket and zipped up the white go-go boots I'd bought at a vintage clothing store years ago. "I know he's only a guy acting a role. But if you had seen him…let's just say he looked a lot like Dracula would have looked if he'd really lived."

"According to history, he really did live." Bill knotted his tie. "Not Count Dracula; the historical person Bram Stoker based him on. His name was Vlad the Impaler. Had a real taste for blood."

"Since when are you studying the history of vampires?" I asked.

"I read that article in the *Etonville Standard*. Preshow publicity. Quotes from Walter and Lola. And Penny." He chuckled. "She claimed vampires exist in parts of Europe today."

"She said that?" I tied a gold headband around my wavy auburn hair, the result of Irish ancestry on both sides of my family, and studied my reflection in the mirror. Not too bad.

Bill put his arms around my waist and kissed my ear. "What's it going to be like engaged to Wonder Woman?"

"Step out of line, buster, and I'll show you," I teased, twisting in his arms. He planted a good one on my lips. *Yowza!*

"That should hold you until tonight," he said.

"Speaking of tonight, you'll make it to the costume shindig, right?"

"I'll try. I have my first Police Chiefs meeting in Trenton late this afternoon."

"You have to wear a costume—"

"I'll go as—"

"And you can't go as—"

"—a cop," we both said in unison.

Bill put on his pouty, little-boy face. "I hate wearing costumes."

"Didn't you trick or treat as a kid?"

"Back then there was candy at stake."

"Think of the grand prize as a ten-year-old's bag of goodies."

He looked skeptical. "What's the grand prize?"

"It's a surprise." I trailed Bill out of the bedroom. "I put the Superman costume in the front hall closet."

"Superman? Oh no—"

"You said you'd go as my hero," I said sweetly.

"I thought that meant I could wear my uniform," he complained, hunting for his car keys.

"There's a shirt, cape, boots…"

"I might have to work late." He kissed me quickly and darted out the door.

"…and tights," I said to his disappearing back. Bill was as bad as Henry when it came to dressing up. Hell might have to freeze over before the town of Etonville would catch sight of Bill in tights and the equivalent of Speedos.

As I climbed into my MC and drove from the north end of town, where Bill's two-story Colonial was located, to Main Street, I considered his comments about the real Count Dracula—Vlad the Impaler. In the bright sunshine of this morning, it was hard to envision Carlos as anything weird even if he did unnerve Lola. And me. Good thing the show opened tomorrow night. The sooner it was up, the sooner it would close. Hopefully without incident and with a healthy box office.

Etonville had awakened early this morning. Main Street was already jammed with cars stopping and starting as they crept into and out of town. By three o'clock the main drag would be blocked off to allow the youngsters' parade to proceed from the Municipal Building down several blocks past Coffee Heaven, the Etonville Little Theatre, and the Windjammer, ending at the Etonville Library. The littlest tots might not make it all the way, but for the kids who did, the library was handing out its own special treats: books and DVDs.

I had arranged to meet Lola for breakfast at Coffee Heaven, Etonville's nod to the old-fashioned Jersey diner. A handful of booths and a wide variety of comfort food. My go-to favorites were heavily iced, warm cinnamon buns and caramel macchiato, my obsession. Enough sugar to accelerate my day. I found a parking space directly in front of Coffee Heaven, put some coins in the meter, and, in keeping with my costume, strutted into the diner. The welcome bells jingled as I entered, and heads turned and stared at my boots and miniskirt.

I smiled bravely as I accepted comments on my way to a back booth.

"Morning, Dodie!"

"That's some getup."

"Who're you supposed to be?"

"I know! A cheerleader!"

"Where's your pom-poms?"

Geez. Maybe Wonder Woman wasn't such a terrific idea—

"Love the costume," said Lola. She sat opposite me. "Wish I had the nerve to wear something like that. In public."

Was it that revealing? I eased my leather jacket closed to conceal exposed chest. "You're going as Cleopatra. Not too shabby in the cleavage department."

"She's a queen. My costume's royal," Lola said serenely.

"You're in a better mood. Must have had a good tech rehearsal."

"That and a full night's sleep. Forget what I said about Carlos yesterday. My imagination was on overdrive. He's doing a spectacular job and is a nice guy. An *ordinary* nice guy," she said.

Who was creepy in the moonlight. Never mind, no sense in revving Lola's engine with *my* overactive imagination.

"In fact, Carlos offered to help clean up the props."

"That's unusual?"

"For an actor."

"So you all left the theater together last night?"

Lola yawned. "Actually, I cut out with most of the cast. Walter and Carlos and a few others stayed behind." She picked up a menu.

"You gals want your regulars?" It was Jocelyn, the Coffee Heaven waitress. She pulled a pencil out of her red French twist.

"Absolutely," I said.

"Make my coffee black and my eggs over easy."

Jocelyn wrote up our orders, then scrutinized my costume. "Hmm. Tried to get Walter to saddle up with me and go as zombies."

A zombie? Jocelyn had decided last summer that she was gunning for Walter—cranky, anxious, full-of-himself, insecure Walter. She was a woman on a mission. Walter, gobsmacked by her attention, tended to run the other way when he spotted Jocelyn. She was nothing if not persistent.

"That's sweet," I said. "Zombies…"

"Nope. Walter had another costume in mind. He keeps me on my toes. Must be why we're so good together." Jocelyn sashayed her buxom self to the kitchen.

"Poor Jocelyn. What parallel universe is she living in?" I asked. "She still thinks Walter has it bad for her."

Lola tittered. "Anyway, his costume has nothing to do with zombies." She raised her coffee cup and eyed me over the rim. "Wait and see."

* * * *

By four o'clock Main Street was packed with ghosts of all sizes, cowboys with and without ten-gallon hats, princesses galore—including Benny's daughter—and ninja warriors. Plus a variety of animals and characters from popular movies. They popped in and out of shops, loading up brown bags and pillowcases with treats. I manned the refreshment table, handing out doughnuts to hungry kids and providing apple cider for their thirsty parents. I'd told Benny to go and have fun with his own little princess while Gillian kept an eye on the dining room. Early diners wouldn't surface for another hour. Henry had resolutely remained in the kitchen, preparing tonight's rollout of the garlic specials: roasted garlic and anchovies on focaccia bread, garlic mashed potatoes, and shrimp in garlic sauce. I hoped I hadn't gone overboard with the theme food.

Ralph Ostrowski, a member of the Etonville Police Department, was usually assigned traffic management and crowd control. He sauntered over and sized up the doughnuts, putting his hands on his hips, and selecting three. Ralph was a walking cop cliché.

"Mmm." He gave his seal of approval and headed back into the crowd.

Benny's little girl, swathed in pink, flouncy layers of taffeta and tulle, had tired of the parade and promptly sat down in the middle of Main Street. She waved her wand at her dad. He ran over to the doughnut table, his pirate costume complete with frilly shirt, eye patch, hoop earring, and a mascara-drawn mustache.

"Cute. And the princess too," I smirked.

"Funny." Benny picked up two doughnuts and a cup of cider. "Like she needs more sugar! I'll be back in time to handle dinner."

"Take your time. I can cover for a while. Before the dress rehearsal."

He looked at his daughter slapping her magic wand on the ground. "Gotta rescue the street." Benny raced away.

Henry stuck his head out the door of the Windjammer, harried. "Georgette is asking about the garlic ice cream!"

Georgette's Bakery supplied the desserts for the Windjammer, and she'd graciously offered to handle the ice cream as well. "Coming." The parade was winding down, the last of the kiddie procession dragging their tails as well as their candy. They could help themselves to the remainder of the doughnuts.

On to the next event.

* * * *

"Hey, these have garlic in them too," said Vernon, stabbing a fork into a mound of mashed potatoes.

Mildred, choir director at the Episcopal Church and Vernon's wife, poked him gently. "That's the point. All of the specials have garlic in them. It's part of the theme." She delicately speared a shrimp dripping garlic sauce. "You'd better not breathe on anybody tonight."

Etonville might be hit with an epidemic of halitosis.

The Banger sisters pulled out their ropes of garlic, dangling them over their dinner plates. "We're protected!" said one.

"From what?" Vernon was truly mystified.

"Vampires," said the other Banger sister.

Vernon shook his head.

"The Hanratty place is supposed to be haunted," Mildred said.

"I wouldn't be caught dead in that old rattrap. Gives me the willies. They should have declared it a 10-7A," Edna said firmly. As dispatcher of the police force, she loved her codes.

"Translate please," begged Mildred.

"Out of service."

"It must be livable. Carlos and Bella have been there for three months," I said.

"Who knows where they lived before." Mildred's tone was ominous.

Abby had been silent until now, chowing down on one of Henry's special burgers. No garlic for her. "What's that mean?"

Vernon defended his wife. "It means we don't know where they came from. What kind of place they lived in before."

"You mean like a coffin? You believe in this vampire stuff too?" Abby asked, not amused.

So it wasn't only Lola who was bitten by the vampire bug…

"That's nuts," Abby added.

"You can't be too sure," said a Banger.

The conversation was in danger of going off the rails. "You all have your costumes for tonight?"

Mildred and Abby nodded. Vernon ploughed into his potatoes. Only Edna was truly excited. "Got a feeling I might haul in the grand prize."

"Who're the judges?" Mildred asked. Everyone exchanged looks that said *not me.*

Roving anonymous judges had been chosen by the city council. After roaming through the crowd for most of the night, they would announce the winners: funniest, most dramatic, most creative, scariest, and the grand prize.

"That's a 10-36," Edna said. "Confidential information."

"Dodie, what do you think about Carlos and Bella?" Mildred asked, sincere.

"Me?"

"Yeah, you. Wonder Woman!" Abby cracked.

"I don't know them. He's certainly terrific in the role of Dracula, according to Lola."

"A real natural," Edna announced.

Silence for a moment.

"What's for dessert?" asked Vernon. "I hope nothing with garlic."

Yikes.

3

"Go without it!" roared Walter, fidgeting, while Chrystal fussed with his cravat.

"Without it?" Penny was aghast. "We've never done that before."

"And we've never done *Dracula* before either!"

Everybody milled about the stage—Walter and Vernon and Romeo in period suits, Edna the Maid in a black skirt and white apron, Abby, as the Attendant, in a uniform, the young man playing Renfield, tousled and unkempt, and Janice as Lucy in a filmy negligee. Carlos stood alone upstage in his black tux and cape. The cast looked believable, timely, and twitchy. All but Carlos.

I had left the Windjammer in Benny's assistant manager hands and hurried to the theater intending to watch the first act. I assumed the run-through would start around six, giving the ELT time to complete the rehearsal and make an appearance at the party by eight thirty. But when I arrived, I was met with the theater in crisis mode.

"What's going on?" I asked Pauli, who sat in the house, digital camera in hand, transfixed by Janice in her semi revealing nightgown. She was, no doubt, responsible for Pauli's transformation: his floppy brown mop was replaced with a trim, gelled haircut, his worn-out hoodies exchanged for casual sweaters and knit shirts. Pauli had become handsome.

"Hey, Dodie." He didn't take his eyes off his girlfriend.

"Walter's steaming."

"Some mix-up. Like a prop missing," said Pauli, dragging his attention away from Janice. He gave me the once-over. "Nice costume." He grinned.

"Thanks. What's missing?"

"The stake."

"What stake?"

"The one they, like, ram through Dracula's heart," Pauli said.

Penny corralled the actors backstage, alternately blowing her whistle and flapping her arms to get their attention. "I guess the show must go on. With or without the stake," I said.

Pauli held the camera to his eye. "Like yeah." He was the ELT photographer, more motivated than ever to take pictures with Janice in the cast.

I plopped into a seat next to him. "Haven't seen much of you lately. College keeping you busy?" Pauli was a freshman at a local community college.

"And new online classes." He perked up whenever the topic of digital forensics cropped up. "This semester it's file system analysis, data artifacts, evidence collection. Awesome."

"Wow. I'll let you know if I need your help," I joked.

He sat up straighter. "You have…something for me?" His eyes glowed.

Pauli had been my go-to tech guy when I'd gotten involved in murders in the past. He employed a variety of tools—facial recognition software, unique search engines; he'd even done a little email hacking when necessary. But those days were behind me. I had a wedding to plan. "No, no," I said hastily. "All good."

Chrystal hustled up the aisle.

"All ready backstage?" I asked.

The usually unruffled costume supervisor looked worried.

The stage went black, the house slowly dimmed, and in the dark, howling wolves raised goosebumps on my neck and arms. *It was make-believe,* I reminded myself. The lights rose on the library of Dr. Seward's Sanatorium. Edna led Romeo, Lucy's love interest Harker, into the room and the dialogue began. Then Vernon as Dr. Seward entered, frantic over his daughter Lucy's strange symptoms. Before long, Walter/Van Helsing strode on stage, already agitated. Either from the anemia killing Lucy or the missing stake. Hard to tell. Renfield, the fly-eating patient, zipped around the set grabbing imaginary bugs out of thin air, chased down by a Cockney-spewing Abby as the Attendant. Beside me, Pauli snapped photos when Lucy entered, unsteady, leaning on her fiancé's arm, unnaturally pale, a scarf around her neck. She was totally convincing as the dying ingénue. Even more so when she collapsed on the sofa and recounted her nightly dream: a mist in the bedroom, two red eyes in a white face staring at her. Van Helsing unwrapped the scarf to reveal two small marks on her throat. *Yikes.*

A clap of thunder, a flash of lightning. I jumped involuntarily. Dracula appeared in the doorway.

"Wow!" I whispered to Chrystal. "Those effects are bloodcurdling."

"I'll say."

Pauli leaned my way. "Janice is awesome."

He had it bad. "Yep."

Dracula explained how he loved England and his ruin of an estate, even though the dust was deep and the walls were broken. Sounded like the Hanratty place to me. Carlos didn't mind living there either...

The dogs barked again, Dracula exited, characters discussed the existence of vampires, and plotted to use Lucy as bait to capture the "Thing" that haunted her. And sucked the blood out of her! The stage lights dimmed, Lucy reclining on the divan in firelight. Dracula's hand, then face stealthily materialized from the back of the couch. Lucy screamed, Dracula disappeared through the trick bookcase, and chaos broke out. Act One ended.

Whew. I was stunned. I'd seen bits and pieces of rehearsals, but not a whole act. The ELT had a winner on its hands and Carlos was sensational, realistic... Too realistic? I did a mental head slap: *knock it off!*

* * * *

The basement of the Episcopal Church was swathed in orange and black. Crepe paper streamers looped and dipped from one end of the room to the other. Black paper cloths covered the banquet tables and plastic pumpkin centerpieces held candles. Even the paper plates and cups were orange. The decoration committee had taken its task seriously.

The entertainment committee was no slouch either. We'd set up games—a guess-the-number-of-candy-corns-in-the-jar at the entrance to the room, bobbing for apples in one corner, and a pumpkin-carving contest in another. At the back of the basement, we'd fashioned an improvised booth with spotlight, curtains, card table, and chairs for Bella to read palms. There was something to suit every taste. Perfect.

This was the first time Etonville had experimented with an indoor town event. Summer picnics in the park usually focused on softball games or movie nights. Getting a substantial number of citizens in one location dressed in Halloween costumes was no small feat. I was thrilled.

I drifted over to the makeshift bar where La Famiglia had set up drinks and food. I tried not to appear too interested, although the Halloween-themed tidbits looked delicious: meatball and marinara mummies, graveyard taco dip, cheesy pumpkin quesadillas. I circumvented the orange spiked punch in favor of a glass of chardonnay and mingled.

"Dodie, this is such fun!" It was the Banger sisters, dressed as two peas in a pod in green tights, green turtlenecks, and green tunics with large, stuffed peas around their midsections. They held hands.

"You ladies went all out!" I gulped my wine to keep from giggling.

"We think we might get the prize for most creative. Don't you think so?"

"Absolutely." Really?

The room was filling with outstanding getups as the actors wandered in. Theater folks knew how to dress up. Mildred and Vernon came as Robin Hood and Maid Marian, Romeo was a truly frightening zombie, and floating into the party at nine o'clock was Lola, sexy and queenly as Cleopatra accompanied by—surprise!—a stalwart Walter as Julius Caesar. I was shocked. Lola hadn't even hinted that she and Walter had made plans together. Did this mean something? I hoped Jocelyn wouldn't get her nose out of joint …

Pauli had come dressed as a 1940s' newspaper reporter: baggy suit, goofy tie, pad and pen, and a sign in the hatband of his fedora that said "PRESS." With his digital camera around his neck. Janice was a fairy with wings, a wand, and a flouncy ballerina outfit.

I wandered over to the pumpkin carving. Penny had gouged out teeth and a grin. "This is hard work, O'Dell." She took her witch's hat off her head.

"Hey, Act One was great tonight. Did you find the stake?" I asked.

She frowned. "We had to improvise. That's the theater for you. You gotta be ready to follow your feet and think while you're standing. Wherever they go."

I coughed into my drink.

"Want my opinion?" Penny said seriously.

Did I have a choice?

"I think somebody's trying to sabotage the show."

"Other than the theater ghosts?" I joked, but I was curious. "Why would someone do that?"

"O'Dell," she sighed. "The theater's full of competition."

Didn't I know that. I'd spent Labor Day weekend witnessing the rivalries among New Jersey community theaters. "Who would stand to gain from interfering with *Dracula*? The actors want to see the show open without a hitch. So do Walter and Lola. That leaves crew members."

"Or someone from outside." She squinted at me. "Lots of outsiders in town lately."

I assumed she meant Carlos and Bella. Or Gabriel, who played Renfield. "True but—"

"Keep your ears open and eyes on the ground, O'Dell." Penny slapped her pointed hat on her head, hiked up her witch's skirt, and trotted off to Bella's cubicle to have her palm read.

Speaking of outsiders, I caught a glimpse of Renfield/Gabriel, dressed as a clown with an orange wig and a bulbous red nose, next to Romeo, their heads together, laughing mightily. Must be some good joke. I'd love to be a fly on the wall for that one.

Lola gestured from the bar, waggling a glass of wine.

"You look amazing," I said to her and motioned to the bartender for a refill. A jeweled neckpiece and flimsy gown with side slits made my Wonder Woman look modest. "Queen of the Nile. Love the wig." It was pitch black with straight bangs and a gold circlet.

"Chrystal helped me put it together."

"Walter's too?" I asked slyly and sipped my drink.

Lola grimaced. "He was at a loss and said he wasn't coming because he couldn't think of a costume, and in a moment of weakness I said why not Julius Caesar and blah, blah, blah. Next thing you know, we're a couple. A costume couple. That's all. For tonight," she added hastily.

"Right."

"This is an excellent turnout," she said.

"I don't see Carlos."

"He'll be here. Said he had his costume all ready." She grasped my hand. "C'mon. Let's get our palms read. I can't wait to hear what's in store for my future."

Lola pulled me across the basement toward Bella's stall, where a line of customers had formed. Clearly, the most popular entertainment of the night. At least that's what I thought her palmistry was: a diversion. Pure and simple. I'd only had one previous experience with a psychic on the Jersey Shore boardwalk. When I was seventeen an old woman with a crystal ball told me I'd be married twice with four kids by the time I was thirty-three. That ship had definitely sailed.

In front of us, Mildred and Benny waited for Walter to finish with Bella. I scanned the crowd to see if Carlos had made an entrance. A Grim Reaper loitering by the candy corn jar at the entrance to the basement caught my attention. I hadn't seen him before. His black hood and skeleton mask hid his identity, unlike most partygoers.

Walter emerged from the booth, dazed, his two hands in front of him, palms facing upward.

"What did she tell you?" Mildred asked cautiously.

Walter stared at his palms and stubby fingers. "My heart is broken easily and my life is filled with emotional trauma."

I could have told him that without even peeking at his hands. His chill pills were blatant confirmation.

Lola rolled her eyes, which was hard to do with gobs of mascara on her lashes. "It's only for fun. Nobody takes this stuff seriously."

Walter did. "I'm going to the bar," he sniffed. "Good thing I'm also creative, spontaneous, and down-to-earth, even if I can be manipulated by others." He flipped his Julius Caesar robe over one shoulder and marched off.

As a member of the entertainment committee, I could cut the line to visit Bella. I smiled apologetically to Mildred and drew the muslin swag aside to reveal the psychic in full gypsy regalia: a bandanna covering her head, tons of necklaces and bracelets, a flowing, multicolored gown. I found her intriguing. Bella touched an extraordinary necklace at her throat. A multicolored, iridescent pendant surrounded by a thin gold band. Then she tucked it away into her shawl. As aloof and distant as her husband was, Bella, on the few occasions we had spoken, was approachable and friendly. She opened her hands and invited me to sit.

"No, thanks. I wanted to see if everything was fine."

Bella tilted her head, her hands remaining extended in my direction. Her eyes probed my face.

Not wanting to offend, I sat. "Well…" I laughed awkwardly, and she took my hands in hers.

She turned them over, then back, then over again, staring into my palms. Releasing my left hand, Bella traced several lines in my right. "Heart line, head line, life line," she said earnestly.

"Glad to see I have all three." I attempted playfulness.

Bella was anything but playful. Was that a bad sign? Her bracelets jingled as she moved her fingers around my palm. She was a sturdy woman, her torso robust. Yet, at the moment, she appeared fragile. She shrank back into her seat. Was this part of the act?

"I see that you are not content with your love life and are looking for a change." Her voice was barely above a whisper.

I leaned in. "I am?"

"You have an enthusiasm for life while you are confronting an emotional crisis. See these?"

Bella pointed to crosshatching on my palm. "Be careful. You are about to make momentous decisions."

I tugged gently on my hand. "I'll let the next person—"

She hung on. "This line? Your fate. Do you see where it joins with the life line? At this point, your interests must be surrendered to those of others."

I was speechless. In my head I had convinced myself that reading palms was a parlor game; in my heart, however, her talk of "discontent with my love life," "momentous decisions," and "surrendering my interests" brought me up short. Bill? In the midst of the excitement about my coming marriage, had I given enough thought to how my life might change? Permanently? And what was that "discontent" about? I resisted the thoughts. Another mental head slap. *Calm down!*

"Remember, your palm doesn't control your fate. You do." Bella's concentration sharpened as she studied my expression.

I thanked her for donating her time, said folks were enjoying her readings, and scurried out.

"What took you so long?" asked Lola, lifting her empty glass. "Now I have to go back to the bar." She floated away, Cleopatra on her barge, limping a little.

"I'm next," Mildred said. She peeked around the curtains and tiptoed inside.

"Hey, what happened in there?" Benny flipped up his pirate's eyepatch and gave me the once-over. "You're white as a ghost."

"Must be the fluorescent lights." I pointed to Bella's stall. "Have a good time."

"Uh-huh." Benny wasn't fooled. He'd guessed something must have unnerved me. "It's just a game."

"Right." I waved to Vernon, who was bobbing for apples and dripping water onto his Robin Hood outfit.

The atmosphere in the room shifted a bit. Heads turned to the entrance of the basement, the assembly inhaled a collective gasp. Not that there weren't plenty of fantastic costumes in the room. But Carlos's Phantom of the Opera was incredible. White tie and tails and black cape, the half mask and slouch hat covering his face. Though he was barely identifiable, the posture and presence could only be his. He held a single red rose. Everyone near him broke into spontaneous applause. There was an arrogance about him as he moved easily through the crowd, greeting people, bowing as his character until he stood a few feet away. Carlos approached and extended the rose. I was slightly embarrassed to be singled out.

"Thanks," I said and smelled the flower. The perfume was pungent.

"You are most welcome." He inspected the room. "A fine get-together."

"Your wife is very popular. Everyone is enjoying having their palms read."

"You?" he asked.

"Sure. Interesting having Bella dig into my life."

He laughed. "I understand you have done a bit of digging yourself. Murder investigations."

Had Etonville been talking about me? "I had a little input on a couple of cases."

"Input? I think you are being modest. I hear your participation was much more than that."

"I trust my instincts." *Why did I tell him that?*

"Hmm. I'd like to talk to you about your instincts some time," he said. My little hairs danced. "Uh…okay."

He bowed smoothly and drifted into the crowd.

What was that about?

* * * *

The throng was raucous, thoroughly enjoying the music—a mix of oldies and Motown and newer tunes—wiggling and bouncing, costumes flying. The La Famiglia menu was a rousing success, all of the food having been scarfed up. I assumed the incognito judges had made their decisions and would be announcing winners soon. I stifled a yawn. It had been a crazy-busy day. I was sorry Bill had not shown up in his modified Superman outfit, but I understood. This NJ Police Chiefs assignment was a significant appointment and I was proud of him.

My Wonder Woman spandex top was chafing my upper torso and the boots had worn out their welcome. I glimpsed the clock on the church basement wall. We had only an hour and a half to go; midnight was the witching hour. The temporary dance floor was clogged with partiers. Romeo danced with Lola, Mildred and Vernon waltzed to Motown, Pauli and Janice swayed slowly, and the Bangers held hands, bouncing their peapods off each other.

Carlos and Bella huddled together outside the palmistry booth. He had removed his hat and she had tied a shawl around her shoulders. Their body language was troubling. Unlike the folks on their feet, enjoying the merriment that pervaded the festivities, the Villariases were arguing. She firmly gesticulated, he shook his head opposing whatever she had suggested. Too bad they were fighting in the middle of the party. Bella pivoted abruptly and vanished.

As if in slow motion, Carlos swiveled his head and stared across the basement. The mass of bodies was too dense to pinpoint the focus of his attention until the dancers spread out, forming a large circle into which individuals leaped, shimmying and shaking.

Now I could see what had attracted his notice: the masked Grim Reaper I'd spotted earlier by the candy corn container was standing by the bar being served a cup of punch by a waiter from La Famiglia. The Reaper looked at Carlos, who in turn took a few steps toward the Reaper, then hesitated. He must have thought better of his plan because he replaced his hat and walked away. The Grim Reaper lifted his mask far enough to down the punch in one gulp, then headed to the entrance, where I lost sight of him. Some kind of drama?

I was about to seek out the rest of the entertainment committee to confirm the judges' progress when I saw Gabriel behind Bella's makeshift cubicle, holding his clown's red nosepiece in one hand, a beer in the other. From that vantage point he could clearly see the at-a-distance silent communication between Carlos and the Grim Reaper. And he could see me watching the moment play out. Had the Bernridge actor observed me observing the others? *Why?* A chill ran down my spine. I stuffed my dread inside my Wonder Woman red, white, and blue and waved nonchalantly to Gabriel. He stuck the red ball back on his nose, melting into the boogying mob.

* * * *

"Fooled you all!" Edna cackled into a microphone set up on the small stage at the end of the room. "I'm doing a 10-61. For you civilians, that's a 'miscellaneous public service.'"

The assembled partygoers chuckled and applauded Edna, in a white sailor suit complete with a cap perched atop her graying bun, being a surprise costume judge, along with the mayor's wife in a nurse's uniform, a stethoscope around her neck.

"So if everybody will gather round, we'll announce the winners. Cause I know some of you think this part of the night is a Code 2. That's 'urgent!'"

A murmur flitted through the gathering as the crowd bunched up, edging toward the stage. Edna and the mayor's wife proceeded to acknowledge all the magnificent costumes before announcing the winners. Without further ado, they got to it: funniest went to husband-and-wife duo Abby and Jim as a pair of sneakers connected by oversize shoelaces; the most creative was awarded to the Banger sisters for their two-peas-in-a-pod getup; the most dramatic prize went to Lola for her regal and sexy Cleopatra. Without her Julius Caesar. The scariest was obvious: Romeo as a bloodcurdling zombie. The mayor's wife handed out little gold trophies. The ELT was cleaning up in the awards category.

"And now for the final award of the night. The grand prize…" Edna made a fuss of opening an envelope as a hush fell over the room. She beamed as though taken aback, even though she'd been the one to choose the winner. "…goes to Carlos Villarias as the Phantom of the Opera!" She scanned the crowd. "Come on up!" She hefted a larger gold trophy.

The partyers clapped and cheered and hooted. And waited. And waited some more. Carlos was gone.

"Bella, do you want to claim the prize for him?" Edna asked, swinging her head back and forth like a searchlight.

Again clapping and cheering until it was obvious that there was no Bella either. They'd left. Too bad. They might have enjoyed being recognized by Etonville.

"Leaving the bash before it's over is a 10-30," Edna said mock-seriously.

"What's that?" someone yelled good-naturedly from the audience.

"Doesn't conform to regulations!"

The throng laughed heartily, then broke up, collecting their costume pieces, saying good night to one another, and heading out. It had been an astounding success. Now it was time for the cleanup crew to get to work. So grateful I was on entertainment… I would have liked to thank Bella for her palm reading tonight. Odd that the Villariases had cut out early. I inspected the gathering making their way to the exit. For that matter, where was the Grim Reaper?

4

It was midnight. The streets in Bill's neighborhood were deserted. Trick or treaters had long since dragged their weary bodies and sacks of candy home. I pulled my MC into his driveway and switched off the ignition. The light from a streetlamp shimmered around the nearly bare branches of the weeping willow in Bill's front yard. A gentle wind sent the limbs bending and swaying, throwing shadows on the ground below. In the distance, a car door slammed, a dog howled, a shout then laughter drifted into the clear air. The night had an eerie quality. I knew the first annual Etonville Halloween gathering had been a success—my feet were killing me.

Bill's front door opened. "It's about time," he said.

I tromped delicately into the house. Bowlegged.

"Why are you walking like that?" he asked.

"Have you ever spent fifteen hours in go-go boots?" I bypassed the kitchen, resisting a late-night snack in favor of bed.

Bill shut the door and trailed behind, his mouth curving into a grin. "Can't say I have."

Upstairs, I stripped off my boots, miniskirt, red spandex top, and jumped into the shower. Oooh, the hot water was just what the post-party doctor ordered. I closed my eyes and let it roll off my back.

"How did it go?" Bill called out.

"People came in all kinds of costumes…" I toweled off. "No Superman, though."

"Sorry about that. After the commission meeting a few of us had dinner in Trenton, and by the time I got home it was too late to come."

"Right," I said skeptically.

"Honest." Bill raised a hand to swear an oath and I took the opportunity to grab the other hand.

I peered into his palm. "Oh no! See these little Xs? You're about to make momentous decisions," I muttered.

"What little Xs? That's a scar."

"You missed the best part of the evening. Madame Bella's palmistry. She can tell the future, you know."

"Oh yeah? Me too." He enveloped me in a bear hug, partly lifting me off the ground, kissing me firmly. "I've got a pretty good idea how we'll spend the next hour!"

Yowza!

* * * *

I ran and ran, the crumbling walls of a mansion closing in on me. At my back, twin zombies, their faces bloody, eyes gouged out, grasped and clawed at my Wonder Woman costume. I gasped for breath, desperate to reach a door into the castle. At the last minute, when I was about to be sucked into the waiting arms of the undead, the door swung open and a figure in black emerged. It was Carlos, and he handed me a red rose. I stretched out my hand to take the flower and he laughed. "Momentous decisions. Surrender to others! Surrender to others!" He slammed the door in my face and I jerked awake, my breathing ragged.

"Wha'?" Bill rolled over.

"Shh. Go back to sleep," I whispered.

He did.

I tossed and turned, afraid to close my eyes for fear I'd see the zombies chasing me again. I shuddered. The creatures made sense. Even the mansion and Carlos in evening dress with a rose. My subconscious was reliving the Halloween party. His words? "Surrender to others!" Was I overreacting to Bella's reading of my palm?

I gave in to exhaustion.

* * * *

A loud jangling yanked me out of a deep sleep. *Not again! No more zombies!*

Next to me, Bill had clamped on his cell phone, clearing his throat, running a hand through the spikes of his brush cut. "Chief Thompson." His voice was like sandpaper, then he listened.

I was wide awake now, the bedroom suddenly filled with the kind of tension that accompanied trouble. Big trouble. I squinted at the digital alarm: 3:00.

"Give me ten minutes," Bill said and immediately stood, grabbing clothes. He clicked off his cell.

"What's wrong?" I asked, dreading the answer.

He shoved his legs into pants, plucked a uniform shirt from a chair where he'd lain it last night.

"Bill?"

"Bunch of kids were messing around in the cemetery."

The Etonville cemetery was an historical landmark, some of its graves dating from the American Revolution. It hosted the gravesite of Thomas Eton, the town founder. Every once in a while, area teenagers got caught roaming the grave markers, generally getting into mischief. And last night would have been an especially great time to "mess around."

"Halloween night. Kids like to go to the graveyard. Scare each other silly."

"They're scared all right. They stumbled on a body. Male."

Oh no! "Dead body?" I murmured.

"Yes."

"Did they...know who it was?" I asked, trembling.

"No." He clapped a baseball cap on his head. Located his wallet and car keys. "Suki's there now."

"Cause of death?" Hoping against hope the victim died from natural causes.

"Waiting for the coroner. Go back to sleep," he said.

As if that was possible.

"I'll call you later." He kissed me.

"Maybe it was a heart attack?" Although why someone would suffer a cardiac arrest or a brain aneurysm in the cemetery in the middle of the night was—

Bill hesitated. "He had a metal stake in his chest."

Murder.

Seconds later, the front door slammed, the engine of Bill's BMW turned over, and then all was quiet. A metal stake...like the one missing from the *Dracula* prop closet? How many metal stakes could be running loose in Etonville on Halloween night? I shut my eyes to avoid the image of ELT folks once word of the murder boomeranged around town. Which it would within hours, driven by the efficiency of the gossip machine.

I climbed out of bed, slipped into a sweat suit, and padded to the kitchen. I debated: coffee? tea? a snack? I rummaged around in Bill's refrigerator. Way more appealing than mine. There was the end of a gourmet tuna casserole and some spaghetti carbonara, not to mention the artisanal cheeses Bill kept on standby. I removed a jar of olives buried behind the Greek yogurt and systematically ate half a dozen before I replaced the lid. I scoured the pantry and settled on herb crackers and a jar of peanut butter. I brewed a cup of tea and hunkered down in the living room, wrapping myself in an afghan Bill's aunt Josephine had knitted for him last year. Speaking of relatives, Bill and I had yet to consider a possible guest list for our wedding. We'd only been engaged for two months, but as Lola, my matron of honor, reminded me, "we have to pick a date, choose a venue, and get cracking." The thought of planning a wedding made me tired. Maybe it was the hour—three a.m.—or my crazy nightmare, or the disturbing news from the graveyard. My mind was a jumble of discombobulated notions.

Who was the victim? A local resident? A stranger? Did he have a connection to the Etonville Little Theatre or the *Dracula* production? I remembered a discussion with Penny last week, when I'd inquired about the eighteen-inch metal rod supposedly thrust into the heart of Dracula. What if Romeo misjudged his blows when he pounded the stake? I'd asked.

"O'Dell, it's all fake. Theater's fake. None of it's real. Haven't you learned that by now?" She'd cackled at my ignorance.

I knew it was all "fake." Yet I'd seen a rehearsal as Walter and Vernon jockeyed for positions near Dracula's coffin to witness the delivery of the fatal wallops. The stake was set carefully in "Dracula's heart" before Romeo raised the hammer. What if he missed the stake?

"O'Dell, that's a dummy in the coffin. Carlos is backstage. Anyway, the point of the stake is blunt. Walter sticks it in a hole in a sand box before Romeo whacks it. It couldn't cut butter."

So the *Dracula* prop couldn't have been a murder weapon, right?

I forced thoughts of the dead man out of my head and opened my laptop. I needed a matrimonial to-do list. The clock on the wall was inching toward three thirty. I yawned and typed: date, venue, guests, food, photographer. Maybe we should elope? My parents would be devastated. My mother had been waiting for this day for years. Lola was right. I had to get cracking.

Lola! I had to let my BFF know about the death. Anything that could disrupt opening night should be on her radar. Since I knew Lola kept her phone on 24/7, it was too early to text. I had to wait at least three hours. I hoped it wouldn't be too late. My cell phone pinged. A text from Bill: *going to be a long night and day. I'll call later.*

* * * *

Sun poured into the living room, forcing my eyes open. It was seven a.m. I pushed the afghan aside and headed for the bedroom, calling Lola on the way. It was still early, but I couldn't wait any longer.

After five rings, a sleep-deprived Lola answered. "Hullo?" she rasped.

"It's me. We gotta talk. Can you meet me at Snippets in an hour? I have an appointment at eight thirty. I'll call Carol and ask her to come earlier."

"Dodie?"

"Lola, get moving! I'll bring coffee."

"Fine," she muttered before clicking off.

* * * *

We sat in the swivel salon chairs sipping caffeine, all of us half awake after last night's revelries, yet jittery after my bulletin about the homicide. Until the body was identified, we'd be sitting on pins and needles.

"So it's good news, bad news."

"What's the good news?" wailed Lola, erect in her seat, eyes gaping, wildly twisting a strand of blond hair.

"Yeah, what's the good news?" echoed Carol, who scanned her appointment calendar for the day. I was at the top of the list.

"They found the missing stake?" I tried to lighten the situation. "Assuming it's the prop used in *Dracula*." Which they'd have to replace for tonight's opening because the metal rod was now a primary piece of evidence.

"How did it get to the cemetery?" Carol asked.

Or into the hands of the murderer?

Lola closed her eyes and rested her head against the back of the chair. We were all probably thinking the same thing: someone connected to the show had removed the stake from the prop closet. "It couldn't have killed anyone. Penny said the tip was blunted." Though Bill did say the dead man had a stake in his chest. And who was the victim? I winced inwardly to think it might be someone from the theater. From the cast of *Dracula*…

"I don't know. I just don't know. How are we going to open tonight when all anyone is going to be thinking about is this murder in the cemetery? And what if the victim…?" Lola didn't need to finish her thought. "I have to call Walter before word spreads around town." She leaped to her feet, grabbed her bag and coffee.

Too late.

The door to the salon burst open. A winded Edna stood in the frame. "Have you heard? It's a 187 in the cemetery—"

Homicide.

"Those kids were guilty of a 594—"

Malicious mischief.

"—and nearly had the pants scared off them."

"Have they identified the...deceased?" I asked tentatively.

"Don't know. It's a 10-55," she said grimly. "Gonna take some time to—"

"Edna! The codes?" Lola shrieked. She was over-the-top angsty and not in the mood for Edna's shorthand.

The dispatcher blinked, taken aback.

I, however, was used to Edna's codes by now and knew most of them. A 10-55 was a coroner case. "Maybe you should go to Walter," I said soothingly.

Lola gestured apologetically at Edna and hurried out the door.

Carol sighed. "She's got a ton on her plate today."

Edna and I agreed.

"It would help if we knew who the victim was," I said.

Edna looked around the empty shop as if we might be overheard and murmured, "You thinking about solving the murder?"

"No!" Because I'd done a little investigating in the past didn't mean I was ready to—

"I'll keep my ears open for any scuttlebutt I pick up today," Edna said knowingly. "We gotta know if the vic was connected to the ELT."

True.

"Hard to have a murder hanging over an opening," Edna said.

Again.

"Gotta go. I'm on a coffee run for the chief and Suki," she said.

"Is B...uh...the chief in this morning?" Edna may be my only source of info on Bill's whereabouts today.

"Came in right from the crime scene at about three a.m. I hear." Edna smiled slowly. "Guess he didn't get much sleep last night." She winked and disappeared out the door.

Geez. Etonville's general interest in Bill's and my love life had gotten worse since our engagement was announced last month.

"Speaking of which..." Carol grinned. "What are we doing with your hair today?"

A trim to get the bangs out of my eyes. My waves were going wild. "The regular."

"Oh." Carol eyed me critically. "How about something a little different? Maybe we could experiment with an eye toward the wedding."

What? The wedding was months away. I assumed.

"Never too soon to be planning." Carol swung my chair in an arc to face a mirror. "I'm thinking an inch or two off the length…" She fussed with my hair. "You could wear a wreath of flowers. Or else pin it up so a few curls drift down like this." She demonstrated with a handful of bobby pins.

With the hair off my neck, I felt cool and light. *Uh-oh.* My pinned-up, prewedding, experimental coif quivered, giving me notice beyond Carol's styling attempt: something was up besides my hairdo.

* * * *

I zipped my MC into a parking space outside the Windjammer, scooped up my bag and this morning's *Etonville Standard*, catching a glimpse of my new self in the rearview mirror. Not too bad. Henry greeted me inside the restaurant.

"How was last night?"

Which meant "how was the food catered by La Famiglia?" That rivalry would never end. The restaurants were like two bratty kids always at each other.

"The costumes were fun, everybody played the games, even had their palms read, and—"

"What did you do to your hair?" He squinted at me.

"Like it?"

He grunted. "We're out of butternut squash. I had to change the soup special. Better call Cheney Brothers." Henry trudged into the kitchen.

I fluffed my new do; Carol had clipped two inches off the length, resulting in a springy, curlier bob. The wind chimes above the entrance tinkled as the door opened.

"Hi," Benny said, hanging his coat on a wall hook. "Some party last night." He looked as tired as I felt. "What did you do to your hair?"

"Like it?"

Without even a second glance he headed for the bar and began his daily ritual. Wiping down the beer and soda taps, stocking wine, washing a few glasses that remained in the sink from yesterday. "Sure."

I drew myself a cup of coffee and plopped onto a bar stool. I opened the *Standard* so that the front-page headline was visible: HALLOWEEN HAVOC IN CEMETERY: MAN FOUND DEAD. The newspaper had wasted no time. It had even published this special early morning edition. "You heard?"

"Oh yeah. Didn't even need to see the paper. I stopped in the Shop N Go to pick up Cheerios for the princess. You know Betty? The frozen food lady? She was holding court with the cashiers. Her nephew was one of the kids who found the body."

Now this was news. "The article doesn't name names. Guess they were all juveniles."

"Drinking beer and tossing bottles at gravestones. You know, hit the bull's-eye and break 'em. Except one of them didn't break." Benny raised an eyebrow.

It had landed on the victim. "All of the boys local?"

"One from Etonville. The rest from Bernridge," Benny added. He studied the newspaper.

I had skimmed the article quickly on my way to the Windjammer. Long on headline, short on information. A minor reference to the stake found at the scene and the irony of having *Dracula* open this week. No mention of the identification of the man. If he had been connected to the Etonville Little Theatre, word would have been broadcast by now.

"Guess the victim was out trick-or-treating," Benny said.

"Guy's probably a little old to beg for candy," I said.

"Not too old to dress up. Says he was found in a costume."

I missed that detail. "Let me see that." He was in a costume all right. *Whoa. A Grim Reaper.*

"Kind of weird," Benny said. "Dress up like Death and then..." He shrugged.

Something was tickling the back of my mind. "Benny, do you remember seeing a Grim Reaper at the Halloween party?"

Benny thought. "No. I was busy eating, drinking, and dancing. Hey, how about those marinara mummies and pumpkin quesadillas? Delish and clever."

"Mum's the word on the catering."

"Got it." Benny turned his attention back to the bar. "Hope this doesn't kill the opening of *Dracula* tonight."

"Right." I knew I had seen a Grim Reaper last night.

"Game on for the Etonville PD. Again."

* * * *

By noon the Windjammer was full, its customers so enthralled by news of the murder—creating theories on the method and motivation for the killing—that few paid any attention to Henry's specials: grilled three-cheese sandwiches and his gourmet chicken soup. He might as well be serving cardboard on rye. Runner-up topics of discussion were the success of the

Etonville Halloween party and my new hairstyle. I whizzed around the dining room, refilling coffee cups, bussing a table here and there, generally giving Gillian and Benny a hand.

"Dodie, the festivities last night were simply grand," said a Banger sister, bouncing her head.

"Such a shame it had to end on a terrible note," said the other.

"Yes. Really unfortunate."

They leaned together and then tilted their bodies toward me. "Do you think it had anything to do with…?" They fingered the garlic necklaces they'd worn throughout lunch.

"*Dracula*? I don't think so."

"But the man had a stake in his heart!" one gasped.

The word got around quickly. "I think we need to wait until the police investigate."

They stared at me, giggling. "Until Bill investigates."

Sheesh. I smiled and picked up my coffeepot.

"Have you set a date?" the other sister asked.

"Not yet." I turned to go.

"What did you do to your hair?"

I couldn't help myself. "Like it?" I swept a hand through my newly shorn locks.

"Mmm," said one sister.

"Aha," said the other.

I moved on, stopping at a table with Mildred, Vernon, Penny, and Abby. I gestured with my pot. "Refill?"

"Here we go again, O'Dell." Penny handed me her cup. "Another opening, another mur—"

"Don't say it out loud, Penny! It will bring bad luck." Mildred spooned up the last of her chicken noodle soup.

"Like we don't have problems already, with the vampire thing," Abby groused. "If the town's freaked out by a murder, people might stay home."

"Do they know who it is yet?" Mildred asked.

"The vic hasn't been ID'd," muttered Vernon.

"You sound like one of those television detectives," grumbled Abby, unimpressed.

Vernon shrugged away the comment.

"What a terrible way to die," Mildred whispered.

"Like Dracula," Abby said sarcastically.

"FYI, Dracula is a fake person. This guy was real," said Penny with great authority. "Too bad it had to happen on opening night."

The table fell silent, its occupants pondering the fate of *Dracula* now that the murder had been made public. I needed to change the subject. "Loved that costume, Abby. You and Jim as a pair of sneakers? You deserved your prize." I beamed.

"I guess," she conceded.

"It was a spectacular night, Dodie. Especially the palm reading." Mildred tossed her head at her husband, who chewed his grilled cheese perfunctorily. "Vernon doesn't believe in psychics. Bella told me I freely express my emotions and love adventure. That I should take advantage of my wanderlust. I'm thinking of a Caribbean cruise this winter."

"Hmph," said Vernon.

Mildred swatted his arm. "You're upset because Bella said you have a short attention span and are tired all the time."

"I'm *tired* of talking about hands." Vernon was grumpy. Too much Robin Hood.

Penny opened her hand. "I've got a square palm and short fingers. Means I'm bold, instinctive, and insensitive. I'd make a great leader," she said smugly.

Geez.

"Did any of you see someone in a Grim Reaper costume at the party last night?" I asked.

"You mean like the murder victim?" Abby asked darkly.

"Yes," I said.

"Maybe." Abby.

"I'm not sure." Mildred.

"Nope." Penny.

Vernon shook his head.

Abby stared at me. "What did you do to your hair?"

* * * *

The next couple of hours zoomed by. Patrons coming and going, rumor and innuendo about the murder whizzing around the dining room. Speculation on its relationship to *Dracula*'s opening was prime material. What was Bill up to in the Etonville Police Department? He could be with the coroner, or interviewing the teenagers who'd been playing target practice with a six-pack, or coordinating with the state police lab, or creating a list of potential suspects who would require interrogation, or…I paused. Who could possibly be listed as a suspect at this point? So far, no one I'd spoken to had remembered positively seeing a Grim Reaper.

Was I hallucinating? No, I was certain that, for a brief moment last night, Death had paid a visit to the Etonville Halloween bash. And had seemed to disturb Carlos Villarias…

I was behind the cash register when the phone rang. It was Edna, calling in an order for Bill, Suki, and two out-of-town police officers.

"Make that two special burgers…the chief loves 'em," Edna said.

Didn't I know that!

"A chicken noodle soup, a grilled cheese…" Silence on the line as Edna crossed items off a list. "And a Caesar salad for Suki. I'll be by in half an hour?"

"I'll deliver it," I said. Breathing some fresh air would be good.

"Thanks, Dodie."

"Wait a minute." I turned my back on the dining room and cupped the receiver in my hand. "How's it going over there?"

Edna lowered her voice as well. "Crazy. Got a 10-12 from Bernridge PD, two officers from the state police with the chief, bunch of kids cooling their heels in the outer office. With parents in tow," she added.

I could imagine her eyebrows inching upward knowingly.

"Wouldn't want to be in those kids' shoes," I said.

"In addition to underage drinking, the chief's got them on a 594 and a 604."

I recognized malicious mischief. "What's a 604?"

"Throwing missiles."

That made sense. I got a sudden urge. "Did you happen to hear any talk about time of death?"

"You didn't get this from me, but…the coroner called and I happened to be on the line."

"Uh-huh."

"Sometime between eleven p.m. and one a.m.," Edna whispered. Then, as if Bill had walked into the dispatch room, Edna called out, "Copy that, Chief."

"Talk later," I said.

"10-4."

5

Between eleven p.m. and one a.m.. About the time I arrived at Bill's place. I walked briskly up Main Street and down Amber. Last night, while I was washing off the grunge of my day as Wonder Woman, a body lay dead in the Etonville cemetery. Above ground. On a brisk, sunny, fall afternoon like this one, it was difficult to imagine a man, as yet unidentified, stabbed in the dark with a metal spike.

I opened the door to the Municipal Building and immediately faced its ego wall of mementos and trophies celebrating the town's law enforcement and athletic successes. There was an *Etonville Standard* article about Bill's involvement with the New Jersey State car theft unit last summer and a photo of him in uniform. Excellent! I took the hallway to the right, stopping at Edna's dispatch window. I lifted the brown bag. "Lunch."

Edna raised a finger, indicating I should hang on, then spoke into her headset. "Mrs. Parker, we cannot call animal control to catch a bat you saw flying in the park. There's no law being broken." Edna listened, did an eye roll. "It doesn't matter if you think it's actually Dracula. Now, you have a good day." She ripped off her headset. "That woman is three sandwiches short of a picnic." Edna leaned through the window. "Want me to take that?"

"I'll deliver it," I said.

Edna winked. Her phone lit up. "Ralph? Where are you? The chief's been trying to reach you. There's an 11-66 over on Anderson and traffic's backed up in front of Georgette's Bakery. You'd better get a move on." She listened. "Forget the Donut Hole. 10-4."

Everyday mayhem in Etonville.

Suki was at her desk in the outer office, her head bent over a file, her straight black hair swinging forward to cover her face.

I stopped. "I think the Caesar salad belongs to you?"

Suki smiled enigmatically, as usual. "Personal service," she said.

"The walk felt good."

"Yes. It's a nice day." Her expression neutral, expectant. What else did I want?

"Should I deliver this to the chief's office?"

Suki rose and accepted the sandwiches for the two state police officers in a conference room farther down the hallway. She buzzed Bill to let him know I was coming in.

I knocked softly.

"Enter," a tired voice said brusquely.

I stood in the doorframe and took in his office. *Whoa.* This was a change. Bill's normally tidy desk was littered with loose papers and files. One guest chair had a stack of yellowed folders that looked as if they'd been resurrected from dusty archives. He still wore the shirt he'd pulled on at three a.m. this morning, tie undone, sleeves rolled up. He rubbed the blond stubble on his chin. "I'm famished. Nothing but coffee since last night."

He fell on his lunch like a starving man, not pausing until he'd devoured most of it. "Are you making any progress on IDing the victim?" I asked tentatively.

"Working on it. Got the state police from the forensics lab digging into his ID. Fingerprints. Facial recognition."

"I noticed the kids and their parents are gone."

"Edna," Bill said wryly. "I knew word would get out about them."

"There was a mention in the *Etonville Standard.*"

"Newshounds! They were sniffing around the cemetery before I even got there. We let the four teenagers go. They didn't have much to say. They thought the guy was drunk and passed out at first. This black hood thing was draped over his head. His face was covered with a Halloween mask."

The Grim Reaper costume.

"They got scared and ran. Then one of them, the smart one, insisted they call the police."

"Didn't they question the stake in the man's chest?"

"They claimed, each of them separately, that they didn't see any stake," he said.

"Oh?"

Bill stared at the wall opposite his desk. Possibly contemplating this bizarre turn of events or else so exhausted he was distracted by paraphernalia from his NFL days playing for the Cleveland Browns and Buffalo Bills. Caps, banners, and trophies filled bookshelves.

"If they are reliable witnesses," he added.

I had to tread lightly. My history of helping to solve murder cases in Etonville was a double-edged sword. Bill had come to appreciate my instincts, at the same time he bristled when I pushed too hard or crossed the investigative line. "Do *you* believe them?"

He sighed. "We'll see."

"But the stake was there when you arrived? I was wondering—"

Bill raised a hand like a crossing guard. "Please. It's early in the investigation. Too early for hunches," he said wearily. It was a pointed comment on my intuition. He focused on his messy desk.

"Right." My plate was full and I had no intention of sticking my nose into another murder inquiry. Besides, we needed a wedding site. Bill and I had a lot to discuss... Still, I couldn't help one niggling thought. "I saw a Grim Reaper at the Halloween party."

Bill jerked up his head.

"At least I'm pretty sure I did," I continued in a rush. "I asked a few other folks and nobody else admitted having seen him, but there was one point, about an hour before the awards presentation, when I saw him hanging by the candy corn count and then he..." I stopped and caught my breath.

"He what?" Bill asked sharply, all business.

"He had a...moment with Carlos Villarias."

Bill leaned back in his chair, showing more interest. "The guy playing Dracula? What do you mean 'a moment'? They spoke?"

"No. In fact, they were across the room from each other. But it felt like they were..." How to describe the interaction? "Communicating."

"Communicating?"

"They stared at each other."

He tapped a pencil on his desk blotter. "What did this Grim Reaper look like?"

"I don't know. He had the hood over his head. Like the victim," I finished.

"I'll make a note of it. Probably going to have to interview half of Etonville, because the vic wore a costume and it was Halloween night and people were out and about," he grumbled, and ran a hand through his scruffy brush cut. "How many other Grim Reapers were there?"

"None as far as I could tell. See you tonight?" I asked softly.

"I'll text later. Thanks for lunch." He shifted his attention back to his desk, then looked up. "Did you do something to your hair?"

I took a chance. "Like it?"

"Cute."

Yes!

* * * *

I was having mixed feelings about my garlic-themed food. Henry had done a fantastic job with last night's specials and tonight should be no different: garlic-roasted baked brie for an appetizer and pork chops with sweet garlic relish for the entrée. Could the palates of Etonville take this much garlic? As I wandered the dining room as inconspicuously as possible, I overheard diners' remarks:

"Garlic again?"

"What else is on the menu?"

"Think I'll pass tonight."

"Too bad the murder victim didn't eat here last night…."

I smiled as politely as I could and whisked dishes off tables, helping Gillian and Enrico's wife, Carmen, who lent a hand in the dining room on weekends. Murder fever was not going to die down until Bill and his crew determined the identities of the victim and the perpetrator. He didn't have much to go on.

I dropped onto the bench of my back booth with baked brie on a hunk of bread and a seltzer. I intended to work until the dinner rush ended and then catch the third act of *Dracula*. I was curious about the stake-stabbing scene and—

"Thought I'd find you here." Lola slid onto the bench opposite me, dressed for tonight's opening: a black, silky pantsuit, her hair in an updo.

"Hey! Nice outfit. How did it go today? Walter in control?" I asked, savoring the warm brie. It was delicious.

Lola brushed the lapels of her jacket. "He's surprisingly calm. No cancellations at the box office. The murder hasn't dampened enthusiasm for the show."

"You know Etonville…nothing perks this town up like a good, old-fashioned homicide."

"You got that right."

Benny appeared at my back. "Anything to drink, Lola?"

"Or eat? This brie is terrific. Not to mention the pork chops. I think there's some soup left from lunch."

Lola waved off my suggestions. "Just water. I'm not hungry."

Benny ambled off. Something was up. It wasn't like Lola to skip dinner on opening night. In fact, she usually fortified herself with both food and alcohol. "Want to talk about it?"

She tugged on an earring. "It's nothing. Well, actually, it is something, but I'm not sure exactly what." She hesitated. "Maybe I'll have a half glass of chardonnay."

I motioned to Benny, pointed to Lola, and mimicked drinking. "So... this 'something' that has you in a twist; what's it about?"

"I saw something that might be important, or might not be. I'm not sure whether to say something and get someone in trouble or let it alone and see where the chips fall. Know what I mean?"

I hadn't a clue.

Benny set her wine and water on the table and Lola sipped each one in turn. "Should I go to the police?" she asked.

"Let's start at the beginning." It was six o'clock. Lola could afford to lollygag in the Windjammer for at least another half hour.

"When I got to the party last night, I noticed my left heel was a little wobbly. I wanted to go back home and change shoes and told Walter to go in without me. But you know Walter. He insisted that we had to make a grand entrance together. It would be more dramatic, give us an edge for the grand prize, which I didn't care about anyway, blah, blah, blah."

I was familiar with Walter's inclination to play a starring role in most situations. Lola must have given in, because they appeared at the door of the church basement together.

"As the night wore on, the heel got worse and I turned my ankle once."

"Wow. I saw you limping."

"I made it through most of the night but at eleven, I gave up. I had a pair of flats in my car, so I hobbled out to the parking lot to change shoes. The parking lot was lit by the security lights and I had my cell phone flashlight."

I took another bite of the brie.

"I got into my car and found my flats in the back seat. When I looked up I saw Carlos...that Phantom costume was so distinctive...walking toward me. I wanted to get out to say hello, but he passed by as if he didn't see me. He cut across a row of cars and then stopped. And somebody else was... just there. Like out of nowhere." Lola murmured, "The other person had a long black robe and hood and a hideous white skeleton mask."

"The Grim Reaper. Like the costume on the murder victim."

"Yes!" Lola said, agitated. "And the two of them were very...animated. Like maybe they were having an argument."

Yikes! Carlos and the Reaper had done more than communicate across a crowded room.

"Could you hear what they were saying?"

"No, and they must have realized they could be seen because the other person pulled Carlos away and they sort of...vanished. Into thin air."

Or, more likely, into a car. They would have been pretty conspicuous in those getups on a street in Etonville. "I'm torn. What if Carlos was talking to the victim? If I say something to the police, it might take him out of the show. I have trouble believing that Carlos is a criminal. Despite some thinking that he's a...a...you know."

"Vampire?"

"Or at least something paranormal." She gulped her wine. "What should we do?"

We?

"I know you said no more murder investigations, that you had enough to do organizing your wedding, which I know we should be talking about, but we need to clear Carlos of any suspicion so that there's no interruption in *Dracula*. I couldn't handle another canceled production."

"How do you propose to do that?"

"You know how good you are at digging into people's backgrounds—"

"Lola, I'm afraid—"

"—and using your instincts to figure out motives and—"

"I can't get involved. I told Bill that I was done with investigating—"

"—freeing innocent suspects and finding the guilty parties."

She paused. "If you could only talk with him? Maybe nose around in his background? Find something that might explain why he'd be talking to the dead man."

"Lola..."

"That's what best friends are for." She reached across the table and clasped my hand.

I hated to turn her down. How would I explain this to Bill? Wouldn't it be simpler for Lola to relate her story, let him have a few words with Carlos, and put the whole event to bed? "Talk to Bill and explain everything."

As if she hadn't heard me, Lola continued. "What if you never poke around a murder again?"

"First, I hope that's true. That there are no more homicides in Etonville... and second, why wouldn't I ever investigate again?"

Lola shrugged. "After you're married, it might be awkward for Bill's wife to be involved in police matters."

I leaned back in my seat and studied Lola. Was she using a tactic to entangle me in the Carlos situation? Or was she right? Would I have such a different identity in the future that I wouldn't be free to follow my instincts? I felt a chunk of tension in my stomach that had nothing to do with bread and brie. "Let's say I agree to talk to…dig around a little…"

"Thank you, Dodie! You can't believe how much better I feel." She downed the rest of her wine with a water chaser.

"I'm only agreeing to dabble—"

"You can start tonight. Carlos and Bella are hosting the cast at their place after the show. Maybe you could pull him aside." She glanced at her watch. "I've got to run." She blew me a kiss and flew out the door.

Now what?

* * * *

The audience of *Dracula* milled about the lobby, the second intermission underway. It was a nice crowd for an opening. I eased through clumps of theatergoers chatting and nibbling on concession snacks, eavesdropping on conversations.

"That flying bat is something else." Impressed!

"The green light is creepy." Yes!

"I love the way Dracula appears and disappears magically into the bookcase." Yay!

"He's really scary. Do you think it's true what they say about him?" *Sheesh.*

The rumors about Carlos were going to zing around Etonville until *Dracula* closed. I mulled over potential conversation starters with him, as per Lola's plea. *How old are you? Have you ever lived in Transylvania? What kind of a coffin do you prefer to sleep in?* I had to laugh despite the seriousness of his possible predicament. And mine. At what point would I need to share Lola's revelation with Bill?

"Hello, Dodie."

A familiar voice brought me out of my Carlos musing. It was Bella, looking very different than last night. The jewelry, bandanna, and multicolored gown were replaced by a tailored maroon skirt and a white turtleneck sweater. Her flowing brown hair was gathered at the nape of her neck in a smart chignon. If I hadn't seen her reading palms at the Halloween party, I would immediately assume she was a corporate type on an evening out. Come to think of it, I had no idea if she *was* a corporate type, or where she was employed. As with Carlos, none of us knew much about Bella. "Hello."

"Are you enjoying the play?" she asked, her tone as feathery as it was last night, her eyes as penetrating.

"I just arrived. I've seen a few rehearsals, so I'm third-acting it tonight. I'll be back before it closes to see the full production."

She cocked her head. "I sense that I've met you before."

I laughed awkwardly. What was it about the Villariases that unnerved me? "You mean other than last night when you read my palm?" And warned me about surrendering my personality.

She frowned. "Yes. Other than last night. You have a memorable persona."

I do? "You certainly provided memorable entertainment at the party. People loved the palm readings. Even gave a few customers some unforgettable advice." I was thinking about Walter. And me.

"I'm pleased Etonville had a good time. It's a charming little town."

I was on the brink of inquiring whether her future plans involved long-term residence in our "charming little town" when Lola appeared. She slipped an arm through mine, a frozen grin on her face.

"Hello, Bella," she said.

"Lola."

"So lovely of you to host the cast tonight. Is there anything we can bring?" Lola asked brightly. Too brightly.

"It's our pleasure and, no, I think we're all set," she said graciously. "I'm happy you'll be joining us, Dodie."

How did she know that? Had Lola mentioned anything? The lights in the lobby flicked on and off, signaling the impending start of Act Three. Bella headed back into the house.

"What's up? I recognize that fake smile." I had a similar one that I whipped out whenever I was in over my head. Usually about once a week. "How's it going out there?"

Lola tightened her grip on my arm. "The French doors in Act Two were stuck and Dracula had to practically bash his way in. Then Lucy's gown ripped. She almost had an R-rated scene with Carlos. The flying bat ran into a light batten and several instruments wobbled. I'm holding my breath until the curtain call. Wish I could run next door to the Windjammer..." she added wistfully.

"Pull yourself together. I'm sure things aren't as bleak as you make them sound. I overheard people raving about the show." I gave her a thumbs-up.

She straightened and squeezed my hand. I trailed her into the theater, where the lights were already dimming. Lola moved swiftly to her seat down front, while I sat in a chair in the last row next to the ELT photographer. "Hey," I whispered to Pauli.

"Hey," he whispered back.

I settled in as the house lights went dark. In the blackout, dogs howled as they had earlier in the play. Truly a chilling effect. When the lights rose, the play was back in the same setting as Act One—the library of Dr. Seward's sanatorium. Walter and Vernon pleaded with the Attendant—Abby—to find the bug-eating Renfield so they might use him as bait to catch his master, Dracula.

A trick chair swung upstage, then downstage, while curtains fluttered as though some invisible force had entered, stayed for a bit, then exited. Supposedly the vampire. Van Helsing, Dr. Seward, and Harker plotted to kill Lucy, if necessary, to save her soul. When Janice entered, looking healthier and more vital than in the previous act, due to an unnatural transfusion, she fluctuated wildly in a Jekyll-and-Hyde routine depending on when Dracula's influence overcame her. I was transfixed, as was Pauli. He angled his body forward in his seat as if drawn like a magnet to the stage. Janice's Lucy was riveting as she bent her lover's neck, dogs wailing, her mouth heading toward his throat. Walter and Vernon enter in the nick of time to save Romeo's life.

I exhaled. The tension level ratcheted up another few notches when the devil himself appeared in evening clothes, mocking Van Helsing, Seward, and Harker, threatening to take Lucy with him to the other side and make her his bride for centuries to come. Talk about a marriage not made in heaven! When the three heroes attempted to keep Dracula in the room until daybreak—at one point they were down to ten seconds—to destroy him with the metal stake, the Etonville Little Theatre performed its best feat of magic. In a flash of smoke, the vampire vanished through a trapdoor in the floor, leaving his cape behind. The onstage characters were stunned. So was the audience.

In a brief blackout, the house erupted in a vibrant hubbub, releasing the tension of the previous scene.

I turned to Pauli. "Wow."

His eyes were shining with excitement and pride. "Totally. Isn't Janice…" Words failed him.

"She sure is." I patted his shoulder.

The final scene was played behind a scrim, the actors in dim light and shadow. A bright flashlight guided them downstairs and into an underground chamber where the coffin containing Dracula was located. As Van Helsing and Seward hover by the casket, placing the stake over Dracula's heart, Harker swings a hammer and strikes the metal with an awful force. An offstage groan indicated the spike had hit the sweet spot. All executed smoothly, consistent with Penny's explanation of the Dracula dummy and the spike being fitted into a sandbox. Possibly a new spike?

When the lights burst on, the stunned crowd sat in silence for a moment, then erupted in cheering, clapping, and shouts of "Bravo!" By the time Carlos took his bow, spectators were on their feet. The ELT had a bona fide triumph.

Folks drifted out of the house, caught up in the energy and exhilaration of the last scene, the noise level rising steadily. Lola was stuck in the aisle between two enthusiastic fans. I caught her eye and gave her the okay sign. She smiled sheepishly.

After announcing that he'd see me at the cast gathering—he'd wheedled an invitation as the ELT photographer—Pauli squirmed his way through the mob to reach Janice backstage. I was happy for the two of them. For everyone.

As I watched the happy horde exit the theater, something in the first scene of Act Three pricked at my imagination. Something someone said… I reran the scene in my mind. Dracula explained to his three nemeses that the stake-in-the-heart routine only worked if the victim died by day and not by night. Hmmm… The man in the cemetery definitely died by night. If I believed in vampires, which I certainly didn't, I'd have to acknowledge that the victim might have become one of the undead…I gulped.

6

"It sure looks haunted," Edna murmured to no one in particular, to the cast of *Dracula* in general. They were grouped around her on the sidewalk that ran past the old Hanratty place that Carlos and Bella had rented. I'd never been inside, though I'd driven by it once when I first moved to Etonville on my way out of town. The house stood on half an acre of scruffy lawn with patches of dried dirt, surrounded by a few straggly trees—minus leaves at this time of the year—and no neighbors. The nearest houses were on a side street some distance away. The three-story building looked as if it might collapse at any moment, its outer walls covered with weathered, gray shakes, the steps to the front door supported by concrete building blocks. There was no handrail. Light leaked out of windows on the first floor. Curtains covering small, circular panes on the third story—an attic room?—quivered. Was someone up there watching us? I shivered. A turret rose upward from the right side of the structure, giving the house a smidge of outdated dignity. A drainpipe dangled loosely from the gutter.

"Let's go." Penny corralled actors and nudged everyone forward to the front door. There were six cast members, Renfield saying he'd be along later, plus Penny, Lola, Pauli, and me. Strength in numbers.

We crept across the porch cautiously, aware of the creaking beneath us as the flooring shifted with each individual's footsteps. Penny put out a hand to knock on the door. Before she could hit her knuckles to the wood, it flew open. "Welcome, everyone!" Bella stood in the doorway, a silhouette backlit by muted foyer lighting.

Behind her, Carlos stood silently, observing the group huddled in his entryway, like deer caught in headlights.

Lola took the lead, moving graciously into the house. "Thank you. So nice of you to invite us to your home."

I'm not sure what the members of the Etonville Little Theatre were expecting. Given the exterior and location of the Hanratty homestead, I anticipated something out of a late-night, classic horror film. Amityville? Instead, the interior was warm and inviting. Literally. Off the foyer, which boasted worn wood floors, lightly faded Oriental rugs, and a small antique table and chairs, was a roaring fire in a parlor. Carlos escorted his guests into the room, suggested they get warm or help themselves to food and drink across the hall in the dining room, where a large mahogany table was covered with platters of refreshments.

The cast, relieved to find themselves in a relatively normal social setting, babbled all at once. Pauli helped Janice with her sweater, Lola and Walter spoke with Bella, Vernon, and Abby; Penny made a beeline for the eats; and Edna turned to me. "Kind of a shock." She studied the room. "I pictured something out of..."

"*The Shining?*"

"Copy that." Edna grinned, adjusted her bun, and followed the others to the dining room.

"I'm glad to see you joined us for this little outing." Carlos looked down at me from his six-foot-plus height. I hadn't registered exactly how tall he was before.

"I'm more or less an honorary member of the ELT. I tend to tag along to parties."

"Hmm."

Across the hallway, behind Carlos, I could see Walter and Vernon competing for Lola's attention, one on her right, the other on her left. Trapped between them, she had no choice but to gaze beyond them in my direction. Noticing that I was left in the parlor alone with Carlos, her eyes widened, giving the impression she was crying, *go for it!* No time like the present to plunge in. "Too bad you missed the awards presentation last night. I guess you heard you won the grand prize."

He laughed haughtily. "I did hear that."

"And your costume? Fantastic. Did you ever play the Phantom? You must have a theater background."

"No, I never appeared in *Phantom of the Opera*. I do gravitate toward black capes, though."

Oh? "Speaking of black capes, I saw someone in a Grim Reaper outfit at the party. Did you see him?"

"I'm afraid not."

Was he lying? "And then the same costume was on the murder victim. Guess you heard all about that."

"Very unfortunate. Etonville seems like such a safe little town."

If he only knew… "I can understand leaving early. It must have been exhausting. Working all day, dress rehearsal, getting into another costume, talking to strangers from Etonville." I'd left the door open for Carlos to respond to several gambits: his job, exiting the celebration before it ended, meeting someone in the parking lot—

"I don't tire easily. I'm more energized at night."

Did he realize what he was saying?

"I barely sleep. Only a few hours at a time."

Uh-oh…if the ELT overheard this, serious doo-doo would be hitting the fan.

Change direction. "That's such an interesting accent you have. Not at all Jersey." I chuckled.

He studied me. "No, not at all Jersey."

"Because a New Jersey accent is pretty hard to shake. I've tried to a few times."

"Oh? Why?" His gaze narrowed, sucking the energy out of my "memorable persona."

Whoa. I was in trouble now. "Well…let's see…one time…"

"Carlos?"

Saved by the Bella.

"You're monopolizing Dodie." She frowned slightly.

He bowed. "Excuse me." And walked to another part of the house.

I watched him leave. "Your husband is such a gentleman. I'm sure you must hear that a lot."

Bella accepted my assessment quietly. "We're on our best behavior in front of guests."

"Your home is so warm and comfy. The furniture…vintage."

"You mean old." Her gray eyes twinkled. "The house was furnished when we rented it. I think the real estate agent took care of that. Certainly not the owner."

"Right."

"Can I get you a plate of food?" she asked.

"I'll head over. I want to thank you again for reading palms. Have you been doing it for a long time? It takes such skill." Maybe Bella would divulge some personal information if her husband wouldn't.

Bella's laugh was wispy. Ethereal, almost otherworldly. "Not as much as you would think. Certainly not as much skill as tarot."

Aha! "You read tarot cards too?"

"Sometimes." She considered me. "If you'd like to have a reading…" She let the invitation dangle.

Not on your life. "Sure. Sometime. Sounds like fun."

"It can be fun. Also surprising."

Now what did that mean? "Guess I'll pay a visit to your delicious buffet."

* * * *

I scrolled through my texts for the tenth time that evening. No word from Bill. How was his investigation going? He would be exhausted when he finally surrendered for the night. I poured myself another ginger ale from a bottle on a sideboard where the Villariases had set up a minibar. Soda, wine, whiskey, an ice bucket. I was getting antsy and frustrated. I had no more information about the backstories of this couple than I had when I entered the Hanratty place.

"Hey, O'Dell."

"Hi, Penny. Nice spread." I scanned the dining room table with the remains of platters of sandwiches and crudités, bowls of fruit and salad, and a double chocolate layer cake.

"Yep. 'Course, I can only eat certain things."

"The Mediterranean diet. Right. How's that going?"

Penny snatched a chunk of cake. "Chocolate's good for you."

"So the opening went well. Only a few minor glitches, according to Lola." I dipped a piece of celery in ranch dressing. "I guess you had to find another stake to substitute."

"Nope." Penny removed carrots and cucumbers from the veggie tray and stacked them on her plate, pouring the remainder of the dip over them.

I stopped chewing. "Why not?"

"Gabriel found the original one backstage. Stuck under cables and instruments."

Renfield? My pulse picked up. The murder weapon wasn't the stake used in *Dracula*?

"Nope. Not the one used in *Dracula*."

Penny was in my head again.

"Isn't that odd? How would the stake get stuck under equipment?" Wouldn't somebody have to put it there? Had Bill heard this yet? I should text him. I hurried to the foyer and dug my cell out of my bag, which was sitting on a chair. "Was Gabriel searching for the stake? When did he find it?"

Penny pursued me. "O'Dell, you thinking of playing detective again?"

"Who me? No!" How many times would I have to say this?

"'Cause I think there's some sabotage going on." Penny pushed her glasses up her nose.

That again.

I texted Bill: *have information on the stake from* Dracula...*home soon?* I wasn't certain about his schedule, but I intended to exit the Villariases' as soon as I found the ladies' room.

Penny pointed upward. "Top of the stairs."

Geez. "You're getting better at reading my mind," I said patiently.

"Easy came, easy went. Practice makes perfect," she said seriously.

"Here's a suggestion. Why don't you let Bella teach you how to read palms? Put those skills to better use than mucking around in my brain." I tramped up the staircase.

Penny chuckled. "Nah. Too much fun keeping you on your toes, O'Dell. Anyway, I'm already pretty psycho."

I blinked and turned back. "You mean psychic?"

"Whatever." She stuffed a piece of cake into her mouth. Definitely not on her diet.

Penny was correct. At the top of the stairs was a dimly lit hallway, the wallpaper a patterned leafy green, glass sconces sparkling. The first door on my left was the bathroom. I entered, used the facilities, and washed my hands, my mind running off in different directions: the murder weapon, the investigation, Bill...I stared at my likeness in the mirror. My face, flushed from the fireplace heat, contrasted nicely with my green eyes. Another gift from my Irish ancestors.

I smoothed my beige sweater, dabbed at my lipstick. My eyes fell on the medicine cabinet. Habit stopped me in my tracks. Ever since I'd begun my investigative journey, I'd paid special attention to personal choices. Bathrooms were a prime information-gathering location. For example, what kinds of prescriptions did they have, what toiletries did they use, what did they stash away behind the bottles and jars? This was a guest bathroom, I presumed, so its contents might be less enlightening. I flipped open the mirror and examined the shelves. Sure enough, very little of interest. A tube of toothpaste, minty, with whitening added. A bottle of generic aspirin. A package of throat lozenges. I shut the cabinet and went into the hall. To my right was the staircase leading to the foyer. To my left, the hallway extended for a bit. One door on this side, two doors on the opposite one. One of them was ajar.

I hesitated. I'd offered to speak with Carlos to find out what I could about his background. Something that would explain his behavior Halloween night, his exchange with the Grim Reaper. So far, I was batting zero. I glanced up and down the hallway. Laughter and yakking from below drifted up the stairs.

Three doors. I was tempted to stick my head in each room, determine which one belonged to Carlos, do a quick inspection, and beat it back down to the party. As Pauli would say, piece of cake, though that felt like trespassing. However, if a door was already open...

I tiptoed across the hall. Penny had said the bathroom was at the top of the stairs. She'd neglected to mention which side of the hall. I could just as easily have thought this room was the loo and walked in. Besides, the door was partially open.

Satisfied with my rationale, I peeked into the room. Ambient light from the hall sconces threw a shaft of illumination onto a dark carpet. From what I could see without switching on a light—no way was I going to warn anyone outside the house that I was roaming around—the room was simply furnished. A four-poster bed, nightstands, a bureau with a mirror and antique washbasin, an easy chair by a floor lamp next to the window. Nothing in the bedroom that indicated it was occupied by a member of the household. It had to be a guest room.

I eased back into the hallway, leaving the door ajar again. I wavered. Should I check the other rooms? Was I pushing my luck? I tiptoed to the door on my right. It was locked. Lots of reasons hosts would lock doors when a group of almost-strangers traipsed through their home. Two doors done, one to go. I padded quickly across the hallway to the third room. It was unlocked, the door shut. Might as well complete the job. After another glance down the hallway I twisted the handle, nudged it open, and stepped in. A glow of rosy light from a table lamp was warm and welcoming. Larger than the guest room, it held a king-size bed, a clothes closet in addition to a large chest of drawers, a desk and chair in one corner, and a chaise longue in another. A plaid quilt in earth tones with brown throw pillows on the bed, a hairbrush and pins on the bureau, a shawl laying casually on the chaise next to an open book, and a desk with a few papers on it. Though the guest bedroom felt somewhat sterile, this bedroom suggested personality, a human touch. People actually slept here.

Everything was normal, not paranormal. I quickly examined the desktop—issues of the *Etonville Standard*, a *Dracula* rehearsal schedule, and a Chinese takeout menu from Bernridge. Quite a distance for delivery... That was it. Curiously, there was no mail, nothing with the Villariases' address on it. Still, I had a squirrelly feeling. There must be something in this room that provided a clue to their lives. I noticed a wastebasket half hidden by the desk. It held a circular advertising appliances from a Creston department store and a flyer publicizing Etonville's Halloween party. On the carpet next to it was a crumpled piece of paper. Someone had missed the wastebasket. I picked it up.

Footsteps moved down the hallway. I panicked. There was nowhere to hide. I jammed the paper into my bag and sprinted across the room to a spot behind the door. Maybe the person was looking for the bathroom? What if it was Carlos or Bella? My mind went on overdrive, rummaging around for an explanation for my presence here. Somebody paused outside the bedroom, I closed my eyes, as if that would prevent whoever from seeing me. The door slowly opened, light from the hallway leaking in.

"Dodie?"

I recoiled. "Arrgh!"

"Ssh!" Lola hissed.

"Ssh!" I hissed back, and pulled her into the room, shutting the door.

"What are you doing in here?"

"Looking for something about Carlos. What are you doing here?"

"I was walking up the stairs to the ladies' room when I saw you come in here. Did you find anything?" she asked, breathless.

"Only a piece of paper on the floor. Let's go." We stepped to the door, listening, then opening it carefully and checking the hallway. We hurried down the stairs. I tried to look composed.

"There you are," said Carlos as he spied us descending the staircase. He regarded us quizzically. "I thought maybe you'd left." He addressed both of us, but his eyes were fixed on me.

"In the bathroom. Then Lola came up and we got to gabbing." I smiled at Lola, silently requesting confirmation.

"That's us. Gabbing, gabbing." She laughed and glanced behind her. "The fun has moved into the dining room."

Carlos followed her gaze. "Bella is doing tarot. I think you'd like to have a go at it," he said to me.

I would? "I've got to get home."

He persuasively wound an arm around my shoulders. "A quick look. Come."

He was smooth as a baby's bottom, my great-aunt Maureen might have said.

"Okay," I said weakly, sliding my eyes in Lola's direction. She shrugged helplessly.

I joined the group gathered around the table where Bella and Walter were seated, food having been transferred to the sideboard, squeezing in next to Pauli and Janice.

"Hi, Dodie," said Janice, her eyes wide. "Walter is having his fortune told."

Pauli snorted lightly. "Like yeah."

Bella shuffled a deck of cards, explaining that there were four suits, much like playing cards: wands, swords, cups, and pentacles. She added in a little history, how the tarot originated as a gaming deck and only later came to be used for divination. She asked Walter to shuffle the cards, think about a subject or issue, and divide the cards into three piles. Which she designated as past, present, and future.

Abby looked skeptical, Romeo smirked, and Edna eyed the proceedings eagerly. Vernon fingered his hearing aids. As Bella turned cards over and remarked on his love life, noting relationship problems in the past, movement toward new romantic endeavors in the present—possibly Jocelyn?—she warned him about a future card that hinted at a less-than-sincere interest in a new partner. Meaning he was out to take advantage of someone, Bella added. Walter appeared dismayed, the rest of the cast snickering.

I'd had enough of the Hanratty house and the Villariases' gathering. I said a quick goodbye to Carlos, who stood off to the side, taking in both Bella's reading and the reactions of the ELT members. Then stole to the front door. As I pulled it open from the inside, someone pushed it from the outside.

It was Gabriel. "Sorry! You okay?"

"No problem. You're in time for the tarot reading."

"Not what I need. Someone telling me about my future." He laughed good-naturedly. "I've got enough trouble with my present."

I zeroed in on his argument with Carlos the night of the dress rehearsal. What was the nature of their relationship now? "I know what you mean."

"I hope there's some food left," he said.

"A bit."

"Have a good night."

"You too. By the way, Penny told me you found the missing stake."

"Good thing. It would have been a pain to replace it this late." Gabriel took off his jacket.

"How did it get stuck under those cables?" I asked.

Gabriel shrugged. "Not a clue. I had to poke around and dig it out."

"Like it got shoved in there?"

"I guess."

"You must be a little psychic. Knowing where to search," I said lightly.

He studied me coolly. "Not really. I scoured the entire backstage area. Along with everyone else."

Penny hadn't mentioned that. "You're doing a nice job with the role."

He brightened. "Thanks. Renfield's a challenge."

"The ELT's lucky to have you in the show. Congratulations on the opening."

He walked to the dining room, where Walter poured himself a glass of whiskey, a consolation prize, while the skeptical Abby sat down to the hoots and hollers of the cast.

I stood on the front porch. The night air was bracing, clearing my head, filling my lungs. Without streetlights on this patch of road, the slice of moon provided the only illumination. The branches of the trees scattered throughout the yard pointed every which way like bony fingers, reaching out. A breeze whipped up a pile of dead leaves sending them spiraling into the air. November had arrived.

I hurried to my car, slightly creeped out by the shadows and silence. My cell pinged. I jumped into my MC, slapped the door locks, and read Bill's text: *where are you? coming home?*

You bet.

7

Tossing and turning at night should be considered exercise, given how little I'd slept during the past eight hours. Exercise reminded me that I needed to think about fitting into a wedding dress. My great-aunt Maureen's retort, whenever the subject of exercise reared its ugly head, came to mind: *rabbits jump and they live eight years, dogs run and they live fifteen years, turtles do nothing and they live one hundred fifty years. I rest my case*, she'd say.

Sitting at the island in Bill's kitchen, I toyed with my tomato, asparagus, and goat cheese omelet. Usually I loved Bill's epicurean breakfast delights. He loved experimenting with ingredients, sauces, and spices.

"You're not hungry?" he asked and swallowed another forkful of his egg concoction. "Or you don't like the omelet?"

I took a sip of coffee. "Love the omelet. Delicious." I scooped up a mouthful. "Ummm."

Bill was not easily misled. "What's up? Sorry we didn't talk last night. I was exhausted. Could barely get words out of my mouth by the time I got home."

"You had to be worn out."

"You got that right." He finished his eggs.

I knew I had to tread lightly this morning. "Making progress?"

"Not much. Haven't ID'd the victim yet. Waiting for the prelim from the coroner."

"Any witnesses other than the kids?"

"Not so far."

"Penny told me they found the missing stake from the *Dracula* production," I said nonchalantly. "It was backstage, hidden under cables."

"Missing stake?" Bill asked, perplexed.

"You know, the one they ram through Dracula's heart to kill him once and for all?"

"Oh, right."

Bill hadn't seen the show yet, but surely he knew the mythology surrounding the life and death of vampires. Come to think of it, he hadn't eaten a garlic-themed dinner at the Windjammer yet either... "I thought maybe the stake from the show was the same one the killer used to murder the man in the cemetery," I said a little more energetically than I'd intended. I focused on my English muffin.

"Dodie, what's going on in that mind of yours? Your imagination running wild again?" he teased, though his words were tinged with a sober edge. "I thought you weren't going to get mixed up in any more investigations."

"I'm not. I figured you should know, that's all. I don't suppose you have any persons of interest?"

Bill rose from his stool and put his arms around my waist. "Here's what you'd like to know. No witnesses, no ID, no persons of interest. Time of death between eleven p.m. and one a.m."

Which I already knew, thanks to Edna's indiscretion.

"And no stake from the show. It was a metal spike about a foot long. But...and here's the weird part, and the thing you need to keep under your hat. 'Course, the *Standard* will get wind of this in the next twenty-four hours and plaster it all over town," he grumbled.

"Yeah?"

"The vic didn't die from the stake. It was shoved into his chest, but there was only a superficial scratch. The point never broke the skin. The guy's costume protected him."

"He wasn't stabbed to death?"

"Nope."

"How did he die?" I asked.

"To be determined after the autopsy is completed."

I speared a piece of tomato. "The stake was...for what...show?"

"Possibly." Bill planted a kiss on the top of my head and carried his plate to the dishwasher.

"Why would someone do that?" I asked, incredulous.

Bill shook his head. "Why would someone kill a man in a Grim Reaper costume in the cemetery on Halloween night?"

Good point. "Could the kids have planted the stake? You know, a *Dracula* thing?"

"Possibly. We'll see."

We agreed to meet up for dinner at the Windjammer, where Henry was featuring garlic-roasted prime rib. I knew it would be scrumptious, a crowd-pleaser. That is, if the crowd hadn't tired of garlic. Afterward, I planned to take a night off from *Dracula* and kick back at home with my own idea of entertainment...*Yowza!*

My cell pinged: a text from Lola suggesting we meet at Coffee Heaven before I went to work. It was strangely cryptic. I showered and slipped into my skinny black jeans and a red sweater—my power color. I required a jolt of energy to get into the day.

I arrived at Coffee Heaven before Lola and headed straight to a booth in the back, pretending to concentrate on today's *Etonville Standard*, avoiding eye contact with other patrons. On days like this, when Etonville was humming with murder innuendo and everyone assumed I had an inside track on the investigation—which I did—the only safe course was to play dumb.

"Hi, Dodie!" A woman fluttered her fingers at me. "Any news?"

Heads swiveled to face me.

"Morning," I said pleasantly and shook my head.

"Too bad."

Jocelyn appeared at my side with a coffeepot. "Now you all let Dodie alone. Go on. Back to your own business." She motioned to the woman, who was a trifle put out, then ducked her head until we were nose to nose. "Any news?"

"Sorry."

"Heard the cast had a party at the Hanratty place." Jocelyn arched an eyebrow. "Fortune-telling."

"Bella brought out the tarot cards. It's only a parlor game," I said.

"Also heard that Walter might be involved in a new 'romantic endeavor' in his present," she said archly. "I could have told him that without those funny cards."

Poor Walter.

"Hi, Jocelyn." Lola huffed as she plopped into the seat opposite me. "I'll have two eggs over easy, dry wheat toast, black coffee." She intended to get down to business.

"I ate breakfast already," I said. "So—"

"Cinnamon bun and caramel macchiato." Jocelyn wrote up our order. "Extra icing."

I had to seriously think about getting into a wedding dress one of these days. Maybe I should consider Penny's diet—

"I am at my wit's end," Lola moaned.

"What now? The show's a hit, the house was full, the review is terrific."
I pointed to the newspaper. I'd read the first and last paragraphs. Enough
to know that the *Standard* critic had generally given the show a positive
evaluation.

"It's not *Dracula*. Or at least not completely. Walter was so distraught
after Bella's tarot card reading…"

"I saw him down a glass of booze as I left." I chuckled.

"That was last night. This morning he called me at seven a.m. obsessing
about his future."

"You mean him taking advantage of a new love interest?"

"Yes! He's afraid he's going to offend someone…"

That particular horse was out of the barn.

"So he's decided he has to resign from the theater."

"What!" I exclaimed.

"As soon as *Dracula* closes," Lola said.

"The Etonville Little Theatre has been his life for over twenty-five years."
Walter was a real estate agent in Creston, but he spent most of his time in
Etonville. "What's he bothered about? His real love interest is the ELT."

"I agree. This reading really has him spooked." Lola twisted a strand
of hair. "I had a funny feeling about those tarot cards."

"Lola, first it was Carlos, then the theater was haunted, and now it's
tarot cards. I think you might be the one getting spooked," I said gently.

Jocelyn delivered our food and we dove in.

"I got so distracted by Walter that I forgot to ask if you got any
information out of Carlos last night." Lola bit into her toast. "Anything
about his background or the Grim Reaper?"

"No. I tried a few different angles. Carlos sidestepped every question
about work, his previous theater experience, even the Grim Reaper. He
said he hadn't seen anyone dressed like that."

Which I knew wasn't true—I'd witnessed the Reaper and the Phantom
exchanging stares.

"He said that?" Lola's brow puckered. "Could it have been so dark that
night that he didn't notice the costume?"

I savored the last of my cinnamon bun, licking icing off my thumb.
"You were farther away and you noticed the costume. Anyway, the skull
mask was a dead giveaway. No pun intended."

Lola nodded. "What was the piece of paper you took from the
Villariases'?"

I gawked at her dumbly. I'd stuffed the sheet in my bag and totally
forgotten about it until now, other concerns jostling one another for my

attention. "No idea." I dug it out and smoothed the crumpled paper on the table between us. It was a page from a newspaper—the *Daily Herald*. Dated July 23. A little over three months ago. Lola and I scanned the news, which focused on local issues, articles about a parks and recreation scandal in a nearby town, a police action against a drunk driver and a purse snatcher, and a story on a shooting victim who had been identified.

I Googled the name of the newspaper. "Suburban Chicago paper," I said.

"Why would Carlos, or Bella, have a newspaper from the Chicago area?" Lola wondered. "None of these articles are particularly earth-shattering."

"Beats me." I turned over the paper. Nothing on that side but the obituaries and advertisements. I had a sudden flash. "Sometimes when folks move away from an area they still subscribe to their hometown newspaper. My parents read the *New York Times* every day even though they live in Florida."

"The *Times* isn't a local paper," Lola said and wiped her mouth.

"True. But they identify with the northeast. Maybe the Villariases are from Chicago. Did Carlos ever mention where they lived before Etonville?"

"Not that I recall."

"What about his bio for the *Dracula* program?" I hadn't actually seen a program, having sat through rehearsals and only half of a performance.

"He said he didn't want a bio."

An actor who didn't want to toot his own horn? That was odd.

"I persuaded him that the star of the show had to have some sort of presence in the program, so he gave us a few lines about how pleased he was to play the role, thanking Walter, the cast, and the crew."

No mention of any previous acting gigs. "He seems to be experienced. This couldn't have been his first time onstage."

"Absolutely not. No first-time amateur has that kind of poise or confidence. What are you thinking?" Lola asked eagerly.

"Nothing much. I'll read back through these articles and see if anything pops. Otherwise…" I shrugged.

Lola got the picture. "We tell Bill what I saw and implicate Carlos and run the risk that he becomes a suspect and might not be able to complete the run of the show, which will devastate the ELT and sink the box office and ruin our standing with the New Jersey community theater crowd, not to mention how berserk Walter will go considering he plans to quit the theater—"

"Lola! Land the plane!"

She paused to breathe. "Thanks, Dodie. I know you'll do your best." She grabbed her purse. "I have to get to the theater and intercept Walter before he issues a press release to the *Etonville Standard* and all hell breaks loose."

I wished her good luck, arranged to meet for an early dinner to discuss wedding venues—Lola was gently but firmly forcing me to organize our big day—and agreed to text if I discovered anything about Carlos. I finished my caramel macchiato, my mind idly wandering through my to-do list for the Windjammer this morning. I folded the page from the *Daily Herald* in half and was about to fold it in half again when I spotted the obits. My father had made a habit of reading the obituaries in recent years. He'd joke that as long as he didn't see his name there, he was good to go.

I skimmed a full page of remembrances acknowledging folks who'd passed away in the Chicago area last summer. A listing of seventeen deceased men and women, most in their sixties and older, two in their forties, and, sadly, one thirteen-year-old who had drowned in a boating accident. I was mulling over the cruelty of fate when the seed of an idea took root at the back of my mind. What if Carlos hadn't been interested in the local news on July 23 but the obituaries? Generally, each obit provided birth and death dates, surviving relatives, and date and place of funeral services. Most summarized the deceased's past—educational background, military service, and career. A few had emotional reflections on the loss of the individual. Yet there was nothing on this page that seemed out of the ordinary. Had Carlos known one of them? There were no Villariases. Even so, his potential connection to the Chicago area most likely meant nothing regarding his connection to the Grim Reaper. Hopefully, Carlos knew nothing about the murder. Still, these obits warranted some scrutiny.

Time to call in my big gun. Pauli.

* * * *

The Windjammer was busy: a steady stream of customers served, a bungled order of seafood from the Cheney Brothers corrected, next week's vegetable inventory sorted out, and staffing schedules coordinated. By three o'clock I was ready for my afternoon break. The dining room was quiet; Gillian was putting inserts into menus while Benny hauled cases of wine from the basement and polished the soda taps. I settled into my back booth with a seltzer and salad. I *had* to take this wedding dress thing seriously. I'd texted Pauli this morning that I'd like to talk if he had a minute. He'd responded that he had no classes today and would stop by the restaurant this afternoon.

I doodled on an old inventory sheet: guest list, menu, dress, photographer, flowers…*geez*. This would be quite the production. The Etonville Little Theater had nothing on my upcoming nuptials.

"Hey." Pauli slid into the seat opposite me.

"Hi. Thanks for coming on short notice. Are you hungry?"

I ordered a burger and fries for him, another seltzer for me.

"Is this about the dead man?" he asked, his eyes bright. "Got some new DF techniques."

I knew DF was Pauli's shorthand for "digital forensics," besides Janice, the love of his life.

Pauli opened his laptop.

"I'm not sure," I confessed.

He observed me over the lid of his computer. I withdrew the newspaper page from my bag and laid it on the table between us.

"So like obituaries. What am I looking for?" he asked.

What, if anything, would make Carlos save this paper from July? Was it someone in the obits? Or in one of the articles on the reverse side? I needed to keep Carlos's name out of Pauli's search for the moment. The kid was too close to the production. "Pauli, I need your discretion here. Like you say—"

"Confidentiality is the first rule of digital forensics," we said in unison and laughed. "I don't know what I'm looking for. I'm interested in the backgrounds of these people." I tapped the paper. As a result of his online DF classes, Pauli had access to databases and deep searches that the average civilian—meaning me—could never log on to. "If you use your digital forensics tools, you might find something…"

"Useful." Pauli finished my thought. "Totally. I'll see what comes up."

He was no fool, having been around my investigating long enough to know when I was on the hunt. Except I wasn't. This present gig was simply an attempt to lessen Lola's concerns about Carlos's behavior Halloween night. Combing through random obituaries seemed pointless. Yet it was all I had to go on. Sooner rather than later, she might have to go to Bill with what she'd witnessed.

Benny delivered Pauli's late lunch and my tech guru went to work.

"The info in the obits should help you get started." As if Pauli needed help.

"Mmm," he said and bit into his sandwich.

I left Pauli to his own devices while I researched wedding outfits and prices. *Whoa!* Sticker shock! I scanned pages of dresses that would equal several months' rent. Or the gross domestic product of a small nation. A justice of the peace was looking better and better…

The door jingled announcing the arrival of a customer, and I glanced up out of habit. The place was empty, so the man could have his choice of tables. Gillian invited him to sit wherever he pleased. He declined a table or booth and instead seated himself at the bar, accepting a menu from Benny. I refocused on my wedding wardrobe. I yawned and stretched. Pauli was bent over his laptop and I needed either caffeine or fresh air. I opted for both.

"I'm going for a walk. Let me know what you find?"

Pauli bobbed his head, his eyes never leaving the laptop screen. "Gotta bounce in half an hour."

Behind the bar, I filled a carryout container with coffee, snapped on a lid, and swung my bag over my shoulder.

"Here you go," Benny said and deposited a bowl of tomato basil soup in front of the patron. "Your BLT will be up in a minute."

The man ducked his head over the soup and inhaled. "Smells delicious."

"Our chef's specialty soups are always a hit." Benny polished a glass. "First time at the Windjammer?"

"Yep." The man dipped his spoon in the bowl.

"Etonville's close to the highway, so we get a lot of traffic passing through town. Eating here or at La Famiglia."

I exchanged glances with Benny. Any mention of Henry's culinary rival usually set off shock waves in the Windjammer. Fortunately, Henry was in the kitchen, up to his elbows in garlic and prime rib.

"Hmm," the man replied, checking something on his cell phone.

I recognized Benny's polite attempt to make conversation. Pure bartender banter.

"I'll be back in twenty minutes," I said to Benny, and smiled at the man who gazed at me, his spoon halfway to his mouth. Ordinary enough. Late forties, maybe fifty, dark hair, medium build in a suit coat with his shirt collar unbuttoned. It was a habit of mine, describing people to myself. Ordinary except for his eyes. Coal black and piercing. I was startled, uncomfortable as he continued to stare at me.

Benny went to the kitchen for the rest of the man's lunch and I stepped out from behind the bar. "Enjoy your meal."

"Thanks. Nice day out there." He went back to his soup.

"It is. Typical for this time of the year in North Jersey."

"I wouldn't know. It was thirty yesterday back home," he said.

"That's cold! I know Upstate New York was freezing last night."

Benny moved through the swinging door from the kitchen and held a plate aloft. "BLT coming up."

The man tucked a napkin into his belt.

"I grew up down the Jersey Shore. We rarely saw freezing weather." I left the door open in case he wanted to linger over our weather chat.

"Midwest," he said.

"Midwest?" I asked. I noticed the Chicago Cubs logo on his windbreaker.

"My home. Where the temp was thirty," he reminded me, his eyes boring a hole into the center of my forehead.

"Whoo," said Benny. "Too soon to have weather like that. At least wait until after Thanksgiving."

The man chuckled, Benny grinned, and I waved goodbye to both of them. I pulled on my leather jacket. Some coincidence. Carlos with a possible connection to Chicago…a stranger wandering into the Windjammer also with a possible connection to Chicago. The Windy City had invaded Etonville.

8

Lola smoothed an Excel spread sheet on the table between us. "I did a thorough investigation of possible wedding venues in the area."

"Which area?" I asked, wary, studying the list Lola had compiled.

"Etonville. Creston, Clifton. I ignored Bernridge. New York, if you think you want something more glam."

Glam was not in my wheelhouse. "I think local is fine." And less expensive.

"Etonville is limited. There's the Episcopal Church basement, the park if you are thinking warmer weather. I got married on a June afternoon." Lola's face took on a dreamy expression. "It was outdoors under an arbor, the sun setting, a string quartet…"

Lola had been a widow for over ten years. Boyfriend-hunting for most of the time I'd known her. Unsuccessfully. Lately, she'd sworn off the pursuit of men.

"Are you thinking warm weather?" Lola asked, the subtext being "set a date."

"Not sure."

"Oh. Now in Creston, there's the Crestmont Country Club, Pleasant Valley Catering, the Loft, Davino's, One Stop Wedding…" She looked up. "What kind of place do you think Bill will want?"

Bill? He'd as soon get married in the Municipal Building as one of the locations Lola had included on her spreadsheet. However, I was grateful to my BFF for getting the matrimonial ball rolling. "I'll ask him. Maybe we can go over this list next week?"

"Sure. Just remember…"

"I need to get cracking. Thanks."

She ducked her head. "Any progress on the you-know-who front?" she stage-whispered so eagerly I hated to break the news.

"Nothing yet. I'll keep you posted."

"Hi there."

I jerked upward. "B–Bill!" I stuttered. Did I sound guilty? "Nice surprise."

He glanced from Lola to me. "We made early dinner plans. Remember?"

"Right!"

Lola scooted out of the booth. "I'll let you two have a nice, relaxing meal together."

"Don't hurry off on my account. Join us," Bill said.

"Thanks. I have to run next door. Put out any vampire fires before they get out of hand." She looked meaningfully at me. "Let me know about Chicago," she added before bouncing off.

Lola!

"What did she mean about Chicago?" Bill removed his coat and cap.

"We were gabbing about wedding venues."

"In Chicago?" he joked.

"No, silly. We were talking about…" My mind fumbled through a range of possible justifications. "…the ELT season for next year. They're considering *Chicago*. The musical?" I gave myself a mental pat on the back for quick thinking. I needn't have bothered. Bill hadn't heard a word I'd said. He studied a menu even though he knew it by heart.

"Great."

"Maybe we can get married underwater?"

"Okay."

"Or at the top of the Empire State Building?"

"Whatever you think…" He frowned.

"Bill!" I yelled. At the bar, Benny looked up from his crossword puzzle. *All good*, I gestured.

"What?"

"Something must be up. You agreed to get married in a swimming pool."

"I did?" He groaned. "Guess I'm preoccupied."

"Want to talk about it?" I asked tenderly.

He folded his hands. "Things took a strange turn today."

"How so?"

"Might not have been a murder after all."

"What are you talking about? There's a dead body in the morgue."

"The guy died all right. According to the coroner's preliminary report, the victim had heart disease. He died from a heart attack, confirmed by a lack of blood at the murder scene."

Yippee! My pulse soared. That meant Carlos could not have been a murderer. Lola would be ecstatic. I had to tell Pauli that he could suspend his search—

"Problem is, we ID'd the guy. Turns out he's a pro."

I gulped. "A pro...?"

"Professional. As in associated with organized crime. Name's Daryl Wolf."

"Was he a...hitman?"

"Possibly. Not sure yet."

"What would a pro be doing in the Etonville cemetery?" I asked. Or talking with Carlos. "With a stake attached to his body."

"Good question. And all the way from Chicago."

OMG.

* * * *

An hour later, Bill had decamped for his office after raving about Henry's prime rib, telling me he'd be working late and not to wait up. The dinner crowd had begun to drift in, and my mind was in a muddle. I scurried from the dining room, to the cash register, to the kitchen, supervising, managing, and greeting, all the while I sorted through Bill's revelation. The victim's death was almost surely from natural causes—even though Bill cautioned me the coroner's findings were only preliminary—so there was no point in bothering him with Lola's Halloween night observation in the church parking lot. Whatever the conversation between Carlos and the guy in the Grim Reaper costume was about, it didn't result in murder. Which left me off the hook. That fact didn't eliminate troublesome questions, though: What *was* that discussion about? And their previous "communication" during the party? Why did Carlos leave early? Why did he keep the newspaper page from the *Daily Herald*? And, most troubling, what was a mob associate from Chicago doing in Etonville?

I picked up a coffeepot.

"Earth to Dodie...come on down," Benny murmured.

"What?"

"I asked if you wanted me to close up tonight, but I think you were miles away. Am I right?" he asked.

"I guess."

"Is it the wedding? I remember the year we got married. My wife was flying around like a madwoman, trying to get everything done. I wanted to help, but there were some things she had to do herself."

"There's a ton of organization." I was thinking about Lola's Excel spreadsheet.

"You should try those online wedding planners. Like Marrying in Style, Before You Tie the Knot, It's Your Big Day."

"You're familiar with them?"

"My little bro is getting hitched next year. It's all he talks about," Benny said.

"I'll check them out."

The restaurant was full by now, many customers sampling Henry's garlic-roasted prime rib and agreeing with Bill about its flavorful taste. The verdict was thumbs-up, though there were a few rumbles wondering "how long this garlic thing would last." Time to unleash slider week. We'd had it in the past and the mini sandwiches were always popular.

I surveyed the dining room, coffeepot in hand. The one thing all of tonight's patrons *could* agree on was the status of the murder investigation. Which was not a murder any longer. Information continuously leaked out of the Municipal Building and rebounded around town like a loose basketball. The consensus? The murder victim was an out-of-town troublemaker.

Once the actual cause of death was announced in the *Etonville Standard*, the rumor mill could shut down. But until then...

I moved between tables, assaulted by gossip:

"I heard he was on the lam from somewhere out West."

"He'd only been in the country a few days."

"No wonder he was in disguise."

"Grim Reaper. Kind of predicting somebody's death."

"Like his own..."

Folks in Etonville loved to take a molehill of information and transform it into a mountain of hearsay. It was the town's favorite pastime. Yet, out of the mouths of investigative innocents could come a seed of wisdom: it was prophetic that Daryl Wolf chose to wear a Grim Reaper costume.

Across the room, Mildred and the Banger sisters waved at me. Might as well get the day's wackiest chatter out of the way. "Hi, ladies. Enjoying the prime rib?"

"It's delicious," said Mildred. "Rare. Perfect." She chewed a bite and grinned.

"Where's Vernon tonight?" I asked.

Mildred swallowed. "He decided to eat at home."

"He doesn't appreciate garlic the way we do." The Banger sisters were nibbling on soup and a salad, fingering their necklaces.

"Aha." Definitely slider week coming up.

An oversize book sat on the table. "What's this?" The title was *Dracula Through the Ages* and featured a photo of a man in formal dress with a black cape, protruding eyes, pitch-black hair combed back from a high forehead, and a demonic smile.

"Vernon's research for the show. He didn't actually *read* the book. He left it in the dressing room under his makeup kit. I need to take it back to the library." She wiped her mouth and set the napkin aside. "It's the history of all the actors who've played Dracula."

The little hairs on the back of my neck quivered. "Do you mind if I take a look? I'll return it to the library when I'm finished."

"Don't read it before you go to bed. It'll give you nightmares. I flipped through some of the pages. Pretty creepy pictures in there."

The Banger sisters continued to finger their necklaces.

"Thanks for the warning," I said, my eyes glued to the book cover.

"Dodie, have you heard about the murder victim?" One of the Bangers.

"Uh…what exactly?" I asked, distracted.

"The man died from shock." The other Banger. "Not from the stake."

I wrenched my attention away from the Dracula photo to the table. "Shock?" Bill had said a heart attack. "Are you sure?" Then I caught myself. *Really, Dodie? You're confirming rumors with the Banger sisters? You need to get a grip!* I excused myself and hurried to my booth, book in hand. I slipped onto the seat and stared at the cover again. In fine print at the bottom of the picture was a name that neither Mildred nor Vernon had detected: *Carlos Villarias.* I flipped through the pages, bypassing the general history of vampire mythology, looking for the man on the cover. Halfway through the book, I found a short biographical statement and a filmography of Carlos Villarias. A Spanish actor born in 1892 who eventually came to the US and died here in 1976. His list of films was extensive, but by far his most famous was a Spanish-language version of *Dracula.* Forget Chicago. What kind of bizarre coincidence resulted in the ELT's Dracula having the same name as an actor from decades ago whose claim to fame was playing Dracula? A tension headache had reared its ugly head.

I jammed the book in my carryall, told Benny I'd take him up on his proposal to close the Windjammer tonight, reassured Henry that his prime rib was a roaring success, and, once the dinner service was winding down, made my exit. It was overcast, clouds obscuring the moon. Possibly rain tomorrow. The street was empty, the outdoor lights of the theater next door glowing brightly, reminding me that *Dracula* would be well into its second act by now.

I hopped into my MC, already envisioning a glass of chardonnay and my sweats. I drove a block down Main Street toward Bill's place and stopped. Then executed an illegal U-turn and beat it to my bungalow. Maybe it was all of the wedding chatter that had me anxious to hunker down in my own place for the night. Though I loved Bill's more spacious, beautifully decorated home, my five-room, half of a duplex was like an old shoe. Slightly worn down at the heels but comfortable and welcoming. I raised the heat, changed clothes, climbed into bed with my wine, the Dracula book, and my laptop. Then I texted Bill: *spending the night at my place. talk tomorrow. xoxox.* I added a string of heart emojis.

As I sipped my chardonnay, I paged through the book. Aside from the entry I'd already read, there was very little about Carlos Villarias. Mostly photos from his *Dracula* days. Though melodramatic and exaggerated in horror mode, his face was creepy. I picked up my laptop. I'd speculated about Carlos for weeks now but hadn't done a basic Internet search on him to see what materialized. I typed his name in the search bar, and up popped a string of links for the actor Villarias: his IMDb page listing his films, a Wikipedia page with the bare bones of his biography that I was already familiar with, and YouTube videos of his *Dracula* performance. There was even a black-and-white, Spanish-language segment of his work on Vimeo, complete with subtitles, eerie production values, a crazed Renfield, and howling dogs. There was a blog devoted to a discussion of whether Carlos Villarias was even dead. *Yikes*! That was carrying the vampire thing a bit too far.

I also found a video of a Carlos Villarias, bodybuilder.

Facebook yielded only a couple of scary-looking characters. I scanned links on several additional pages, but none provided new "Carlos Villariases." I could find no presence of the Etonville Carlos on the Internet. Odd. Almost everyone had something in their history or biography that landed them on the web. Or maybe Carlos Villarias was simply an uncommon name? I had hit a dead end and set my laptop aside. Maybe Pauli could dig up something. I'd have to broach the topic carefully, of course.

I picked up the latest Cindy Collins mystery—*Murder Most Personal*— from my bedside table, where I'd left it a few nights before. Chapter eight: in the midst of a gruesome homicide investigation, the heroine detective is debating how she'll balance her work life with her private life once she ties the knot with her fiancé. *Sheesh.* Too close for comfort.

I closed the book. I couldn't concentrate. I opened my own Facebook page, saw my brother Andy's posts of his three-year-old son, Cory, on Halloween. Dressed as a minipirate, my nephew held a jack-o'-lantern of candy aloft. I laughed out loud. The pictures reminded me that I owed Andy a call. We hadn't spoken since I told him the news of my engagement last month. He was thrilled for me; Andy loved Bill. As did my parents. I owed them a call too. The whole family was happy to see me "settle down," my father's description of wedded bliss. And especially with someone like Bill, the uber son-in-law. Kind, thoughtful, good sense of humor. It didn't hurt that he had a professional career, was ex-NFL, and knew his way around a gourmet recipe. I loved Bill and felt lucky, as Lola, Carol, and most of Etonville reminded me often enough. So why the recent uneasiness whenever wedding planning came up? I was probably driving Lola crazy.

I avoided my troublesome thoughts and turned out the bedside lamp, early for me. At least I'd get a good night's sleep. Tomorrow I could thrash through my niggling doubts. As my head hit the pillow, my cell pinged from its charger on my dresser. I wavered. It could wait till morning, I decided. I rolled over, pulling up the comforter. My cell pinged again. Maybe I should check it out. Maybe it was an emergency. Nope, I told myself. In emergencies, people called. I closed my eyes and took a deep breath, imagining that I was sinking into the mattress—a third ping made me sit up in frustration. What was going on? My alarm clock read ten thirty.

I threw back the cover and stomped across the chilly wood floor. Three texts awaited me.

I crawled back under the covers. Bill: *miss you 2night. love you.* With a string of emoji hearts back at me. He really was the sweetest thing… and getting pretty frisky. Lola: *late drink? Carlos in strange mood…* I texted back that I was already in bed and would catch up tomorrow. I was about to replace the phone in its charger when I remembered that I had a third text. It was from Pauli. I hated to disappoint him, but tomorrow I would tell him he could suspend the snooping into the obits from the *Daily Herald.* There was no need to decipher the paper's importance to Carlos. Our Dracula could remain a mystery to the town of Etonville, even if he had the same name as a famous actor who also played Dracula….

I stopped my mental rambling and read the text: *hey…you up? found something…* I was going to let this all go, right? My free-wheeling investigative reflexes went to war with my rational, post-engagement impulses. My thumbs fluttered above the keyboard, unsure how to respond. Then: *thanks for searching but no need to now.* Before I hit the Send icon, my little hairs twitched wildly, demanding that I pay attention. I surrendered.

I erased the sentence and replaced it with *come by Windjammer tomorrow afternoon.*

* * * *

Getting seven solid hours of sleep did wonders for my head. I bounced out of bed, energetic and ready to face the day and all of the question marks in my life, including whatever Pauli had found on the Internet. A hot shower, a cup of coffee, and a stretchy black sweater gave me a dose of adrenaline and confidence. I had a fantastic idea. I would swing by the Donut Hole in the north end, choose a few of Bill's favorites—jelly, glazed, and iced bowties—and surprise him with breakfast.

I parked in the driveway next to his gold BMW and let myself into the house. All was silent. No shower running or sounds of him traipsing around upstairs. Could he be asleep? At seven thirty?

"Bill?" I climbed the stairs and peeked into the master bedroom. The bed was unoccupied and already made. My fiancé was a neatnik. No clothes scattered around, no stray shoes out in the open.

He must have driven the squad car home last night.

I descended the stairs and contemplated the bag of doughnuts I'd left on the counter. Who was I kidding? Bill's favorite doughnuts were also mine. My stomach growled; my mouth watered thinking of biting into one of the glazed variety. Then I flashed on the wedding dresses I'd researched yesterday. I placed the bag in the refrigerator—they'd keep better that way—and made up my mind. I needed to get into a workout routine. Expend more calories before I seriously considered wedding garb.

I locked the front door and sat behind the wheel of my MC, contemplating my next move. I could begin with a simple walk in the park. The day was overcast, with gunmetal gray clouds scudding across the sky. They, as well as my weather app, hinted at rain later. For the moment, the temperature was in the midsixties, comfortable enough for taking a hike. I backed out of the driveway and cruised down Bennington Street to Anderson toward the east side of Etonville. Driving along the outskirts of town would save time and the temptation to stop at Coffee Heaven. I passed the former home of Thomas Eton, now the Eton B & B, and La Famiglia, and approached the old town cemetery where the Grim Reaper was found. I slowed down as I approached the entrance gate. The graveyard wasn't used anymore and only remained of interest to history buffs, folks who liked to wander through the markers and appreciate the solitude, and mischievous kids with nothing good on their minds. Especially on Halloween.

On a whim, I pulled to the side of the road. I could as easily tramp through the cemetery as the town park and get some fresh air in my lungs, burn a few pre-breakfast calories. I had no trouble spotting the scene of the would-be crime: yellow police tape outlined an area that included several headstones. I scanned the graveyard; there was no one in sight, and I walked the thirty yards or so until I stood next to the crime scene tape. Worn grave markers—many dating from the late 1700s—stood in parallel rows like ancient soldiers, some leaning, about ready to topple over. The grass around the headstones was neatly trimmed. I assumed the Etonville historical society engaged a landscaper to keep the place tidy and respectable. I'd only been here on two occasions. Once with a group from the Etonville Library, when I had just moved to town and wanted to learn about the history of my new home. And once by myself, on a bright summer day. I'd been overwhelmed by the town chatter and needed some solitary time with my favorite mystery author.

I'd almost forgotten about that afternoon…how pleasant and serene the cemetery was. Not a bit eerie or weird. Simply an attractive alternative to the library in providing peace and quiet.

I also knew what had attracted the teens—a spooky cemetery on Halloween night was like catnip to a group of rowdy kids. What had brought the Grim Reaper out here? In costume? A breeze kicked up, and I pulled my jacket tighter around my waist.

I walked the perimeter of the yellow tape, imagining the vantage points of the kids aiming beer bottles at the largest marker in the area. Large enough to conceal a body swathed in black. I stopped by a patch of ground that had been dug up. Probably where the deceased had lain. The caretaking crew would have some work to do when the tape was removed. Which could be any day now, because the death would soon be declared "natural." But what was natural about a man in a Halloween disguise dying from cardiac arrest in a cemetery? With a fake stake planted on him? Could he have been frightened to death?

I retraced my steps to the car. I glanced around again—no one in sight—and looked down as I unlocked my MC. On the edge of the road, half-buried in the damp grass, was a colorful object. I stooped and dug it out. An iridescent, pear-shaped pendant in a gold frame, its colors swirling shades of red, orange, green, and blue. Very unusual. Where had I seen this before? I pocketed the piece of jewelry. A rumbling from the south suggested that rain could come sooner rather than later. I ducked into my car. My cell pinged as a text materialized. Lola: *where are you? time for coffee?* I answered that I was in the cemetery and would meet her at the Windjammer ASAP.

* * * *

"There's a name for that, you know," said Lola, biting into a piece of rye toast.

I'd unlocked the Windjammer two hours before the official opening time and whipped up simple breakfasts for us—scrambled eggs, toast, and black coffee. The calorie counter's special. I intended to make every effort to bypass the caramel macchiatos and hot cinnamon buns at Coffee Heaven. At least until I found a dress I could live with.

"Taphophilia," Lola added triumphantly, finishing off her cup of coffee.

I retrieved the coffeepot. "What's that?"

"Having a passion for cemeteries, gravestone rubbings, studying the history of famous deaths, reading epitaphs, wandering among the markers..."

"Taphophilia? Are you kidding?"

"I had a great-uncle who was a taphophile."

"Who knew? I'm not a taph—"

"Supposedly, he spent every day in a cemetery once he retired," Lola said.

"Really?"

"Doing gravestone rubbings, taking photos. He was also rumored to be a somnambulist."

I refilled our cups. "Sleepwalker?"

"One night they found him sleepwalking in the cemetery."

"Seriously?" I said.

Lola crossed one jeans-clad leg over the other, flipping her blond hair. Not for the first time did I marvel at her youthfulness: no way her appearance suggested she had a daughter close to graduating college. "What were you doing there anyway?"

I hesitated. What *was* I doing there? "I stopped at Bill's to deliver some doughnuts, but he was gone. Probably an early beginning to his day. Then I decided to up my exercise game before I chose a wedding dress—"

"Great! Not that you need to get in shape," Lola backtracked. "You look terrific as you are, but focusing on the dress will get you oriented toward a wedding venue and we could visit some—"

"—and I was headed to the park." I blew by Lola's fixation on venues. "But passed the cemetery on the way and thought I might walk there."

"Nice idea," Lola said. "If a little creepy."

"I like the solitude. The crime scene's still taped out."

"Even though it's not a crime anymore?" she asked. Lola had read the article in this morning's *Standard,* declaring that the victim died of natural causes. She was relieved Carlos was off the hook. Which meant *Dracula* was off the hook, which meant the ELT box office was secure.

"He was peculiar last night," Lola said thoughtfully.

I brought myself back to the conversation. "Who?"

"Carlos."

"He's quirky. Has been from the beginning."

"Last night was a different kind of peculiar. Before the show, Penny and a few of the actors were in the green room talking about the murder, which, of course, everyone knew by then wasn't actually a murder, and Carlos walked in and demanded that they stop."

"Stop talking?"

"Yes. He said, 'Please stop talking about that man's death.' He was very upset."

"What set him off?"

"I don't know. When Penny tried to calm him down, he turned on his heel and marched off."

We sat silently, Lola wary of rehashing the confrontation she witnessed the night of the party. As if thinking about it might make Carlos guilty of something once again. I pulled the pendant out of my pocket. "Does this look familiar to you?"

Lola took the piece of jewelry and rubbed dirt off it. "It's beautiful. Where did you get it?"

"I found it at the cemetery. Is it familiar?"

She looked up. "Sorry."

I pocketed the piece and checked the clock on the wall. Time to get to work. I cleared our dishes, told Lola I'd catch up with her later, and settled myself in the pantry among the shelves of cans and packages and spices to take inventory.

I'd seen the pendant somewhere before.

9

"Hey, O'Dell. What's for lunch?" Penny slid onto a stool at the bar, decked out in her postal service uniform. "I'm in a hurry."

"Short lunch hour?" I asked. Penny often came by for a midday meal, usually taking her sweet time before sauntering back to work.

"Nah. Got some errands to run."

"I'd go with today's soup special. It's butternut squash. Yummy. And a cold sandwich. Tuna or chicken salad. Quick and easy. Also works with your Mediterranean diet."

Penny nudged her glasses a notch up her nose. "O'Dell, you ever been on the Mediterranean diet?"

"Me? No."

"Too much counting polymonosaturated fats. Too much green stuff. I'll have a cheeseburger and fries."

"You want the bun?" I asked in all seriousness.

She squinted at me. "You yanking my chain?"

I wrote up the order and sent it off to the kitchen. "Heard Carlos had a hissy fit last night."

Penny sighed. "Temperamental actors."

"According to Lola, he didn't want to hear any more talk about the murder."

"Which wasn't a murder anyway," she reminded me.

I had a brainstorm. "Penny, do you think Carlos Villarias is his stage name? You know, the name he uses in the theater? And his birth name is different?" I asked.

"No way, O'Dell. First of all, if Carlos used a sudohym—

"You mean pseudonym?"

"Whatever. I'd know it. Because I'm the—"

"—production manager. Right."

"And second of all, how do you come up with this stuff? You need a hobby." She glared at me. "Why do you think it's a stage name?"

I withdrew *Dracula Through the Ages* from under the bar, where I'd stashed it earlier, and pointed to the cover photo. "This guy played Dracula in a Spanish-language version in the 1930s. His name was Carlos Villarias. Maybe our Carlos liked that idea and changed his name for this production."

Penny stared at the picture, then at me. "O'Dell, people don't go around changing their names for no good reason. Unless they've got something to hide." Her mouth formed an O. "You think Carlos is on the lam?"

"Probably not."

Gillian brought Penny's lunch, and the ELT production manager attacked her sandwich. "I'll keep my eyes and ears on the ground," she muttered.

"Meanwhile, don't mention the name thing to anyone. Wouldn't want to trigger the gossip mill."

"Etonville is nuts about gossip." Penny dunked a French fry in ketchup and cocked her head in my direction. "Didya hear about Walter's ex? Might be taking him back to court," she hooted.

Geez.

* * * *

At three o'clock I settled into my booth for a break, butternut squash soup and inventory sheets in hand. If sliders were the specials for next week's menu, I needed to get Henry on board and up to speed. I opened my laptop and cruised through a handful of culinary websites that were my go-to research sources for Windjammer options. Everyone liked the basic, small burger sandwiches. No issue there. I wanted to shake up the menu, mix in some real foodie alternatives that might up the Windjammer ante. And compete with La Famiglia. I listed slider possibilities: pulled chicken or pork, barbecue brisket, turkey with slaw, cheesesteak, a BLT with avocado, nacho cheeseburgers, pimento cheeseburgers… My mouth watered. Customers would go wild for them.

"Hey."

I looked up into Pauli's cat-who-swallowed-the-canary face. "Hey yourself. Have a seat."

He plopped onto the bench across from me, swinging his backpack off his shoulder.

"Your text was intriguing," I said.

"Like yeah." His laptop was now on the table.

"You hungry?" Benny brought a soda to the table and I smiled my thanks.

"Nah. Having an early dinner with Janice."

"Things are going well in that department?"

"Going to her winter formal next month." He grinned shyly. "We're both exclusive now."

"In the old days, that was called going steady." I studied Pauli. He was a different guy from when I met him a few years ago: confident, more talkative...and in love.

"So you found something?" I asked. Last night, I was ready to cancel Pauli's digital forensics exploration. No need to dig into the newspaper page that Carlos had saved. But in the light of day, I convinced myself that there was no harm in poking around the obits. Besides, Penny's off-the-wall comment about the actor "being on the lam" had fired up my vivid imagination.

Pauli cracked his knuckles and cleared his throat. "So I subjected each data point..." He glanced up. "That's each person who died, to a series of searches in some new, kind of unusual databases. It digs into their backgrounds."

"Got it," I said.

"So the basics. Seventeen obits total. Ten were ancient. Like eighties and nineties." Pauli jammed a straw into his drink. "Four were old. Seventies."

The ages of my parents. Getting older every day. I needed to pay more attention to them...

"Then two people, a man and a woman in their forties. And the thirteen-year-old kid."

"The boating accident."

"Really young to die," Pauli said.

"Yeah."

He refocused. "Everybody died between July 14 and July 21." He flipped his laptop around to show me an Excel spreadsheet with each of the deceased's names listed vertically. Horizontally, he put columns of information that listed birth and death dates, cause of death, surviving relatives, education, military experience, careers, and social media used.

"This is great. A snapshot of the obits on a single day in July in a Chicago suburb." What, if anything, did it tell us?

"With this new algorithm, I deep-searched for cross-references in their backgrounds. Like, did they know each another. Were they related. Come from the same towns. Go to the same schools."

"I'm impressed," I said. "Sophisticated stuff."

He lit up, his face radiant, flushing slightly. "Yeah. So look."

Pauli pulled up a page of notes, cross-references among his "data points." For example, eleven of the seventeen were born and lived most of their lives in the greater Chicago area. Two of the others were distant cousins born in New York City who died on the same day. What were the odds of that? One of the seventeen was a PhD, though all, besides the thirteen-year-old, had completed high school, with half obtaining college degrees. Eight of the seventeen had military service in their backgrounds, with the oldest having lived through World War II. Pauli's program also tracked the geographical patterns of the deceased's lives. Where, in addition to the Chicago area, had they lived? Where had they traveled? Finally, I noticed that he'd been able to create mini family trees for everyone, tracking their immediate relations.

What did it all mean? How did any of it relate to Carlos? Again, I wondered what had made him save this particular listing of deaths. *If* that was what he'd done.

Benny waved to me from the bar. "Pauli, can you hold on? I'll be right back."

He slurped up the rest of his drink.

"What's up?" I asked my bartender.

"Enrico said Henry's having a garlic meltdown. Doesn't want to add garlic to the steamed clams or vegetables." He tossed a bar towel over one shoulder. "Want to handle this?"

We had one more theme night to get through. For the most part, the garlic-infused dishes had gone over well. Yet customers and chef were at a tipping point. "Maybe we can compromise."

By the time I'd convinced Henry to keep the fall vegetables—broccoli, cauliflower, and brussels sprouts—steamed in olive oil and garlic, in exchange for eliminating the garlic in the steamed clams, Pauli had packed up his laptop.

"Gotta bounce. Meeting Janice."

"This is super work, Pauli. Can you send me all of this information?"

"Easy peasy. Already done." He slung his backpack onto his shoulder. "So like...these obits...are they important?"

Pauli knew me well enough by now that if I asked him to do some digital forensics exploration, it wasn't because I was twiddling my thumbs. "I'm not sure. I need to take another look at everything you found."

"Sweet. Let me know if you need more digging."

I smiled. "Thanks. You crushed it."

He ambled off. I checked my inbox and confirmed that Pauli's research had arrived. Though I was dying to drill down on the data, I knew it would have to wait until later tonight. The kitchen door swung halfway open. Enrico poked out his head apologetically. "Dodie?" he called to me.

I looked up from my computer screen.

"Henry needs you in the kitchen."

"What now?" I asked.

The smell of something burning had Enrico scrambling back into the galley. I followed slowly, my mind in a whirl. Who was Carlos Villarias? And Bella, for that matter…

* * * *

Dinner was uneventful, the steamed clams a winner, patrons content, though pleased that next week would bring a variety of sliders.

"I love those little sandwiches," said Mildred. "Don't you, Vernon?"

Vernon laid his napkin on the table and pushed back his chair. It was time for him to head to the theater and get into makeup. "I don't care what size they are, long as there's no garlic in them."

Oops…

"I think they're dainty. A few bites in each one. You can hold a slider in your hand easily," Mildred said.

"I don't need dainty burgers. What's the point? Might as well eat one big one as three small ones." Vernon grabbed his coat, kissed Mildred on the cheek, and saluted.

He had a point. "Have a good show," I said.

Vernon waggled two fingers and exited the restaurant.

The dinner service slowed after eight o'clock, anyone attending *Dracula* having already retreated to the theater. I was tempted to run next door to catch the stake-stabbing end of the play again. I had an itch about Carlos that needed scratching….

"Whew. Glad we're done with the garlic thing," said Benny.

I laughed. "Wasn't my best idea."

"Nope. The menus were terrific. People in Etonville get bored easily. Short concentration spans."

"Except for the Banger sisters. They loved the garlic," I said.

"As long as they could wear it around their necks," Benny added.

We both cackled.

"I guess all the vampire talk was much ado about nothing. First weekend of the play is finished, no bloodsucking in town, no bodies coming back to life." Benny stopped himself. "Only tragedy was the stranger who keeled over in the cemetery." He flipped a bar towel under the sink. "Poor guy. I read he had a bad heart."

"Yes."

"Made me get my cholesterol tested yesterday."

I patted Benny on the back. "I think you've got a long life ahead of you."

"That's what Bella Villarias told me on Halloween night."

"Did she?" Bella…I flashed on her sitting in the makeshift stall, reading palms. In her gypsy costume. I touched the pendant in my pocket that I'd found in the cemetery. Now I remembered where I'd seen it. Bella had worn it Halloween night! She had fingered the piece gently before hiding it away in the folds of her shawl. My pulse jumped.

"You okay? Look like you've seen a ghost. Or a vampire," Benny teased.

"I'm fine." What was Bella doing in the Etonville cemetery?

* * * *

I stole into the theater and slowly opened the door to the house, standing behind the last row of seats. The audience was riveted, all eyes focused on Carlos as Dracula throttled Renfield. Accusing the young man of betrayal while Renfield pleaded for mercy, begging Dracula to spare his life. Had the scene played this realistic before? I could have sworn something passed between the two actors that was more "life" than "art." Van Helsing, Seward, and Harker entered in a rush, forcing Dracula to release Renfield, literally, and confront his three nemeses. Wow! How did Renfield, aka Gabriel Quincey, tolerate that kind of manhandling during every performance? I watched the scene play out, and a moment before Dracula disappears down the floor trap, a movement to my left caused me to look up. In a corner of the house, a man shifted as he took off his coat. How long had he been standing there? I stared at him. It was the stranger from the Windjammer. The man from the Midwest—Chicago?—who sat at the bar and ordered lunch yesterday. Still in town. And killing an evening at a local community theater. Good for him. He was fully engaged with the show.

I turned back to the stage in time for the blackout. In the dark, I could see a pinpoint of light. Mr. Chicago was texting on his cell. Oops…bad theater etiquette. Streaks of light dotted the stage as the vampire hunters swung flashlights back and forth, seeking Dracula's coffin. I couldn't help but notice that the stranger stayed on his cell. It must be important, or else he wasn't completely engaged.

Events moved swiftly to the climax of the drama, with Romeo as Harker, raising the hammer and striking a forceful blow to the stake. The audience gasped softly, as it did every time I saw the ending. When Van Helsing intoned his "dust to dust" line, sprinkling Dracula's ashes over his dead body, the silence in the house was deafening. Except for a slight chuckle to my left. Mr. Chicago was nodding and texting. He found the last scene amusing?

Applause and cheering erupted as lights rose on the cast. They took their bows in stride by now, accustomed to the accolades. I clapped along with everyone else and failed to notice that Mr. Chicago was on the move. He eased along the back wall and when he was next to me, paused to say "'Scuse me," and slipped past.

"Did you enjoy the show?" I asked, stopping him.

He looked back, frowning, his focus clearing. "Restaurant. Jersey Shore."

"Good memory."

He grunted.

"Nice of you to spend the evening at our theater."

"Nothing else to do." He shrugged.

"Good show, yes?"

"If you like this sort of thing. Pretty silly when you get right down to it. Vampires."

Tell me what you really think!

"You know them? The actors?" He jerked a thumb in the direction of the stage.

"Sure. Most of them are veterans. A few are new to the Etonville Little Theatre."

He turned his back to me and took a step away.

"Like Carlos Villarias," I said on impulse.

His head swiveled to face me. "Who?"

"Dracula?"

Mr. Chicago signaled his disinterest and walked away.

I weighed the man's responses, wondering who he was and why he'd chosen to watch the show tonight.

"Dodie!" Lola joined me. "Did you see Act One tonight?"

"I got here in time to see Carlos strangling Gabriel. You know, that looked very real. Do you suppose—?"

"Then you didn't see Walter's breakdown." Lola twisted a strand of blond hair. "I think he's carrying this resigning thing a bit too far."

"Breakdown?"

"He made such a dramatic entrance, changing his blocking, pacing around the stage like he was pouting and demanding that he get his way!"

"Wow. How'd the other actors react?"

"They were all good. Kind of went with it. Like, you know, Walter's in one of his snits." She bit her lip.

"Sorry."

"I had to go backstage during intermission to give him a talking to, the importance of professionalism, being a role model, tarot cards as a parlor game..."

"Could be a chardonnay night? We're keeping the bar open later so the actors can celebrate after the performance now that they've got a few days off."

"Just give me a straw."

I laughed despite Lola's theatrical angst and told her I'd see her next door. I marched into the lobby, my mind on prepping the bar for the onslaught of actors. On the other side of the door, Bella stood alone, separated from the hubbub, seeming lost in thought. I paused. "Hi."

She glanced up, worry lines replaced with a graceful smile. "Dodie. Hello."

"Another great performance. Carlos was fantastic. As usual."

"Hmm," she agreed.

"Well...I'm trying to beat the cast to the bar. Are you joining us?"

She frowned slightly, the worry lines returning. "I'm not sure what Carlos wants to do. It's been a long day. And night."

What did she do all day that made the hours lengthy? "Some jobs take it out of you."

She nodded, apparently agreeing without divulging anything about her daily life.

"That's a beautiful string of pearls," I said.

Bella touched her necklace briefly. "Thank you."

"I meant to ask you about this." I withdrew the pendant from my pocket. "I think I saw you wearing it Halloween night? While you read my palm." I opened my hand to reveal the unusual piece, its colors striking despite the fine layer of dirt on its surface.

Expressions flitted across Bella's face—surprise, bewilderment, then a shutting down of any further reactions. She took the iridescent ornament from me. "It's gorgeous. Do you know what it is?"

"I've never seen anything like it before."

"Ammolite. It's gem-grade, the shell made of marine mollusks that died out with the dinosaurs. Same material as pearl. Ammolite can only be found in the sediment in the Rocky Mountains. It always features intense colors." She held up the pendant to allow more light to flood through the material. The green and blue and orange shimmered. "Where did you say you found it?"

My instincts were on high alert. Best to keep the cemetery part to myself. "One of the cleanup crew came across it the day after Halloween and passed it on to me." Was that too lame? If it was, Bella didn't let on.

She returned the jewelry. "Ammolite is very valuable." Her eyes wandered away to the far side of the lobby, where the actors had appeared and were being greeted by a general explosion of goodwill. "If you'll excuse me..."

Without waiting for any response, Bella reached Carlos, extracting him from some members of his adoring public, and latched onto his arm before shifting toward Gabriel and whispering something in his ear. Perhaps congratulations on a fine performance. It was well-deserved.

I couldn't afford to watch any more of the post-show festivity. I needed to get to the Windjammer. My fingers encircled the pendant. Bella hadn't denied that it was hers or mentioned how she might have misplaced it. Yet, she seemed to know about the origin and history of the material. Something didn't add up.

10

Romeo turned up the volume on his iPod, and music blared through the compact speakers stationed on the bar. What had begun as an after-the-play drink had morphed into an impromptu bash. The only customers left in the Windjammer at this hour were from the ELT, the last of the non-*Dracula* crowd having taken flight half an hour ago. With the next performance of the show several days away, the cast and crew had decided to let their hair down.

"Think the booze will hold out?" Benny grinned and uncorked another bottle of white wine.

"Talk about letting off steam."

Abby and Romeo began to dance around the tables along with Pauli and Janice. Gabriel and Mildred joined them as Edna tried her darnedest to pry Walter out of a booth, where he was morosely skimming through emails and pretending that Edna was not tugging on his arm. She shrugged in defeat and waltzed past me. "Walter's a 10-7. Out of service."

"10-4. Anything new on the investigation?" I didn't add that Bill had been MIA since early that morning.

"Other than the identification? Can you believe it? The mob in Etonville?" She clamped a hand over her mouth. Too late. "Mum's the word."

Though I already had this intel from Bill, I pretended surprise and raised a hand. "Scout's honor." Word would be all over Etonville any day now.

"The tox screen will close the case," she said knowingly.

"Right." I assumed Edna figured that once I knew about the identity of the dead man, being privy to the standard tests screening blood and other bodily fluids was no big deal. I played dumb.

"A tox screen should do it," I said.

"Copy that."

Gabriel twirled a giggling Mildred. "Edna, I have a question…"

"Yeah?" She stuffed a few loose hairs into her bun.

"Does Gabriel get along with the rest of the cast? I mean, he's an out-of-towner, and you know how Etonville can be." I was thinking of the night I saw the argument between him and Carlos.

She followed my gaze. Gabriel and Mildred were now dragging Vernon, protesting mightily, to his feet, Gabriel shouting into Vernon's ear and Mildred mouthing *don't be a stick-in-the-mud.*

"Gabe? Why, he's like one of us. Like a member of the family. The theater family. Walter treats him like the son he never had," she said confidentially.

Cute. That's all Walter needed. A son…

At the other end of the bar, Lola, who was deep in a discussion with Penny, raised her head and lifted her empty glass. I caught Benny's eye, picked up the fresh glass of wine, and maneuvered my way through the wiggling crowd to the stool next to Lola. "Here you go. Penny?"

"No, thanks, O'Dell. I'm driving."

As if the rest of the company wasn't? "They're glad to have a few days off."

"They need a break. This show has been intense," Lola moaned.

We pivoted our bodies to face Walter across the dining room, still holed up in the booth.

Penny stood, rising to her full five-foot-two inches. "He can't resign. He can't! Walter *is* the ELT, and without him there's no theater family. We're all for one and none for all. I know he has a tough hoe to row, but we can't let him get an insult *and* an injury and air the laundry that's the dirtiest. He's got to climb into a saddle even if it is the wrong tree that's barking. He can't choose to be a beggar!" She grabbed Benny's apron. "Give me a dry martini, two olives."

Lola and I gaped at Penny, who strutted her way to Walter's side. She nudged him over and settled onto the seat. Not sure who I felt sorrier for: Penny or Walter.

"I need some sleep," said Lola. She drained her wineglass and gave me a hug.

I watched her exit, then nodded at Benny, who blinked the dining-room lights to signal last call. Within half an hour, the music died, the cast and crew departed, and Benny and I cleaned up the remains of the gathering. I swept and mopped as he scrubbed the bar and emptied the sink.

"Glad we're closed tomorrow," Benny said, zipping his coat.

"Hooray for Sunday! I hated to end the fun, but it's late."

"I'll say. Twelve thirty. Want me to lock up?" he asked.

"No, you go. I'm good."

Benny said good night and took off. I scanned the dining room, all set for the lunch service on Monday. I flicked off the lights, turned the key in the lock, and moved down the sidewalk past the theater to my MC, parked half a block away. Deep in my bag, my cell phone buzzed. I dug it out and saw a text from Bill. I'd messaged him almost two hours earlier, saying I'd be home shortly. That was before the dancing started...*where are you?* he asked; *on my way. long story*, I responded. Had Bill been waiting up for me? I'd expected to find him snoring away. Without warning, my exhaustion took a hike. I slammed the car door shut and switched on the ignition.

As I backed out of my parking space, happy to see that the Etonville meter maids had cut me a break, I noticed a light flicker in my rearview mirror. Someone else was pulling onto Main Street. The road had been deserted when I left the Windjammer. Normally at this time of the night, I would execute an illegal U-turn and cruise to Bill's place. Though it was getting later by the minute, and I had assured Bill I would be home soon, my curiosity was on overdrive. Adrenaline kicked in.

I drove at a snail's pace one block, waiting until the light turned yellow at the intersection. I turned right in a hurry and, switching off my headlights, ducked into the alley that ran behind a bookstore, the theater, and the Windjammer. My MC was small enough that I could squeeze into a space adjacent to the dumpster at the ELT loading dock. I cut the engine and cracked the window, scooting down in my seat as I heard the hum of an engine close by. I imagined that the car had stalked me through the intersection and now sat on Amber Street, trying to decide its next move. I peeked through the rear window. All I could see around the corner of the dumpster was a dark shape. We waited in this standoff for a couple of minutes that seemed like forever. Then the other car blinked first and coasted down Amber.

I realized I'd been holding my breath and exhaled, relieved to be rid of whoever was tailing me. If that was what this was about. I put the MC in reverse and crunched gravel as I drove slowly out of the alley. To my left lay Main Street and the path to Bill's; to my right, the mystery car. I turned right. I had no idea if I'd catch up with the automobile, but my instincts would not give up. I kept the headlights off, picked up speed, passing the Valley Savings Bank and Lacey's Market, and headed for State Route 53, which provided access to highways leading east to New York City and west to more rural parts of New Jersey.

Out of the blackness of the night, two red dots appeared up ahead. Did they belong to my stalker? I had no definite way of knowing, but no harm no foul. The worst that could happen? I'd tail a car that was headed home and I'd be even later arriving at Bill's. I pressed the accelerator, inching closer to the red lights. One thing for sure: I felt more secure being the follower than the one followed.

About a hundred yards from the entrance to Rt. 53, the car abruptly veered to the left onto the access road, driving faster now. So, he, or she, wasn't heading onto the highway. The speedometer inched up as I tried to keep pace. We flew down the street, circling back to town, zigzagging through neighborhoods. Was my pursuer trying to shake me? I knew Etonville like the back of my hand, but so did the other driver, apparently. Within minutes, we'd crisscrossed streets that took us to the outskirts of town. There was nothing much out here. La Famiglia, the cemetery, an open field... My heart thunked. The old Hanratty place. And Carlos.

The car shot forward at the next turn, but I'd lost my enthusiasm for the cat-and-mouse game that was being played out. I gave up and limped back to Bill's. I parked in the driveway, keeping as quiet as possible as I let myself into the house. I didn't want to wake him if he'd fallen asleep. And I didn't want to have to explain what I'd been doing for the last forty-five minutes. I needn't have worried. I slipped under the covers, rolling over to face him in bed, his spiky hair a tangle, his stubble pronounced. Bill snored away. Unfortunately, now I was hyperalert, my eyes wide open. Sleep was not on my radar.

* * * *

"You look like you haven't been to bed at all," Bill said, scooping up the last of his oatmeal.

"Sunday, you know? I thought we could sleep in." I yawned. It was only eight o'clock. I loved having the freedom of a day off.

"I waited up last night as long as I could."

"Sorry," I said, my head planted on top of my fist. "The *Dracula* gang would have partied all night if we'd let them." No need to mention my car episode.

"Couldn't throw them out, huh?" Bill laughed. At least his mouth laughed. His eyes were another matter, taking on the cloudy expression I'd seen before when something was gnawing at him.

"What's up?" I asked.

"More coffee?" Bill rose and retrieved the coffeepot.

I pushed my mug toward him. "Can't talk about it?"

He filled my cup. "It's this Daryl Wolf business."

"The pro."

"The coroner came back with the results of the tox screen...."

Which, according to Edna, would put an end to the investigation.

"Nothing really unusual. No drugs, blood alcohol level normal. Heart medications in the bloodstream. Some stuff for blood pressure and arrhythmia. The autopsy confirmed what the coroner had already established in the preliminary findings. Heart disease."

Which everyone in town knew by now. "So good news, right?"

"I don't know. Something feels off."

"Oho! Now *you're* operating on instincts," I teased. Instincts were usually my bailiwick; not exactly in Bill's wheelhouse.

He ignored my gentle jab. "I've requested some specialized tests from the medical examiner. I'd like him to dig a little deeper."

Just when the death appeared to be wrapped up. I was almost afraid to ask. "Now what?"

"We've got calls into Chicago to see what they know about his associates. Why he might have been in New Jersey. Any way you slice it, knowing about his background only makes things more complicated." Bill sipped his coffee in silence. "I have to get moving."

"On Sunday?" I'd had other things in mind.

"Emergency meeting of the police chiefs commission in Trenton. State budget issues."

"You were going to make chili for the Giants game." As a former NFL running back, this was Bill's default activity for a Sunday afternoon.

"I am. The meeting's at ten o'clock. I'll be home by one. The game isn't on until four, so there's plenty of time for the chili to simmer." He kissed me on the cheek, grabbed his coat and keys, and was out the door before I could protest any further.

I had the day to squander until Bill got back from his meeting, so I weighed my options: I could go back to bed; I could clean my bungalow and catch up with laundry; or... I'd left my laptop in my bag. Pauli had sent me notes about his cross-referencing of the obits from the *Daily Herald*. I opened my computer and clicked on his email. The obvious information—who had lived in Chicago, who had what kind of an education or had done a stint in the military—hadn't been particularly enlightening. What did pique my curiosity was his ability to track the deceaseds' geographical patterns outside Chicago—where else they had lived or traveled to—and the family trees. Maybe there was a scrap of information buried in the notes that would provide a hint to Carlos's interest in the Chicago area newspaper. One more deep dive into Pauli's research might satisfy my craving to sort out his background. Unless this sheet of newspaper meant nothing at all.

I poured my last cup of caffeine for the day and settled onto Bill's comfy plush sofa with my laptop. I opened Pauli's notes and took a leisurely stroll through his findings about these seventeen souls. I bypassed causes of death, survivors, careers, and lingered for a moment on social media. Pauli had discovered that fourteen of the seventeen had either Facebook pages or Twitter accounts. Or both. No Instagram accounts. Six of the accounts were inactive, according to his notes. Which left five people on Facebook and three on Twitter. I skimmed the FB accounts of the five and found nothing that seemed unusual: all were grandparents and posted pictures and videos of children and grandchildren. I smiled, thinking of my own parents' posts of their life in Naples, Florida: pictures taken on the golf course, at my mother's book club, at their favorite restaurant, and in their kitchen as my father attempted to make Bill's gourmet meat loaf.

Next, I studied geographical travel patterns. Interestingly enough, two thirds of the deceased had hardly ever left the Midwest. Their travel had consisted of trips to Ohio, Michigan, Missouri, and the deep South. Two had gone to Europe and one had traveled to China. That left five. One had been a missionary and spent most of her life abroad in Africa; one had a career in international banking in London; two had never left Illinois.

The travel profile of the last person, Barbara Mercer, was the most intriguing. Eighty when she passed away last summer, besides California and the Northwest, she'd been to Australia, Eastern Europe, Asia, and …New Jersey. Not a typical East Coast vacation to New York City or Washington, DC. But New Jersey? Possibly meant nothing, nevertheless my snooping reflexes were triggered. Her visits to the Garden State occurred every other month for a year to an address in Lennox. I'd never heard of the town.

I Googled the name, and up popped a listing of the tiniest towns in the state. Lennox was one of the tiniest. Population 1,150. Situated about forty-five minutes west of Etonville, near the Delaware Water Gap, the town had a general store and a church. I'd thought Etonville was small. Its profile described the municipality as working class, most residents living in apartment complexes and condo units. No full-time police force and one employee in the Department of Public Works. What had attracted Barbara Mercer to Lennox?

I skipped from geographical tracking to family trees. The genealogy wasn't extensive, Pauli's research revealing three generations at most for the obits. I browsed Barbara's relatives. Her husband had passed away, but she had two children—Olivia and Ethan. Olivia lived in California and had never married. Ethan and his wife had raised a son—Mason—in the Chicago area. No record of their current address. None of the Mercers were on Facebook.

I sank into the sofa cushions and closed my eyes. Contemplating. It was a tenuous link between Barbara Mercer's obituary in the *Daily Herald* and Carlos Villarias's wastepaper basket that hid the newspaper. Did Barbara and Carlos have anything in common? Had I forced Pauli to spin his wheels looking for...what?

My musings were giving me a headache. I should have spent the morning cleaning my house. Then I felt a tingle on the back of my neck...something felt strange. No sign of Ethan or Olivia Mercer *or* the Villariases on social media. What did that mean? On a whim, I scanned the White Pages on my laptop for "Mercer" in Lennox and found no addresses.

My cell pinged. Lola: *what are you up to? did you check those wedding venues? hate to bug you.* Poor Lola. As a wedding planner, she had her work cut out for her. I had an inspiration. I texted back: *how about a road trip?*

I had one more text to send. I asked Pauli if his algorithm and deep geographical searching could generate a specific address in a specific town for one of the obits. Two minutes later I had it: 782 Lancer Avenue, Lennox, New Jersey.

* * * *

"Usually we take my Lexus," Lola said.

"I was in the mood to drive." Lola was ecstatic that I had begun the wedding planning process. Except that I hadn't.

"So this place is in a town called...?"

"Lennox."

"I've never heard of it," she said.

"Me neither. The restaurant description was fantastic. Old world charm, dates from the late seventeen hundreds. Family run." Had I said enough? I felt a smidgeon of guilt involving Lola in my Lennox road trip. However, she provided cover for the afternoon in case Bill got curious. I would fill her in later. For now, I simply wanted to drive by the address Pauli had located and see if anyone by the name of Mercer lived there.

"Do they host many weddings?" Lola asked, skeptical.

"I think so."

"Have you and Bill decided how big you intend to go?"

Bill and I hadn't had an in-depth talk about our nuptials since our engagement at the Jersey Shore in early September. We'd been busy, or tired, or distracted…were we avoiding the topic? "We're still discussing it."

Lola folded her hands and laid them in her lap. "Dodie?"

My GPS Genie said we were fifteen minutes away.

"Are you getting cold feet? About the wedding?" she asked.

"Me? No!"

"Because it feels as though you are…dragging your heels."

"Bill and I are good to go. Things are hectic. And now with the death of that man in the cemetery…"

"The Grim Reaper? There's a rumor swirling that the guy was a hitman from out of town."

Already the word was out? "Lola, that's supposed to be confidential information. Of course, Edna spilled the beans last night…"

Lola mimed zipping her lips. "What would he be doing in Etonville?"

"Good question."

The highway through rural New Jersey guided us past small towns and farms. The day was sunny and pleasant, so I didn't mind the ride.

Lola was another matter. "Are we lost?"

I pointed to a roadside sign that read "Lennox, Population 915." It had lost a few residents since the last census. "Almost there."

"How much business could they do, stuck way out here?" Lola asked.

I took the exit from the highway and drove a mile to the center of town—the general store, the church, and blocks of apartment buildings. I scanned the GPS until I found the street I was looking for: Lancer Avenue. I made a left turn.

"Dodie? What is going on? Where are we?" Lola asked, a little impatient.

I should have been honest with her from the beginning. "I have to confess. There's no wedding venue out here."

"Uh-huh." She crossed her arms.

"I had to make this trip. I can explain it to you after…"

"After what?"

I pulled up in front of 782 Lancer. It was a two-story, yellow-brick apartment building that had seen better days. The exterior was scruffy, the windows dirty. No resources had been devoted to the landscaping of the front of the building, which consisted of a patch of dry grass and a leafless tree. Barbara Mercer traveled from Chicago to this address. Why? An elderly woman exited the front door and stared at us as we stared at her.

I vaulted out of the car. "I'll be right back," I said to Lola.

"Oh no, you don't."

Before I could object, she'd joined me on the sidewalk that ran past the apartments. "Excuse me," I said to the woman who was sweeping the entranceway. "Do you live here?" Possibly the super?

She paused and grasped the edges of an oversize gray sweater, as if for protection. "Why?" she asked wearily, her face a mass of wrinkles from her forehead to her chin.

"I had distant relatives who lived here some time back..."

Lola did a double take, her jaw dropping.

"...and I was wondering if they were still in the area," I finished.

The old woman regarded me suspiciously. "Relatives? And you don't know if they're here?" She continued to sweep.

I ignored the implications of the question and played my ace in the hole. "Mercer. Their name is Mercer."

The woman stopped and looked up. "Nobody lived here by that name."

"Are you sure?" I was disappointed

"I ought to know. I've been the super here for forty years."

I whipped out my cell and showed the super a photo of Carlos and Bella I'd taken on opening night. "Do you recognize him?"

"You mean Johnson. Mark Johnson."

Johnson!?

Lola looked at me as if I'd gone bonkers.

"Crazy persons, if you ask me." She pulled dead leaves off her broom.

"Crazy? Why do you say that?"

"Him creeping around at all hours, her with those nutty outfits. Claimed she could read fortunes. Reminded me of vampires. Or zombies. One of those two."

Lola stiffened beside me.

"Did they live here long?" I asked.

"You from the police too?"

Too? "No..."

"Everybody's interested in the Johnsons lately."

"So I guess they had a lot of visitors?"

"Only the old lady came regularly. Until last summer."

My pulse shot up; my mouth went dry. "Barbara," I said.

"That's right. I think she was his mother."

"She passed away last summer."

"About the time they skipped out," the old woman said.

"Did the...Johnsons leave a forwarding address when they left?" I asked.

"Address?" she hooted. "They didn't even leave the last month's rent."

"Must have been in a hurry," I said.

Was Mark Johnson related to Barbara Mercer…and eventually became Carlos Villarias? "Thank you. Have a good day." Lola appeared stuck to the ground. I tugged on her arm to get her to move.

"What happened to the son?" the super asked, leaning on her broom.

"The son?"

"Nice kid. Normal. Too bad he had wacky parents."

11

I practically dragged Lola to my MC. Once we'd slammed the doors and I eased away from the curb, the old woman watching us make our escape, I said, "I can explain." On the ride back to Etonville, I filled Lola in on the digital forensics work Pauli had done with the obituaries.

"I can't believe it. Pauli got all this information on those seventeen, then you happened to find that one of them…Barbara Mercer…made regular trips to New Jersey. We come here on a whim… and now the 'Johnsons' might be…?"

"The Villariases?" I said.

"And Barbara Mercer was Carlos's mother." Lola was bewildered. "What does it all mean?"

When you put it that way… "Not a clue," I admitted. "It started with that sheet of newspaper we found in his bedroom, and then it kind of mushroomed from there. Especially when I found out that he had the same name as that Spanish actor who played Dracula." I apologized for deceiving Lola about the purpose of our trip to Lennox.

"When I asked you to look into Carlos's background, I was hoping for an uncomplicated explanation for his meeting with the guy in the Grim Reaper costume. Who turned out to be a hitman from out-of-town." She tugged on a strand of hair. "But this…"

"I know you're worried about Carlos and the show. The cause of death of the mob guy has been made public…" I had no intention of sharing Bill's concerns about the tox screen and his intention to delve into Daryl Wolf's blood tests. "…so there's no need to worry about Carlos's meeting with him Halloween night." I fervently hoped that was true.

"It's so bizarre. Carlos with the same name as the Spanish actor. Carlos and his supposed mother, Barbara Mercer." She paused. "And *his* real name is…"

"Mark Johnson."

"But you said the obit listed her son as Ethan Mercer," Lola persisted.

"Maybe she had two sons?"

"With different names?" Lola asked.

We rode in silence until we'd arrived at the periphery of Etonville, the Lennox experience having disturbed both of us.

"What happened to Mark Johnson's son," Lola said.

"You mean Carlos's son."

"Why would Carlos and Bella change their names?" she asked. "If they did."

That was the sixty-four-thousand-dollar question.

Lola turned in her seat to face me. "What do you plan to do with what you discovered?"

"Nothing. It's not a crime to change your name. There might be a ton of good reasons the Johnsons became the Villariases." I wondered about that.

"Can we keep this between us for now?" Lola asked.

I took Lola home, then stopped at the Shop N Go to pick up salad fixings for Bill's chili dinner and cruised the streets of Etonville. Pauli's digging had resolved one issue—the probable significance of the *Daily Herald*—but had raised another huge one. The true identity of the Johnson/Villarias family. It had no bearing on Bill's investigation of the victim, so there was no harm in honoring Lola's request. But the accumulation of "data points," as Pauli would have said, was unsettling. The name change, the Chicago connections, the Grim Reaper on Halloween… Never mind, I told myself. I needed to refocus my energy on wedding plans and leave the Villariases to work out their past and present.

* * * *

By the time I got back to Bill's place, he was already settled into his favorite recliner, beer and chips in hand. The delicious aroma of chili bubbling in a pot wafted out of the kitchen.

"Hey, it's kickoff time. Where've you been?" he asked.

I planted a kiss on the top of his head. "Chili smells delicious. Lola and I did a little reconnaissance—"

"Don't tell me. A wedding venue, right?" He chuckled. "You two have had your heads together on this."

Wow. That was easy. I was prepared to tap dance around my disappearance this afternoon. Lola and I *did* have our heads together today…just not about our nuptials. "How'd you guess?"

I perched on the arm of his easy chair. "We should decide how big we want this thing to be. Fifty people? A hundred? A hundred and fifty?"

Bill hit the release arm on the recliner and popped forward. "A hundred and fifty? We're not inviting the entire town of Etonville, are we?"

"Nope. And I'm good with a small affair." I ruffled the spikes of his brush cut, now standing at attention. "If it wasn't for my mother, I'd be into a trip to Vegas. And we need a date."

Bill peeked over my shoulder. The game was underway. The New York Giants had taken the field against one of their archrivals, the Philadelphia Eagles. Bill was a convert to Giants fandom, having lived in Philly for many years. New Jersey was his home turf now. I'd lost his attention until halftime.

"Let's decide this week? And make Lola's life easier."

"You got it," he said and smiled at me. "C'mon, get a drink and join me."

I had an unexpected thought. "Bill, what happened with the stake?"

"That was interference," he cried to the television. "Did you see that? The Philadelphia guy had his arms all over the wide receiver. Where's the refs?" He looked at me. "What did you say?"

"I asked about the stake."

"What stake?" He groaned as the Giants missed a crucial third down completion.

"The one at the crime scene. Any fingerprints? Any idea how it got there? Why someone planted it on the victim?"

A car commercial came on, and Bill muted the game. "Why are you asking? Not getting the investigative itch, are you?"

"I'm curious, that's all."

Bill pulled me onto his lap and wagged a finger in my face. "I recognize that look. So…here's what you want to know. One, no fingerprints. Two, don't know why it was at the crime scene. Other than it fit a Halloween vampire theme. Three, it's a standard metal spike. Could have been bought at any hardware store. The kind used on construction sites or landscaping. I don't need to tell you to—"

"Keep it quiet," I said.

"Especially from Etonville's ears…and from your teenage high-tech authority," he added with a knowing look.

Pauli. Based on my escapade down the shore in September, Bill knew what my digital forensics expert was capable of.

"Anyway, I'm heading to Chicago tomorrow." Bill munched on a potato chip.

"Chicago?"

"I'm meeting with an organized crime unit of the Chicago Police to get a handle on this Daryl Wolf. Probably an alias. Lots of fake IDs out there now."

Tell me about it. "Can't you talk over the phone or email?" I asked.

"Possibly, but Chicago has a model for police chief mentorship and I've been tasked with observing their process. I'll be back by Wednesday or Thursday. Hopefully with more information on Wolf or Smith or Johnson. Whatever his actual name is. Anyway, whatever I find will help me unlock the victim's last hours. Where he went, who he might have met. Who saw him. What he was doing in Etonville." Bill unmuted the game. "Can you check the chili?"

"Yep." I headed to the kitchen.

I could hear Bill yelling at the television again. I busied myself at the center island with the salad. What if Bill's trip to Chicago revealed something about Etonville's star actor, and Mark-Johnson-aka-Carlos-Villarias might be about to have his identity changed from a "data point" to a "person of interest?" Bill would be away three days. Three days until *Dracula* hit the stage again. I'd intended to stay out of the investigation business and here I was, back in the middle of the mess. Why? One, I wanted to ease Lola's fears about Carlos. Two, my curiosity about the actor had gotten the better of me. Three, I had to admit I might have something to prove. If, as Lola suggested, my identity might change as Bill's wife and I was about to wrap up my investigative career, I was going out in style.

In the future? Whatever life threw at me, I was ducking.

* * * *

It took all of my considerable performance skills to spend the rest of the afternoon and evening pretending to share Bill's joy as the Giants beat the Eagles by five points. I complimented his culinary talents and praised his taste in expensive red wine, all the while I, distracted, fielded a mental flurry of questions. Why did Carlos change his name? Did it have anything to do with Daryl Wolf? What if Bella knew more than she was saying? Who else had been interrogating the super in Lennox about the Villariases?

Bill was on his way to Newark Airport by seven a.m. I'd awakened to see him off and there was no way my head was hitting the pillow again. I made a pot of coffee, grabbed a legal pad and pen, and wrote. Even though

Daryl Wolf's death was not a homicide, there were too many loose ends. Maybe we should have a conversation with Carlos....

I texted Lola, who was in the middle of a mani/pedi at Snippets, and offered to pick her up for a late breakfast. She agreed and added a string of emojis that featured a thumbs-up, a smiley face with one eye winking, and a cup of coffee. Next, I took a long, hot shower, shampooed my hair, and rummaged through my half of Bill's closet for clean jeans—laundry had to be a priority later—and pulled on a T-shirt and hoodie. The weather in New Jersey in the fall could be anywhere from the low forties to the high seventies. Today it was a mild seventy-one.

I studied my hair in the bathroom mirror. It was curlier and bouncier than before, and I was relieved that Etonville had ceased to be fascinated by my appearance. Still, I had doubts about my wedding hairdo. By the time Bill and I settled on a date, my hair could be down to my shoulders again. Or gray, for that matter.

Benny had agreed to open the restaurant, and I assured him I'd be in by noon. I climbed into my MC and cranked the engine. As it purred, I reviewed my plan of action. Lola and I were going to visit the old Hanratty place to speak with Carlos. Tell him that he was seen with the Grim Reaper, arguing; that we discovered Carlos Villarias was a twentieth-century Spanish actor; that Bill and the Chicago Police were decoding the last hours of the victim. If he had anything to confess about his relationship with Daryl Wolf, at least one of those disclosures should rattle Carlos's seemingly agitation-proof cage. No need to mention Barbara Mercer or Mark Johnson or Lennox. Yet.

I hoped Lola was on board.

I eased my MC to the curb on Anderson, where I could see into Snippets salon. Carol was on the telephone, handling appointments, while her assistant manager trimmed Penny's bangs. Edna was having her hair styled. The Banger sisters waited patiently in the reception area, riffling through magazines. It was a cross section of Etonville's gossip machine. I had to be careful what I said.

I pushed open the door to the loud whirring of hair dryers and the chatter of customers.

"Dodie!" called the Bangers.

I waved. "Morning, ladies."

"We're thinking of getting our hair cut like yours, dontcha know," said one of them.

I stopped in my tracks. What did their beaming faces mean?

"We like your curly, short bob."

It wasn't that short.

"Or else we're thinking of going Jane Fonda." The other sister flipped the magazine to show me a layout of the actress in a variety of hairstyles. "A layered look or a sassy shag with curvy side bangs."

"It's kind of sexy, don't you think?" They looked at me expectantly.

I studied their gray permanents. "Sure. Go for it."

Edna motioned to me. "Heard the chief is off to Chicago. Code N," she whispered, loud enough for Penny to hear her.

Code N. A newsworthy event. "A quick trip," I said casually. How did she find out so fast? I only learned about his travel last night.

"That's a euthanasia for 'police biz,'" Penny snickered.

"A…euphemism?"

"Whatever. That dead hitman is going to put Etonville on the criminal map, O'Dell."

Geez. I hurried to the back of the shop. "Hi, Lola. Almost ready?" I said, my widened eyes signaling that we had to make our escape.

"Got my last coat of lacquer." She studied her nails. "I'm not sure about this color. Afternoon Delight."

"It looks great." I cocked my head toward the door.

"Hi, Dodie," said Carol. "Any more thought about your wedding hairdo? I can lend you some magazines with ideas if you want."

"Thanks. I'll get back to you." I returned to Lola. "We'd better get going. I need to stop at the Shop N Go for floor wax."

Lola stared at me.

"*Johnson* and *Johnson*?" I said meaningfully.

I could see the light bulb flicker on. "Oh yes!" She withdrew bills from her wallet.

"Dodie, are you all right?" asked Carol. "You look a little tired lately. Planning a marriage ceremony and reception can be exhausting."

It would be if I was doing that. The other ladies agreed. I thanked Carol and hugged her, and gently escorted Lola out the door. "We've got about two hours."

"That should be enough time for break—"

"Here." I handed Lola a cup of coffee. "Breakfast."

She removed the lid. "Aren't we going to Coffee Heaven?"

"Nope. I brought you a jelly doughnut from Bill's fridge. Might be a little stale."

Lola regarded the coffee and days'-old doughnut. "What are you not telling me? We're not taking another road trip to some unknown part of New Jersey, are we?"

Been there, done that yesterday. I explained my plan of action and promised Lola a free lunch at the Windjammer if all went well. If it didn't...I shuddered.

"Are you sure this is the right thing to do? Asking Carlos to explain his past and his actions on Halloween night?"

"It's either this or wait till Bill shows up and questions him about Daryl Wolf. Someone is going to find out that the Johnsons are the Villariases. Unless they have already."

Lola removed the lid of the container.

"Remember, if all else fails, I say 'Johnson and Johnson'—"

Lola giggled. "That was so smart, Dodie. You are one clever detective." She patted my arm and sipped her lukewarm coffee.

I smiled my appreciation. "—and we see his reaction."

I drove alertly to the other end of Etonville, slowing as I approached the turnoff to Carlos's rented home. Even on a sunny day like this, the Hanratty house loomed large and eerie, ghostlike, as if it held secrets that had never been divulged. Curtains fluttered at upstairs windows. There was a dark green Subaru parked in the gravel driveway, and the front door appeared to be open. I came to a halt and switched off the engine.

Lola had finished the jelly doughnut and was now downing the rest of her coffee. She smoothed her hair and adjusted her denim jacket. As usual, she looked like she belonged on the cover of *Cosmopolitan*, her leggings topped by a light knit sweater, her blond hair in a casual ponytail.

"Ready?" I asked.

Lola slipped on her designer sunglasses, completing her model-like ensemble. We walked across the porch and approached the front door. Which was, indeed, open. Only the screen door blocked our entrance. From within, we heard classical music playing and smelled the rich aromas of herbs and spices.

"He must be home. The car's here, the door's open, and something smells in the kitchen." I peered through the screen and rapped on the doorjamb. "Hello?"

No answer. I knocked again, more firmly, and we waited.

"I guess they must be busy. We should go," said Lola, and turned away.

I plucked at her arm. "Don't you want to see an end to the Carlos mystery?"

"If it means going back in there, then no," whispered Lola.

"Come on. No guts, no glory."

She got a lungful of air and repeated: "No guts, no glory."

I tapped on the door a third time, then gently twisted the handle. It wasn't locked. I opened it a smidge and surveyed the entrance hall. No activity in the parlor or dining room. Only the music originating from somewhere else. The kitchen? "Carlos?" I called out, taking one step into the house.

"Where are you going? This is trespassing!" Lola said.

"I'm not breaking in. The door's open," I rationalized. A windy gust caused the bare branches of the trees in the front yard to clack against each other.

"I'm staying on the porch," Lola said.

I poked my head in farther. A plastic bag on the chair where I'd left my purse the night of the cast party had "Halloween Costumes Super Store" written in gold lettering across the front of it. I recognized the name of the shop, which was located in Creston. "Keep a lookout and let me know if anyone approaches—"

"Can I help you?"

Startled, my hand flew into the air and slapped the open screen door as Lola jerked upright, backing into the doorjamb. We collided. Bella, a basket in one arm, a shears in the other, stood in the front yard and regarded us warily. "Can I help you?" she repeated.

My face flushed crimson, embarrassed. Why hadn't I anticipated Bella being in the house? Lola lowered her eyes, equally mortified.

"Hello," I said as offhandedly as I could manage. "We were looking for Carlos."

Bella laid the shears on the pile of greens in the basket. Her curly hair fell freely, her eyes open and inquisitive. An apron covered her T-shirt and jeans. "I see," she said quietly. The two words spoke volumes. "Would you like to come in?"

"No! We need to be going—" Lola stuttered.

"Yes, thanks," I said.

Bella brushed past me, indicating that we should follow her. "Have a seat." She pointed to the parlor. "I need to take these herbs to the kitchen. The last of the season."

Lola and I sat uneasily on the worn velvet upholstery of the chairs.

"Now what?" she hissed.

I shrugged. I had to think of something.

By the time Bella returned a few minutes later with a tray holding a steaming teapot, cups, and a plate of cookies, Lola and I had calmed down and I had gotten my bearings.

"I don't think I thanked you formally for hosting the cast on opening night," Lola said serenely, accepting a cup of tea and an oatmeal cookie.

"It was our pleasure." Bella eyed Lola and me over the rim of her cup.

"This is delicious," I said.

"Rose hips. From my herb garden. I keep a pot brewing all day long."

"That must be the pleasant smell coming from your kitchen," I said.

"That and a few other herbs for my business," Bella said.

"You grow herbs for…?" I asked.

Bella's face expanded in a smile. "I make lotions, shampoo, healing salves, tinctures."

"That's ambitious. You sell online?"

"Certain products. I have a list of customers." She sipped her tea. "Herbal beauty products and healing remedies are very popular now."

"I'm hooked on chamomile," Lola said. "In the morning I need my caffeine, but there's nothing like a cup of herb tea for a pick-me-up midafternoon."

A momentary pause, while we all nodded agreement and swallowed the hot liquid. We chatted for a few minutes about the weather in New Jersey this time of the year, no hint about anywhere else they'd lived, about *Dracula* and how well it was going. About Bella's tarot card reading and Walter's over-the-top reaction. We laughed, and once again there was a momentary pause.

"You said you wanted to speak with Carlos?" Bella asked.

"If it's not inconvenient." I glanced around the parlor as if he might appear out of thin air.

"I'm sorry, but he's at work."

"Work?" Lola asked, surprised.

"Of course. He left early this morning." Bella looked at me, then at Lola. It was a Monday morning after all, she seemed to be saying.

"Of course," I echoed her. "Carlos never did say where he was employed."

Bella frowned. "It's a new job. At an office in Clifton. Management."

"That's nice," Lola said.

"What did you want to see him about?" Bella asked.

I hesitated to ask her the same questions I might ask Carlos about the Villariases' name change and Carlos's mother and Lennox.

"We are considering changing the time of the brush-up rehearsal Wednesday," said Lola in a rush.

I could have kissed her for coming to our rescue. "Earlier," I said.

"Later," Lola chimed in simultaneously.

We were dangerously close to becoming the Keystone Kops. I set my cup on Bella's tray and rose. "We've kept you away from your garden long enough. Thanks for the tea and cookies."

Lola followed my lead. "Please tell Carlos that Penny will be emailing the revised schedule." She paused. "Oh, I forgot. Carlos doesn't have email…"

That was news to me.

"Penny will call him."

"I'll let him know," Bella said, ushering us to the door.

"Thanks again." Lola's relief was palpable.

"By the way, has Carlos ever played Dracula before? In another theater?" I asked.

Bella's warm smile dissolved into a thin, tight line. "Why do you ask?"

Lola's features displayed the same question. "He plays the role so… naturally. It fits like a glove," I said.

"Carlos had a lot of acting experience in college. Now, if you'll excuse me…"

We moved down the front steps and into my car, Bella watching our progress. As the engine of my MC came to life, she closed the door. And locked it, I imagined.

I backed out of the driveway, Lola shivering. "Talk about uncomfortable. And what was that about Carlos playing Dracula before?"

"Trying to pry some backstory out of Bella. Where he went to college. Where he acted before. He *is* a natural when it comes to Dracula." Lola herself had said the same.

"Yes. He's very realistic."

Lola never said acting was "natural," only "realistic." It was a Walter thing. Naturalism involved mumbling and stumbling around the stage, according to the director. Realism required the actors to incorporate the details of life with precision and planning. I didn't see much difference. Any way you sliced it, Carlos inhabited the role of the vampire as if he was born to it. "No email? Who doesn't have email these days?" I mused. "It's almost like he doesn't have a past, doesn't want anyone to trace his whereabouts."

"Except for his mother," Lola reminded me. "Surprised he has a job in management."

I knew "management" was the generic term for positions in many different kinds of businesses. I'd had a degree in management and I ended up in restaurants. Bella might have been deliberately stonewalling us. "He's gotta work somewhere. Somebody has to pay the rent on the Hanratty place." I had a sudden brainstorm. "Rent!" I shouted.

"What about it?"

"Maybe the rental agent knows something about the Villariases. I remember Walter saying someone in his office found it for them," I said.

"I suppose I could ask Walter who the agent was."

"Perfect!"

I dropped Lola off at Snippets to retrieve her car. I had about an hour before the lunch rush and another stop to make. I was determined to flush out the Villariases/Johnsons....

12

I headed for the highway that ran between Etonville and its next-door neighbor, Creston, a larger city with a variety of neighborhoods from upscale to blue collar. I had gotten to know its downtown shops—a café for out-of-Etonville getaways, a jewelry store that played a part in one of my early investigative adventures—as well as its soup kitchen, where the Windjammer had donated food. Older, run-down areas with small, single-family homes and faded apartment buildings were mere blocks from multimillion-dollar houses. Creston included it all. I also knew that Halloween Costumes Super Store, the location printed on the bag in the foyer of the Villariases', boasted hundreds of outfits to buy or rent, suitable for any dress-up occasion.

I left Route 53 and drove to Gardiner Avenue, two streets over from the central shopping area. I found a space a few doors from the costume business and marched briskly to my destination. I had no time to kill.

I entered the store, nearly empty this morning, and scanned the aisles of costumes. Racks of movie-inspired clothing, zombies, vampires, ghosts, and traditional pirates, cowboys, and nurses outfits. There were also heaps of clothing scattered around the place. No one was at the checkout counter, so I ambled down an aisle until I found a young man with a clipboard, taking inventory. He counted sailor uniforms, gave the costumes a once-over, made notes, and moved on to the next items.

"Excuse me."

The clerk looked up and swept one hand over his half-shaved head, then tugged on a large gold hoop in his ear.

"I'm looking for a Phantom of the Opera costume."

He studied me skeptically. "Halloween's over, lady."

"Right. But I have an event…a theater thing, and I need to go as a famous stage character. I figured the Phantom was a great idea."

He frowned. "What about a princess from *Frozen* or a witch in *Wicked*?"

"I'm kind of set on *Phantom*," I answered.

The young man gestured for me to join him at the checkout counter. He tapped keys on his computer, tugged on his earring some more. "We had four full costumes. One bought, three rented, all of 'em out."

I knew where one of them was located. "What a shame. My good friend rented one from here and we were going to wear them together." Did that even make sense?

"Two Phantoms?" he asked, confused.

"Maybe you remember him? Carlos Villarias? Tall, dark-haired, handsome. In fact, he's playing Dracula at the Etonville Little Theatre right now. Maybe you've heard about it?"

"Nah. Not into theater." He typed on his computer again. "Carlos Villarias. Phantom costume. Still outstanding."

"Did Carlos pick it up or did you ship it to his office?"

"Picked it up."

"I thought maybe he gave you his work address…he has a lot of stuff delivered there."

"No work address. Do you want to see other costumes?" he asked, getting impatient.

"I'll wander around."

The clerk pointed off to the left. "Show costumes are in aisle three." He stepped from behind the counter, then stopped. "You said Etonville?"

"Yes."

"If you know the guy who rented the Grim Reaper costume, tell 'im I need it back this week."

Yikes. That train had left the station, seeing as it was locked up in an evidence box in Bill's office. It wasn't my place to remind the clerk of that fact.

"We've got a *Walking Dead* party we're doing and I have to pull together the wardrobe."

My instincts kicked in. "What's his name?"

He consulted his computer. "Mr. Smith."

Guess the kid had no reason to be suspicious about the name. "Did he give you an address?" I asked.

He shrugged. "Said Etonville and threw a coupla hundreds on the counter."

"He bought the costume?"

"Nah. Said he didn't want it beyond Halloween. Said he'd bring it back. Go figure." The guy tapped a few computer keys. "We don't usually do cash transactions, but he was okay. Said he didn't have a credit card. Left me a huge tip." The clerk finally smiled.

My mind calculated as the kid kept explaining how the store was responsible for some high-end shindig next weekend and was attempting to collect the inventory they'd rented out for Halloween.

"Do you remember what day Mr. Smith rented the Grim Reaper costume?" I asked casually.

He once again consulted his laptop. "Halloween morning. Had it in stock because somebody returned it. Changed their mind."

So Daryl Wolf got his costume at the last minute. What did that mean? He didn't know about the Halloween party until…when? "Think I'll pass on the costume for today," I said.

He tried to convince me to look into the witch from *Wicked*, but I waved him off and left.

I dashed back to the Windjammer in time to open the door to a crush of Etonville folks. You'd have thought it was coupon Monday, the way customers scrambled for their favorite booths, bumping the competition aside to claim their territory, settling arguments by pointing to other tables.

"What is going on?" I asked Benny.

"Beats me," he said. "Could be the change in the weather? Everybody out and about because the mercury hit seventy?" He chuckled.

Or maybe it was the slider specials that had lured patrons out of their homes. Today's menu featured the seven-layer, Tex-Mex version. On top of the mini burger, Henry had piled refried beans, guacamole, tomatoes, spicy sour cream, salsa, and a smattering of olives. Only a couple of inches wide, the slider was stacked tall.

I spent the next two hours gliding around the dining room, seating customers, riding herd on the servers, and accumulating compliments for Henry's mini sandwiches.

"Henry's outdone himself with these." Right.

"It's so high I can't get my mouth open wide enough." Yep.

"Like a burger and a taco all in one." Kind of.

"And no garlic." Oops!

"I'll sit at the counter," said a voice behind me.

Gillian handed a menu to Mr. Chicago. He plopped onto a bar stool, asked what the special of the day was, and made the same decision as most everyone else in the restaurant. The Tex-Mex slider.

"Still in town," I said, leaning against the bar.

"Kind of like Etonville. Nice people."

"True. No place to get back to?" I asked, trying for total nonchalance.

Mr. Chicago tore the paper off a straw and slowly took a sip of his soda. Equally nonchalant. "Not at the moment. So...what else do you do besides manage this place?"

"I help out next door sometimes. At the theater."

"The theater. Yeah."

Two could play this game. "What do you do? Besides eat at this place?"

Mr. Chicago laughed, appraised me like an expensive piece of jewelry in a glass case. "I'm in regional sales. Plumbing," he said.

"Plenty of that action in North Jersey. Enjoy the rest of your stay. I hear Chicago can get slammed with icy rain and sleet this time of year." I was sure I'd read that somewhere. Which made me think about Bill...I wondered how he was doing and what he had unearthed, if anything.

Mr. Chicago stirred the ice in his drink. "Can it?" As if he wasn't aware of the Windy City's weather patterns. As if he didn't live there. Hmmm...

Benny delivered his lunch, and he fell on it like a starving man, wiping the salsa and sour cream from his mouth.

My cell pinged. I peeked at the text. Bill: *how are u? brrr cold here. productive trip. C u in two days. miss u.* Bill's simple, heartfelt message made me think of my great-aunt Maureen's assessment of romance: *Love is a lot like a backache...it doesn't show up on X-rays, but you know it's there.* I missed Bill too. I needed to tell him that more often.

"You do?" asked Mr. Chicago.

"Sorry?" I said, noticing Benny was bobbing and nodding. "What?"

"I told him what an excellent detective you are," said Benny. "Solving murders in Etonville."

I didn't mind the town nattering on about my investigative instincts...that was a given. Total strangers? I hated to throw shade on Benny's supportive accolades, but I had to put a plug in this leaky boat of a chatfest.

"My fiancé's the police chief. Sometimes I give him a few opinions."

"Now you're selling yourself short," Benny said.

Mr. Chicago scrutinized each of us. "Must be nice having a *private* private eye in the family." He kept one eye on the contents of his slider and the other one on me.

"Benny, could you check with Henry about the soup special?" I asked.

"Sure thing." He sauntered off.

Before I could walk away, Mr. Chicago said, "Any hunches about that guy who died in the cemetery? Read about it in your paper."

"Heart attack, from what I read," I said politely and moved away. Something about the man set my teeth on edge. What was he doing, meandering around Etonville and its environs anyway? Managing the sale of plumbing supplies in the Northeast?

I pushed the stranger out of my mind. I had bigger things on my agenda. I texted Lola: *grim reaper info.*

Benny brought me a seltzer. "Hope I didn't blow your cover with that detective talk," he said apologetically.

"No problem."

"I think you're too modest. Nobody else in this town could have done what you did these last years." He walked away.

Except the Etonville Police Department, right?

Lola rang my cell, and I brought her up-to-date on my visit to the Halloween Super Store.

"So the victim rented the costume Halloween morning. Last minute," she said. "And paid cash."

"Bill said the hood was draped around Daryl Wolf…"

"Creepy name. *Sounds* like a hitman. I saw this show on TV last week—"

"Lola! Focus!"

"Okay." The line went silent.

"The victim wasn't actually wearing the hood. Maybe somebody put it around him…" I said. "Like the kids?"

"Why would they do that?"

"That's the puzzle. A Grim Reaper and a vampire stake. What was someone trying to say? After the guy dies from a heart attack?"

"Dodie, I think we might be in over our heads with this one," Lola lamented. "I know I asked you to dig into Carlos's background. Now I'm sorry I did. It's all too complicated. Maybe the Villariases will leave town after the run of *Dracula*, like they did in Lennox."

Possibly. What would send them on the run again?

Before Lola ended the call, we agreed to meet later tonight at my bungalow to catch up and have a drink. She had a meeting with Walter and Penny earlier in the evening to hash out budget issues, now that the box office was flush. She clicked off, and I hauled myself out of my booth. After I checked on inventory with Henry, I planned to take a walk during my break. To the Municipal Building. I needed some fresh air and a tête-à-tête with Edna.

* * * *

Main Street's sidewalk was noticeably busier than usual. It had to be the weather. I sidestepped a sniffing dog and a meter maid writing out tickets. Good thing I'd parked in a spot around the corner. I inhaled and exhaled deeply, letting the scents of late fall fill my lungs and clear my head. The walk to the Municipal Building was only twenty minutes. Already I felt invigorated as I pulled open the front door.

Edna was speaking into her headset, punching buttons on a console. She stuffed a pencil into her bun. "Hey, Dodie! The Tex-Mex sliders were dee-licious. Ralph brought back a sackful. It's a shame the chief had to miss them."

"He'll be back in time for Thursday's special," I said.

"What is it?" Edna whispered.

"Wait and see!" I laughed.

Her console lit up, and she raised one finger. "Etonville Police...Ralph? Where are you? Suki's been on the warpath. You were supposed to handle the 11-84 after that 11-66."

It was difficult for me to imagine the serenely om Suki on any kind of a "warpath." However, I knew Ralph's antics often drove Bill to distraction. Suki was human after all.

Edna lowered her voice. "You better get your daughter's birthday present on your own time." Edna listened. "I know. I know...and you'd better get back here by five. 10-4." She ripped off her headset.

"I was wondering about something," I said. "During the Halloween party, while you were choosing prize winners..."

"We had a ball! The mayor's wife and myself. It wasn't an easy task, what with all the bea-utiful costumes," she said.

"Right. Do you remember seeing a Grim Reaper wandering around?"

Edna frowned. "You mean like the vic?"

"I guess so. It was Halloween, and practically the whole town was there. Maybe the victim had come too. I mean, why else have a costume?" I hoped my logic made sense to Edna.

"Hmm...can't speak for the mayor's wife, but I can't say as I saw any Grim Reapers." She crossed her arms and leaned forward into the dispatch window. "What are you thinking? Does the chief have you working under the radar on something?" she asked eagerly.

Edna, like everyone else in Etonville, now thought of me as a part-time detective.

"No!" I said quickly. That's all I needed...Edna spreading the word that I was "under the radar." Bill would not be pleased. "Got to get back to the Windjammer."

Edna stuck her head out the window. "I did see a *Star Wars* Yoda and a Mad Hatter from *Alice in Wonderland*."

"I saw them too." I waved goodbye.

"You know who we didn't see?" Edna added.

I turned around. "Who?"

"The chief!" She winked at me.

"Copy that," I said.

* * * *

I sat on a bench in front of the theater. I had half an hour to kill before I had to return to work. I rested my head on the seat back and closed my eyes. I knew I'd seen a Grim Reaper at the punch bowl on Halloween night, and that same Reaper receiving ocular death rays from Carlos. I visualized the party, creating a mental snapshot of the church basement…the bobbing for apples, the candy corn count, the pumpkin carving, the palm reading.

Snapshot! That was it. My head popped up, my eyes flew open. Pauli had come to the party dressed as a newspaper reporter. He'd spent the night interviewing people and taking photos for an article in the *Etonville Standard*. Maybe he had captured a Grim Reaper… I texted him immediately: *could I see your pictures from Halloween night?*

* * * *

I had arranged with Lola to meet at ten o'clock. By then, she'd be finished with Walter and I would have closed down the dining room. Henry intended to work late in the kitchen and offered to lock up tonight. The sliders had been such a lunchtime success—attracting a huge crowd—that Etonville had chosen to stay home for dinner. Gillian sat at the bar texting, Benny worked on a *New York Times* crossword puzzle, and I reviewed inventory sheets for the meat and seafood for the coming week. At nine, Gillian cleaned tables, Benny prepped the bar for tomorrow, and I decided we'd close the dining room at nine thirty because there hadn't been a customer in the restaurant in over an hour.

"You might as well head home," said Benny.

"I'll close for you tomorrow."

"It's a deal. Going to the princess's recital tomorrow night."

Benny described his daughter's dance performance as a flurry of pastel tutus with kids streaking on and off the stage. He loved it.

I pulled my jacket off the wall hook and walked out the door. The mild day had morphed into a chilly evening, the sky a blanket of clear black dotted with bits of light. Hopefully, it would be another sunny day tomorrow. I turned up my collar. Might as well hang out in the theater. There was always a chance Lola and Walter would blast through the budget decisions quickly and my BFF and I could enjoy some girlfriend time earlier than planned.

The street was deserted. I had the same unnerving sensation I'd experienced on other nights after closing the Windjammer during the last week. As if I was being watched. I shivered and walked quickly to the theater. In the lobby, a strip of light was visible under Walter's closed office door—the location of the meeting. Not wanting to bother them, I slipped into the theater. The house was dark, the stage lit by Penny's "ghost light" and a large scoop. Behind the night lights, much of the furniture from *Dracula* had been stacked and arranged against the back wall of the set. Prominent was the coffin used in Act Three.

I wandered down a side aisle and sat in the front row. The trick door in the bookcase was open. Possibly JC was tinkering with the mechanism. The trick chair was turned on its side. Ditto there as well. The walls of the set had been covered with flocked paper and a series of framed period photographs. Once again I marveled at JC's artistic talent; he had created a beautiful backdrop against which the actors of the ELT could present *Dracula.*

As I stared at the scenery, I mused on the stake-stabbing scene. Penny had said there was a dummy version of Dracula in the coffin so that when Romeo, as Lucy's love interest, Harker, pounded the stake, it was being driven into a hole in a sandbox. As if drawn by a magnet, I got up from my seat and crept to the lip of the stage. The scoop light caused my shadow to loom large behind me. This might be my only opportunity to examine the inside of the coffin.

I'd always been fascinated by caskets. Not because I had a death wish. When I was about seven years old, I had accompanied my great-aunt Maureen to the viewing of a dear friend of hers. My parents were at work and I was spending the day with my aunt, so her visit to the funeral home meant I was going too. She asked if I had a problem with this, and being the adventurous type—who'd never seen a dead body before—I saw it as a lark and told her I was in.

I can remember vividly the face of the elderly woman in the casket. Her gray hair, her face made up with bright-red lipstick. I was anxious as I approached the coffin with my aunt, my hand inserted firmly in hers.

She had told me I could sit in the back and wait for her, but I wanted to see what all the fuss was about. I'd considered how they'd gotten the woman tucked into the box, which was lined with shiny white satin. I didn't bother to ask my aunt; I simply let my imagination go to work. In fact, I visualized myself in the casket.

Now I stood by the open box that JC had constructed, its outline suggesting the shape of a body. The dummy and sandbox had been removed for safekeeping; the missing stake incident had probably forced the set crew to lock up props. JC had lined the coffin with black duvetyne, a cotton material with a velveteen nap on one side, which I'd seen him use to build curtains for the wings.

I climbed into the coffin and sat down, as if I was in a grotesque bathtub, my arms dangling over the sides. There wasn't much room in here. Romeo's aim when striking the stake had to be good to avoid hitting the wooden sides of the box.

I couldn't resist…I scooted down until I was lying flat on the bottom, staring overhead at the lighting fixtures on battens in the space above the stage. So this is what it felt like lying in a casket. Of course, by the time someone *did* lie in a casket they wouldn't be able to feel—

Instantaneously, the scoop light went dark. Before I could react, the lid of the coffin closed with a sharp snap, the latch clicking into place. I was stunned. Was someone playing a joke on me? I pushed on the cover of the coffin. It didn't budge. The ghost light went out.

"Hey! Knock it off," I yelled, slamming my hand on the bottom side of the lid. I knew the latch on the coffin had given JC trouble. Lola had revealed that the day before the dress rehearsal. Because no one was in the coffin during the play, the latch was basically a minor issue. Until now.

I continued to thump the lid of the coffin. Might I run out of oxygen? I forced myself to calm down. There had to be a simple solution. The seam between the body of the casket and the lid was not a tight fit. Some air could squeeze in there. And surely someone would do a final check of the stage before leaving the theater, right? Walter or Penny would have to notice that the scoop light was burned out—or unplugged. I wasn't normally claustrophobic. But the lack of air and the tight fit sent me into panic mode.

My heartbeat accelerating, I panted as I banged the lid of the coffin, bruising my hand, shouting until my throat ached. "Help!" I screamed.

Minutes later, light leaked in around the seams of the coffin's lid.

"Who's there?" Penny demanded.

"Get me out of here! The lid is locked!"

A jangling of the latch was followed by a creak as the lid was raised and overhead light poured onto the box.

"O'Dell? Funny place to take a nap," Penny said.

"Penny, help her out," insisted Lola. "Are you okay? We thought we heard noises from the stage, and I've been so on edge ever since this show went into production that—"

"I'm fine." I sat up, my pulse throbbing, my ego taking a beating.

Walter stood apart, glaring at me. "No one is supposed to be playing around with the props and furniture."

"I wasn't playing around exactly."

Penny stuck out a hand. "C'mon, O'Dell. Time to go home. *Not* Dracula's home. Your *own* home." She guffawed at her joke.

Geez. I would hear about this for a while. I stepped over the side of the casket. The whole experience had left me shaky and apprehensive, my legs wobbly, my voice raspy.

"Someone shut the coffin. I couldn't raise the lid. Something must be wrong with the latch," I said, borderline hysterical. "It must be broken."

Walter crossed his arms. "There's nothing wrong with the latch. Except for the fact that you shouldn't be messing with it."

"What about the scoop light?" I asked.

"I think the lamp burned out," said Lola.

Too convenient.

"Next time, try the couch in the green room," Penny chortled.

"Next time, stay off the stage!" Walter added icily.

"Come on, Dodie." Lola put an arm around me. "You need a drink."

I nodded numbly, trembling. Yes, a drink would help. What would really help, however, would be discovering who had tracked me into the theater, turned off the lights, and locked the lid of the coffin.

13

"It must have been frightening," Lola said sympathetically.

"It was." I refilled our glasses with a chilled chardonnay and cut a handful of cheese slices. I nibbled on a cracker.

"What *were* you doing in the coffin? Did it have something to do with Carlos?"

Did it? "I was waiting for your meeting to end and I wandered into the theater and it took me back to the first time I saw a dead body in a casket. I don't know…I wondered what it would be like."

"I'm glad we heard you yelling."

Something wasn't right. "Someone else was in the theater. Besides you and Penny and Walter."

"Who?" Lola asked, alarmed.

"I don't know. I do know that latch was locked. I don't think the person was trying to…" I gulped. I couldn't say it. "I think someone was trying to scare me."

"I'll have JC take a look at it," Lola said hastily.

"Odds were you would hear me and come running."

"Which we did." Lola touched my arm.

I took a big drink of wine. "Maybe someone wanted to threaten me somehow?"

"I don't know who that would be." Lola's brow wrinkled.

Someone who'd noticed I'd been asking questions about Carlos?

"I'm happy we came into the theater when we did."

I smiled my thanks. I'd left my cell in my bag, which was sitting in the first row of seats.

"With Bill out of town, would you like to stay with me tonight?" Lola offered.

"I'm okay by myself." My cell buzzed. It was Pauli: *sent pix. more work?* He certainly was eager.

"Pauli sent me photos from the Halloween party."

"I know he took one of me." Lola swished her hair off one shoulder. "Didn't make it into the *Standard*'s article."

"I heard the town is posting some in the Municipal Building. You know, 'Etonville's inaugural Halloween bash,'" I said.

Lola yawned. "Sorry to desert you. I have to write up budget notes before I go to sleep and I have an early yoga class."

I hugged Lola goodbye and tested the locks on the doors and windows. I wasn't totally freaked about tonight's coffin scene. I knew I was right about the latch; I also had the strong sense that whoever had tailed me into the theater was not out to do me in. Just warn me off.

I climbed into bed, missing Bill terribly and counting the hours until he'd be back in Etonville, and tugged the comforter up to my chin. Then I opened my laptop and scrolled through Pauli's photographs. He had done a good job documenting the event: Lola and Walter, looking royal; Edna and the mayor's wife, skulking around the perimeter of the church basement; Bella in her gypsy getup, holding the Banger sisters' hands. I squinted at the picture. I couldn't see Bella's pendant, but I was certain it was there. There was a group of pirates and sailors and nurses all mugging for the camera. And that Yoda from *Star Wars*. He even had one of me—Wonder Woman!

I was two thirds through the album when I noticed something. Pauli had snapped Robin Hood, aka Vernon, dunking for an apple for the second time with Maid Marian, aka Mildred, cheering him on. In the background, half cut out of the frame, was a somewhat blurry figure in black with half a skull mask visible. The Grim Reaper. Yes! I wasn't imagining that I'd seen him. The time stamp read 10:15. What had Lola said? She went to her car to change her shoes at eleven and then proceeded to witness the argument between Carlos and a Grim Reaper. In between, Daryl Wolf and Carlos had had the "moment" of recognition in the church basement.

* * * *

There was a black hood over my head. I was suffocating. Then a hideous skull mask appeared in front of my face. I screamed for help. I woke with a jolt, my heart banging in my chest, the nightmare a mash-up of the coffin and the Grim Reaper.

The alarm read 5:30. Too early to rise. I hunkered down under the covers. It was over an hour until sunrise, the middle of the night as far as I was concerned. I shut my eyes and did one of Walter's breathing exercises to shift my system into low gear. He tended to foist them on his actors during rehearsal warm-ups. The cast usually rolled their eyes. I would never reveal the fact that I had begun to find his rehearsal drills useful. Especially after his snarky comments to me last night. He could have been a little sympathetic to my having been locked inside the coffin. I *was* locked in, right? Was I doubting my own experience?

Despite the calming workout, my mind began to leapfrog over one thought after another—the Grim Reaper, Carlos, Bella, Barbara Mercer, Mark Johnson, Daryl Wolf…the list of dodgy names was growing day by day.

Staying in bed was pointless. I took a quick shower, dressed in leggings and a hoodie, and strode to my car. A brisk walk in the park and a visit to Coffee Heaven would settle my soul. Or else rev me up. Either way, I needed to move into the day.

The sun was rising as I crawled down Main Street, then turned right on Amber past the Municipal Building, wondering what progress was being made in the Daryl Wolf investigation, if any, with Bill out of town. When I reached the edge of Etonville, something clicked for me. Bella had said Carlos left the house "early" for work that morning. What did early mean? It was almost seven a.m. If he commuted to Clifton, as she'd revealed, he might be leaving home in the next hour.

If I intended to see what Carlos was up to, I had to be cautious. His rental house stood out in the open; anyone who came near the place would be seen. I swung down the closest side street, almost a hundred yards from the Hanratty place, did a U-turn, and pulled to the curb. I could just make out the front door of the house. It was seven fifteen. I slid down in my seat until I was barely visible. And I waited. Across the street, a woman left her home, hurried into an SUV, and drove off. I waited some more. Behind me, the door of a house opened and a couple I recognized from the Windjammer walked to their car parked in the driveway, laughing and talking animatedly. In no great hurry and apparently in a good mood despite the fact that they were probably heading to work.

My eyes felt heavy and drifted shut. I blinked hard a few times and opened the window. I needed oxygen. The cool air was like a shot of adrenaline. More alert now, I evaluated my mission. Doubtless a fool's errand, to quote my mother. What did I expect to discover? Even if I managed to follow Carlos somewhere—presumably to his job—what would that tell me? And what if Bella was fabricating a story to protect her husband for some reason?

Carlos exited the Hanratty house. He wore a suit coat, an open shirt—no tie—and carried a briefcase. Carlos looked like many other ordinary folks leaving home for a day at the office. Except that he was not an ordinary individual. He hesitated on the front porch, as if he was waiting for someone. Then he turned back to the house and leaned into the open door. Saying goodbye to Bella?

Seconds passed, and Carlos shifted his briefcase from one hand to the other. Then a black sedan zoomed down the lane leading to Carlos's home. This was someone not afraid to signal his or her presence. The car swerved onto the Hanratty property, gravel flying out from under its tires, and came to an abrupt stop in front of the actor, who had descended the steps. Without missing a beat, Carlos jumped into the front seat. I switched on the ignition, and my MC crept forward. In a flash, Carlos's chauffeur backed up and made a sweeping turn off the driveway and onto the lane. I eased down in my seat again as the two of them sped past me. They were in a hurry. I darted onto the lane after them.

The black car turned onto Fairfield Street, a stone's throw from my home. We were headed back into the town center. But instead of turning down Main or another road in Etonville, the car shot down Fairfield, past the entrance to my street and Lacey's Market, and raced onto the access road leading to the state route. Where were the two of them going? I kept my distance while craning my neck to see around anyone who got between us. Once they darted onto the highway, I was in safer territory. Morning commuters had clogged the route, most likely either traveling to Route 3 and Manhattan or to Bernridge—home of the actor playing Renfield, the teenagers guilty of pitching beer bottles in the cemetery, and the Chinese takeout menu I saw on Carlos's desk. My money, for some reason, was on Bernridge.

The black car swerved in and out of traffic, cutting off other motorists. I leaned forward, squinting at the sun coming through the windshield, my hands tensely gripping the steering wheel. It was the Indy 500 in suburban New Jersey. This driver had to be crazy, most definitely reckless. I stayed two car lengths behind my target, changing lanes when necessary to keep up.

Then, without warning or blinking an indicator light, the black sedan veered to the right and the exit to Bernridge. I was correct. Little comfort, though, as Carlos's driver ignored honking horns and one braking SUV to rocket off Route 53 down the exit ramp. I followed slowly, afraid to get too close. The sedan barely slowed at the stop sign at the end of the ramp, making a quick right into Bernridge's rush hour. We proceeded at a snail's pace through town until we reached the far end, an industrial area. Warehouses lined the street, delivery trucks backed up to loading docks. Despite the shining sun and brilliant blue sky, the area felt dark and dingy.

I tailed the black sedan until it moved through the warehouse area, and the driver tapped the brakes. *A first.* I eased to the curb behind a van. Up ahead, Carlos and companion pulled into the parking lot of a run-down, two-story building. Could this be where he worked? Was this his office? Bella had said Clifton, not Bernridge. I left my MC behind, kept the sedan in sight, and maneuvered my way around the parked cars on the street until I was within a dozen yards. I crouched down behind a pickup truck. As far as I could tell, neither Carlos nor the driver had gotten out. Minutes passed. I was getting tired, hunched down and afraid someone was going to come by and blow my cover, asking who I was spying on.

The passenger side door opened and Carlos emerged, reaching back inside for his briefcase. He walked around the back of the sedan and stood adjacent to the driver's side door. It swung open, and a man stepped out. He wore a brown coat, a baseball cap, was of medium build, shorter than Carlos. They faced each other for a moment, then the driver burst out laughing and slapped Carlos on the back. The actor bobbed his head and shook the driver's hand, like an old friend. In the past weeks, I hadn't seen anyone get that personal with the Dracula star. Neither on nor offstage. Until they drove the stake through his heart…

Carlos walked into the building. The driver pivoted to his left. I ducked down, my vision blocked by the hood of the pickup. I heard an engine rumble and assumed it was safe to look up again. As the sedan squeezed between two cars and turned to exit the lot, I scooted to the back of the truck to keep hidden. But before he moved onto the street, the driver looked right, then left, and I caught his face. Those eyes were familiar. *Mr. Chicago.*

* * * *

"Regular, hon?" Jocelyn asked.

I confirmed the order.

"You look like you could use extra icing this morning." The Coffee Heaven waitress sidled away, filling coffee cups, taking another order or two.

I drove to Etonville in a daze, remaining in the slow lane. The plumbing salesman from the Midwest who had been hanging around Etonville for the past few days, who didn't acknowledge at the performance of *Dracula* that he knew Carlos, apparently did know him. Well enough to drive him to work.

Jocelyn appeared with my breakfast. "Looking a little peaked, Dodie. Maybe you should take it easy."

I smiled my thanks and picked up a napkin.

"You should hire a wedding planner. Take a load off your mind."

Etonville was full of advice about my upcoming nuptials. It wasn't my wedding that had me disturbed this morning. I couldn't get the image of Mr. Chicago out of my mind. "Lola's helping plan my big day," I said brightly.

"Lola." Jocelyn's eyes narrowed. "Think she's still after Walter?"

"Lola? No!" I said a mite too forcefully.

"I saw them together at the Halloween party." She sighed. "I wouldn't blame her if she was. Walter's some kind of man."

Agreed. I was curious. "What do you like about him the most?"

Jocelyn's face took on a dreamy expression. "His cute little ears, that smile, his dimple…"

Walter had a dimple?

"Walter's the perfect man. Anybody'd be lucky to have him." Jocelyn moved on to her next customers.

Love certainly was in the eye of the beholder. My cell buzzed. A text from Bill. Speaking of the perfect man… *hi…miss u…freezing here. finding interesting stuff. want to talk later?* I answered that it was nice and balmy here yesterday and I'd love to chat. We agreed on ten thirty tonight. I was closing, but the Windjammer would be quiet by then. I wondered about that "interesting stuff." I'd have to wait to get the scoop.

I finished my cinnamon bun and doodled on a paper napkin. I'd also discovered some "interesting stuff" this morning. Should I tell Bill about tracking Carlos? Seeing Mr. Chicago with the actor? What would he make of it, if anything? Mr. Chicago was a puzzle. What was his relationship with Carlos anyway?

"Get you anything else?" Jocelyn asked.

"No, thanks."

She slipped into my booth and leaned across the table. I was taken aback; she'd never joined me before. Jocelyn lowered her voice. "Heard something strange." She arched an eyebrow for emphasis.

Strange? This was Etonville. Where strange things happened on a daily basis.

"Bella Villarias was in here this morning."

"Okay."

"We got to talking about the weather, *Dracula*...Did you know Carlos did a lot of acting in college?"

"I'd heard that."

"Anyhoo, I took her order and was walking away when she got a call. Now, I didn't intend to listen, but the Banger sisters were sitting there." Jocelyn pointed to a nearby table. "And they wanted more coffee, so I had to fill their cups...."

"Right. And...?" I was getting antsy. A lot on my plate today.

"While I was standing there pretending to listen to the sisters...you know they can go on and on," she said.

They weren't the only ones. I had to move this along. "You heard Bella say something?"

Jocelyn shifted position, so that her head was inches from my face. "She was talking real low, but I have good hearing. Always have." She paused for effect. "Daryl Wolf."

"Daryl Wolf. The victim from the cemetery?"

"Yep."

"What about him?" *This was like pulling teeth.*

"Well...Bella said...now let me get this correct... 'Daryl Wolf died of a heart attack.'"

"That's been in the *Etonville Standard*. Nothing strange about it," I said. I placed a ten-dollar bill on the table, thrust one arm into my jacket signaling that it was time to leave, and stood.

Jocelyn tapped the table. "But then she said... 'his medicine?' Like that. 'His medicine?' It was a question."

Bill had said there were blood pressure and arrhythmia meds in his bloodstream.

"Most folks with heart conditions are on a variety of medications."

Jocelyn glanced around the diner. Satisfied that no one was paying us any attention, she continued. "After that, she said '...would kill him,' real tenselike." Jocelyn looked at me expectantly. "'Would kill him,'" she repeated.

I sat. "When did you overhear this?"

"About a half hour before you came in."

After Carlos had been dropped off by Mr. Chicago. It wasn't abnormal that he might call Bella and relate his experience with the stranger from the Windy City. They had also talked about the death of the hitman. Across the diner, a customer waved a coffee cup at Jocelyn. She whispered, "Do you think it means Daryl Wolf's medicine killed him?"

As per Bill's confidential disclosure, a deeper dive into the tox screen was coming. "Probably a general conversation about medication. Maybe she has relatives or friends who've had heart attacks." I rose again. "You might not want to repeat what you heard. It could get back to Bella that you were..." Spying? Snooping?

"Listening in." Jocelyn heaved herself out of the booth. "You know, Bella offered to read tarot cards for me. I said 'nope.' I already know the future." She waltzed away.

Yikes. Jocelyn's eavesdropping complicated Bella's role in the Daryl Wolf drama....

* * * *

I could hardly believe my eyes. The lunch rush was underway, the second day of sliders attracting even more patrons than the first one had. Barbecued pulled pork. I had scarfed down a couple of the mini sandwiches before we opened. Yummy. Henry had outdone himself, and the town appreciated it. Which they told him in person, because at one thirty he relinquished the kitchen to Enrico for a bit and happily mingled with the customers. They could hardly believe it either because most of them gawked at the chef, exchanging comments with one another before they congratulated Henry on his success.

"What's that sweet-and-sour taste?" Vernon asked.

"Balsamic vinegar, honey, and brown sugar," Henry said proudly.

"I like the spiciness," Mildred said, licking some sauce from her finger.

"Worcestershire and Dijon mustard." Henry actually grinned.

Benny and I exchanged looks. "What is *that* about?" I asked.

"Dunno. He's never liked to reveal his recipes," Benny murmured.

"I'll bet it has something to do with La Famiglia. Like their chef is dining room friendly..."

"Game on." Benny uncorked a wine bottle.

By three, I had been running nonstop for several hours and my feet were killing me. Henry had retreated to the kitchen, his ego roundly massaged. Enough to last him until Christmas. I collapsed into my "office" with coffee and chicken soup. I hoped the rest of the day was quieter. I loved the business, and the Windjammer's bank account, but between my very early rising, tailing Carlos, and unsettling news from Jocelyn, I was ready for a nap.

I was midway through examining staff schedules for the coming weekend when the jingle bells at the door tinkled. I didn't bother looking up. Gillian could seat whoever.

"I'll have those special sliders. Pretty good yesterday."

Mr. Chicago. He was still in town. And sitting at the counter again. I studied him from the corner of my booth. In the brown coat from this morning, but he now wore dark sunglasses. If he was up to something nefarious, he certainly wasn't worried about keeping a low profile. Should I make myself known? I weighed the pros and cons of saying hello.

"Dodie," Gillian called from behind the counter. She was studying the Windjammer's iPad.

Mr. Chicago looked over, my cover blown.

"Yes?" I ignored his casual glance.

"Just got a big reservation for tonight, and they want a table in a corner, away from the door."

"Who is it?" I asked

"The garden club," she said.

Geez. We'd hosted them once before. About ten or twelve women who had organized Etonville's chapter of the Garden Club of New Jersey. Usually they held their monthly dinner meeting at La Famiglia. Something must have come up at our competition. "Better tell Henry." Good-sized groups were always welcome; however, the garden club presented complications. They were picky about their location in the restaurant and the menu. They disliked too much noise, other customers eating too close to them, kids crying, etc., etc. Somehow we'd have to make them happy.

My cell rang. "Hi, Lola. What's up?"

"Walter's dander. Ever since that tarot card reading, his confidence has gone down the drain."

Walter had apparently called for a speed-through tonight at the last minute. I'd learned a lot of theater lingo over the past few years and I knew that a "speed-through" at the Etonville Little Theatre often resulted in a train wreck. It meant that the cast had to speed through their lines as fast as they could. Between the actors getting carried away and Penny blasting her whistle to maintain some discipline, the whole affair seemed a waste of time to me. According to Walter, it was a test to see how secure they were with the script. Did he think their brains turned to mush because they had a few days off between weekend performances? He had already scheduled a brush-up rehearsal for tomorrow.

"Can you stop by the theater later?" Lola asked. "It would be nice to have you around for moral support."

"I'm closing. And we have the garden club here…"

"Oh them," Lola said.

"I'm sure Walter will settle down once the show is back in performance." I hoped.

We agreed to text once rehearsal was over and I had closed up the Windjammer and spoken with Bill, maybe catch up with a chat at her house.

Mr. Chicago was finishing his meal, digging into his wallet, when I eased out of my booth and walked to the cash register. "Hello there," I said when it was obvious our paths would cross. "Glad to see you're enjoying our menu."

He appraised me coolly. "Not many options in this burg." I must have reacted because he laughed. "Kidding. Like the specials this week."

"They're certainly popular. Do a lot of driving around these days?"

"Some."

"There's a plumbing supply store in Bernridge. Is it one of your clients?" I asked, all innocence.

He dropped some bills on the counter. "Never been to Bernridge."

14

At ten p.m. the dining room was empty except for a few stragglers, two couples drinking at the bar…and the garden club. Once Benny had left at six, I handled the bar while Carmen and Gillian waited on tables. There had been a manageable flow of trade since seven thirty. Then the club arrived.

We'd set up a long table against one wall, away from the front door. One of the group claimed to be bothered by kitchen smells whenever the swinging door opened. So we quickly rearranged two tables and sat them on an angle. Then the club president complained that our gluten-free options were minimal, and I persuaded Henry to create dishes to suit her diet while the club weighed the pros and cons of keto versus vegan versus paleo regimens. Penny should have been here to witness the conversation… Then one of the women copped an attitude because she demanded her pasta be replaced because it wasn't hot enough. I offered to heat it, but apparently that wasn't good enough.

They'd eaten their way through the main course, had ordered desserts and coffees, and were now chitchatting. I couldn't wait until they paid their bill.

My cell buzzed. Lola: *crazy over here…Walter did circle of light for an hour…*

Sheesh. I was familiar with Walter's "circle of light." Intended to create trust among company members, the only thing I'd learned from participating was that you *couldn't* always trust the rest of the cast. Lola:…*then finally started speed-through!*

None of the garden club members appeared ready to head out. At ten thirty I needed to call Bill. Club or no club.

"Can I clear the rest of the table?" asked a bored Gillian.

"Give them ten more minutes," I said.

The stragglers and drinkers had departed, and Henry had shut down the kitchen. I was drawing wedding gowns on a napkin. It was ten twenty-five. My trigger finger was at the ready to place the call.

"Dear, could you re-add this bill?" asked the treasurer of the garden club, handing me the group's check.

I smiled politely. "Of course." I dutifully toted the items. Yep. It was accurate.

"Could we get a take-out menu for future reference?" asked another member.

"Sure."

They slowly made their way to the coat hooks, dawdling over whose outerwear belonged to whom.

It was ten thirty-five. I motioned to Carmen to close down the dining room, retired to my back booth, and tapped Bill's number in my contacts. His cell rang. I counted five rings. *Where was he? Did I have the time wrong?* I left a text message asking him to call me. No immediate response. I followed Henry, Gillian, Enrico, and Carmen out the door, locking up as the last person standing. We said good night and took off in various directions. I walked to the theater, in case the rehearsal ran late, and tried the front door. It was locked and there were no lights on in Walter's office in the lobby.

I walked to my parking space down the road from the restaurant. Main Street was deserted; off in the distance, a dog barked, then howled. I shivered. Ever since *Dracula,* howling animals and walking alone in the dark gave me the willies. I pressed the remote on my key chain and my lights blinked, unlocking the door. I reached for the handle and grabbed a crumpled piece of paper instead. Someone had left me a message. I wasn't illegally parked and Lola would have texted me if the speed-through ended early. I could see Walter madly orchestrating the actors, who spewed lines at warp speed. Penny was right. Much of the time, the Etonville Little Theatre was a hot mess. I laughed to myself and climbed into my MC. The streetlight provided dim lighting, so I could barely see the block letters on the piece of paper. Then I read the message. My pulse jumped. *I know what you are doing. It ends now.* With an exclamation point.

* * * *

"What ends now?" Lola asked, pouring wine in our glasses.

We sat on her brown leather sofa, feet tucked under an array of pillows, sipping and munching chips and dip, careful to avoid dropping crumbs on her Persian rug. Lola was particular about her living room furnishings, the décor spare and stylish.

I studied the note. It was written on plain white paper—the inexpensive kind I used for my printer—that could be bought in bulk at any Staples. The lettering was black, penned with a thin marker. I couldn't foresee any fingerprints left behind. "Well...my snooping around Carlos Villarias's bedroom. Digging into his recent past in Lennox. Finding out about his alias. Walking into his house, though in all fairness, the screen door was unlocked. Following him to work this morning." Not to mention Pauli's Internet deep diving, my visit to the cemetery, calling on the costume shop...I'd been busier than I realized.

"You what?" Lola asked, surprised.

"I woke up early, couldn't get back to sleep, and decided to see if I could find out where he worked and maybe that would clue us in about him." I was a little shaky from encountering the message on my car door.

"And did you find out?"

"A run-down building in Bernridge's industrial area. Not very promising." It occurred to me I was so obsessed with Carlos and his driver that I neglected to take note of any signage on the building.

"What does he do there?"

"No idea. He carried a briefcase and wasn't wearing a tie."

For some reason, I hesitated to introduce Mr. Chicago into the discussion. Maybe my subconscious was afraid of what his presence would imply. After all, a Chicago hitman had died in Etonville. I didn't want to think what possible connection the two men might have.

"I don't understand." Lola's brow furrowed. "Who would know what you've been doing? Carlos? Bella? Wouldn't they just confront you? Anyway, nothing you discovered is particularly incriminating. It's not illegal to change your name or your address."

"What about Halloween night? Carlos having a conversation with a mob guy who turns up dead?" I asked.

"There is that," Lola said. "I don't know. It's all too confusing. Oh, I forgot to mention...Carlos and Gabriel got into a..." Lola formed air quotes. "...heated discussion this evening."

"About the show?" I remembered another "heated discussion" I'd witnessed at rehearsal last week.

"Not sure. Walter did his warm-ups for over an hour. Everyone was burned out by the time he was finished. I've got to talk to him about his pre-rehearsal exercises. Actors are too—"

"Lola?" I gently interrupted her.

"So they all took a break in the green room. When Penny called them out to start the line-through ten minutes later, everyone responded but Carlos and Gabriel. Penny had to go after them, and she said, quote 'Gabriel went postal. Carlos yelling back at him. Almost had a fistfight on our hands.' I guess they were really angry."

Whoa.

"When they got onstage, they both acted as if nothing had happened."

"And the rehearsal?"

"The usual. Abby and Edna competing for fastest time, Romeo and Vernon goofing around, Walter—eyes closed—into his character so deep, he couldn't see what was going on. Janice was a gem, trying to keep up. Carlos and Gabriel took the work seriously. Amazing, considering minutes before they were at each other's throats."

"What were they fighting about?"

"Penny didn't say. I think the shouting was so distracting, the content of the conversation got lost."

My cell buzzed. Bill: *ok to talk now?*

I'd forgotten about our phone call. I texted back: *where have you been?* My cell rang.

"What do you mean, where have I been?" Bill asked, tired and a bit annoyed.

Lola mouthed *Bill?* and I nodded. She tiptoed out of the room to give us some privacy.

"You were supposed to call at ten thirty."

"I know. Got caught up in a meeting. I'm only ten minutes late." He sounded defensive.

"Ten? It's twenty to midnight here."

There was a pause on the line. "It's ten forty here. Different time zone." My fault. "Sorry."

"No, I'm sorry. Things have been nuts here. Meeting with the Chicago PD, talking to the organized crime unit, interviewing some administrators about their mentoring program. Squeezing everything in has been a challenge. I expected to leave tomorrow morning. Now it might be a little later in the day."

I did my best to hide my disappointment. Not only did I miss Bill, I had to come clean with him about my nosing into Carlos's past. And present. What would Bill have to say about Mr. Chicago? He'd tell me I was allowing my overreaching imagination too much authority. "Are you making progress?"

Bill exhaled. "Yes and no. The Chicago PD is being helpful. The organized crime guys less so. It's like they've got information they're not eager to share. I don't think they trust a cop from a small town in New Jersey."

"Hey," I said, "you're not just any small-town cop. You're a police chief. And a former decorated deputy chief from Philly. And you sit on a state commission."

"I guess I'm done in."

"Have you waved your NFL career in front of their faces?" It usually garnered a fair amount of respect from manly man types.

He chuckled. "I should try that next."

"What about that famous Chicago deep-dish pizza? Or those Chicago-style hot dogs I've read about? Yummy."

"I had one of those Italian beef sandwiches. Everybody raves about them here. Not bad. But I prefer Henry's version of a Philly cheesesteak. Or a Taylor Ham and cheese sandwich." His voice oozed into his husky zone. "Served by my favorite restaurant manager."

Yowza! "Then you'd better beat it back here, buddy," I said.

"As soon as I finish with the organized crime unit. Daryl Wolf was known to them."

"Yeah?"

"Keep this on the down low. Apparently, he's been on their radar recently. Turns out he was a high-level enforcer for a mob boss. They're not one hundred percent on why he was in Jersey, but they think it had something to do with his having a contract on a former Chicago native now on the run."

I felt a ball of tension in the pit of my stomach. "Why the contract? What's the runner done?"

"It's not what the runner's done. They think it's what the runner has. Evidence."

"So...this person knows something incriminating about some mob figure?" I asked.

"Apparently big-time."

"And where do they think Etonville fits into all this?" My pulse inched upward.

"Not sure. Hope to find out tomorrow morning. I'll text from the airport," Bill said.

"Can't wait to see you."

"Me too. Sleep tight."

"Love you," I said.

"Back at ya. By the way, you'll never guess Daryl Wolf's nickname."

"What?"

"The Grim Reaper."

* * * *

I spent a couple of restless hours at home, double-checking the locks on doors and windows. In bed, I did Walter's breathing exercises, I counted backward from one hundred by threes—my version of sheep—I tightened and released body parts, toes to head, to relax. Nothing worked. I couldn't settle down after the message left on my MC and the phone call with Bill. *Daryl Wolf was known as the Grim Reaper.* He was found with a Grim Reaper costume. He was in New Jersey, and most probably Etonville, tracking down a potential target who had evidence that was lethal for a mob boss in Chicago. I had prevented myself from admitting what was now jostling its way to the forefront of my mind: Could Carlos be the runner, and was Daryl Wolf after him because Carlos had valuable intel on a mob figure? And who was threatening me? Who would want me to back off?

I hopped out of bed, thrust my arms in my chenille bathrobe—a gift from my great-aunt Maureen many years ago. It was threadbare but comforting; I kept it at my place for late nights like this one. Definitely unsexy. I padded to the kitchen and opened the refrigerator door. Ordinarily, I might go for peanut butter, or cheese and crackers, or any leftovers I'd liberated from the Windjammer stock. Tonight called for the nuclear option. Sweet stuff. I found half a quart of cherry vanilla ice cream, the tail end of a jar of hot fudge sauce, some maraschino cherries, and an old can of whipped cream on its last legs. The combination was perfect. I took my sundae back to bed and scrunched down under the covers. After all, "desserts" was "stressed" spelled backward. The sugar might keep me awake; I didn't care. I needed a soothing end to this night, which was quickly turning into morning.

As I dipped a spoon into the ice cream, wedding dress be damned, I mulled over my next moves. If Carlos's life had been in danger from Daryl Wolf, was he safe now that the Grim Reaper was dead? Or would he and Bella feel compelled to run again? Did he have valuable information on the crime boss? In sorting out Carlos's behavior in recent days, I faced facts: He was guilty of being arrogant on occasion, arguing in the parking lot on Halloween night, looking like a modern-day vampire, and fighting with Gabriel Quincey. Whatever that was about. Mental note: Penny being Penny, she most likely had picked up odds and ends of the quarrel even though she might have been sidetracked by the yelling. I needed to ask her what she'd heard…

None of this added up to anything earth-shattering. Even if he had assumed another identity and his name was Mark Johnson, not Carlos Villarias.

Despite my massive intake of sugar, my eyes were heavy. My alarm read three a.m. Time to shut down if I was going to get any rest before morning. I flicked off the light on my nightstand.

* * * *

My cell pinged. A text coming in. Buttery yellow light streamed through my windows forcing my eyes open. Should I get out of bed and retrieve my phone? It could wait, I decided, and rolled over, clasping the pillow and dragging it over my head. Another ping. Either I was popular this morning or someone was not giving up. I threw back the comforter and glanced at the clock. Eight a.m. I had to get moving anyway.

I checked the text. Lola: *you okay?*

I assured her that I was all right and would see her later to discuss a bona fide wedding venue she'd found. I showered, slipped into chinos and a beige sweater. I had about two hours to complete my morning's mission. Or rather missions. I grabbed a piece of toast and my car keys—my Cindy Collins heroine never investigated on an empty stomach.

I thought twice about my first stop. I was still agitated about the note on my car door. At the same time, I resisted admitting to anyone other than Lola that I had been prying into Carlos Villarias's life. I was too far into the Carlos-Daryl mystery to stop now. But common sense, and a healthy respect for my safety, prevailed, and I drove to the Municipal Building. Leaving the note—securely tucked into a plastic Baggie—with Deputy Chief Suki Shung to have it analyzed for fingerprints was my only rational option. I knew she'd quiz me about the meaning of the warning. Yet, I would have far more luck dancing around its message with Suki than I would with Bill. Besides, I didn't have to pick a wedding date with Suki, and by the time Bill found out what I had been up to, the Daryl Wolf-Etonville connection might be solved. I had to bite the investigative bullet.

I swung my MC into a parking space and hurried down the hallway of the Municipal Building toward the Etonville police station. Fortunately,

Edna was not at dispatch. I was saved from having to explain my presence. I walked into the outer office of the department and tapped on Suki's door.

"Enter."

She sounded more like Bill every day.

I poked my head inside the office. "Hope I'm not interrupting anything too important."

Suki lifted her head from paperwork on her desk and capped a pen. "Have a seat."

Suki and I had a curious relationship. We'd bonded over our common experience of having once been assault victims of jewel thieves. And both of us were Bill's cheerleaders—loyal, devoted, steadfast. Unlike me, Suki was an enigma, rarely letting her emotions show, usually cool and unruffled. "Thanks."

She regarded me expectantly. I pulled out the plastic bag. "I found this on my car last night." No point in beating around the bush. I set the Baggie between us on her desk blotter.

Suki looked from the note to me. "What is it?"

"I think it's a warning of some kind." I assumed my most innocent expression.

She wasn't fooled, picking it up, turning it over. She read the message. "Where did you find this?"

"Stuffed into the door handle of my car."

"I assume you touched it?"

"I assumed it was from someone at the theater and then I read it…"

Suki frowned. When she looked at me again, she had her owl-like face on. I knew it meant she was putting two and two together and getting way more than four. "What do you think it means?"

I shrugged. "Someone wants me to stop something." That was as close to the truth as I dared to tread.

"What might that something be?"

"Not sure." Also pretty much the truth.

Suki crossed her hands and rested them on her desk. "I'll send it to the state lab and see what comes up." She sat back. "Meanwhile, I suggest you don't do anything that might put yourself or others in danger."

In other words, lay off investigating. "Thanks," I said cheerfully. I rose to leave.

"Dodie?"

"Yes?"

"I know you operate on your instincts. Which have proven to be pretty useful to you in the past," Suki said, a smidge of a smile forming.

"I suppose." Where was she going with this?

"It's good to trust your intuition. Still, be careful," she said quietly. "Wouldn't want anything to happen to you."

Me neither. I strode away.

"Hiya, Dodie," Edna called out from dispatch, where she removed a lid from her takeout coffee container. "What's today's slider special?"

I waved as I walked to her window. "Mini cheesesteaks. Philly by way of Etonville."

"The chief would love those. Take him back to former days in the City of Brotherly Love." Edna winked.

"Guess so." I had a sudden inspiration. *Mr. Chicago.* "Has there been an increase in parking tickets by the Windjammer?"

Her forehead wrinkled. "What do you mean?"

"We had an out-of-town customer several days this past week, and each time he parked illegally in front of the restaurant. You know how the town meter maid is about Main Street."

"Hmmm; 586s. Don't know, but I can check." She grinned slyly. "You looking to have Bill fix them?"

Yikes! "No way! I was thinking if he had gotten tickets, I might persuade him to park elsewhere."

Edna picked up a pen. "What's his name?"

"I don't know, but I'll bet the car is a rental. He's been a good customer." At least a consistent one.

She leaned through the window, her eyes sparkling. "I'll see what I can find out."

"10-4." I breezed down the hall and out of the building.

It was a long shot, but maybe Edna could come up with a name and address for Mr. Chicago without my having to request that Suki, or Bill, run his license plate through a rental company. At least I'd gotten past my visit to Suki without having to reveal anything too problematic.

I hadn't had my first hit of caffeine for the day, so I popped into Coffee Heaven for a takeaway caramel macchiato. Jocelyn took my order, then whizzed around the diner. The place was packed. I took out my cell to check for texts or emails just as a flurry of motion behind me caused me to look up.

It was the Banger sisters, waving from a booth to beat the band. Impossible to ignore them. "Dodie, we've got new hairstyles, dontcha know," said one, patting her head.

"Just like yours," said the other.

Like mine? Their still-identical cuts *still* featured gray permed hair. I couldn't see any difference.

"Attractive," I said.

"Sexy and sassy!" said the first. They beamed.

Sheesh. I grabbed my drink, gestured that I had to leave, and rushed out the door. With a little over an hour before I had to report to the Windjammer, I had one more errand on my agenda. Carlos's place of work. I retrieved the address from my cell phone and set my MC in the direction of Bernridge. Traffic was light on State Route 53, and I made it to the exit in record time. It didn't compute for me. Carlos going to work in a shabby building in an industrial part of Bernridge. Bella had said he was in "management." What was he managing in that location?

Within minutes of arriving at the town center, I was sitting in the same parking lot where Mr. Chicago had brought Carlos, thanks to having avoided the morning rush. I peered out my windshield. From this angle, I could see the front of the two-story structure. The exterior of the first floor was covered with faded gray paint. The second story had a beige exterior with two windows. Painted over, from the looks of them. There was a sign atop the door into the office that read "Speedwell Auto Parts." I could easily concoct a reason for entering the building—I was lost, I needed directions, etc., etc.—but what if Carlos was working behind a desk in the space? What would I say to him?

Before I could decide, Carlos appeared in the parking lot. Once again, I found myself ducking behind the wheel to avoid being seen. But I needn't have worried; he darted out of the building, hopped into his car, and took off. I could either tail him to who-knew-where or check out his work environment. The work won.

I straightened my clothes and walked to the entrance. The distinct odor of oil and machines—factory smells—hit me the moment I pulled the door open. A woman of indeterminate age—fifties to seventies—sat behind an old metal schoolroom desk, a cigarette in one hand, a pencil in the other, as she studied a sheaf of papers. A bad henna dye job covered short, straight hair. She jammed the cigarette in an ashtray and stubbed it out.

"Help you?" she asked brusquely.

"Hi. I think I'm lost. I was looking for..." I made a show of taking a Coffee Heaven carryout receipt out of my bag and scrutinizing it. "Hawthorne Street."

"Hawthorne Street? Kiddo you're on the wrong end of town."

"I am? Oops! I get confused whenever I'm in Bernridge."

"Go left out of here until you hit Main. Then hang a right, drive for a mile or so. You can't miss it." She smirked wryly as if to add "well, maybe *you* can."

I had to laugh. "Thanks." I got a glimpse of the shop behind the tiny, crowded office space. "Auto parts."

"Yep."

"I'm from Etonville, but I had a neighbor who worked in this part of Bernridge a few years ago. He was a business manager."

She grunted. "Didn't work here. No managers."

"Must have been another business."

"Yep. There's only me, Johnny, his brother, and Carlos."

My pulse accelerated. "Small enterprise."

"Family owned and operated. Except for Carlos."

"Oh? What does he do?"

"Bookkeeper. Good with numbers."

I thanked the "receptionist" for her help and ran to my car before the "bookkeeper," Carlos, returned. So he was good with numbers... Not exactly the employment picture Bella painted of him. Surely she was aware of his job at Speedwell Auto Parts?

15

So Carlos Villarias was a bookkeeper, probably from the Chicago area. Where he might have been referred to as an accountant. Was there something about that occupation that drove him to New Jersey, first, and to change his name, second? I'd seen enough movies on TCM to recognize the-accountant-on-the-run-from-the-mob character. Was that why Daryl Wolf was in Etonville? To track Carlos down because he was familiar with shady accounting practices? And then what...? I shuddered. I was letting my powers of invention run too freely.

"Getting a cold?" Benny asked as he filled two glasses with soda.

"Don't think so. Is it chilly in here?" I asked.

Benny examined me. "No. Do you need an early night to go home and hit the sack?"

Come to think of it... "I thought I'd run next door at about seven. Dress rehearsal."

"No problem."

"How was the dance recital?"

Benny whipped out his cell and spent the next ten minutes sharing videos of his princess tapping away in her tutu and spangles. He certainly was a doting father. Which reminded me: my father's birthday was at the end of the month. Time to think about a gift.

From behind me, I heard, "Set me up with today's special sliders."

The voice made my skin crawl. "Good choice. Mini cheesesteaks," I said perkily. Benny wrote up his order and went to the kitchen.

Mr. Chicago flipped through his cell phone, ignoring me.

"Hope you didn't park illegally today. The meter maid was on the prowl earlier," I said.

"Hah," he barked. "Haven't gotten a ticket yet."

Damn. Edna would spin her wheels for nothing. Benny sauntered out of the kitchen with a plate of cheesesteak sliders and set it in front of the plumbing salesman, drawing a soda for him without even asking what he wanted to drink. He smiled his thanks, set the phone aside, and took a large bite of his sandwich.

I had a brilliant brainstorm. I whipped out *my* cell and snapped a photo.

"Hey!" Mr. Chicago said, holding a napkin to his mouth.

"We're redoing the Windjammer website. Featuring specials. Would you mind letting me take your picture with the sliders?"

He stopped chewing for a second.

I hastened on. "With Benny?"

"Got it." Benny moved around the counter, standing next to Mr. Chicago before he could refuse. I clicked away.

"Perfect!" I praised the two of them. "These will be terrific on the site. Enjoy your lunch."

I drew a cup of coffee and retired quickly to my back booth. My impulse not only included getting a snapshot of Mr. Chicago, but sending it to Pauli for some of his facial recognition exploration. I'd seen him do age progressions and regressions with photos in the past. I forwarded it to my tech guru with a request to run it through his law enforcement software for matches. Maybe the out-of-towner had a past too.

Which brought me back to a central point. What was Daryl Wolf doing in Etonville? Was he there to find Carlos? Bill would be coming home—great news—with intel provided by the Bureau of Organized Crime that might link Carlos to Daryl Wolf. What would happen then?

I stared at a Cheney Brothers inventory sheet, not even seeing the print on the page. I had to get a grip and prepare the kitchen for next week. I'd been encouraging Henry to experiment with some hearty one-dish specials, like chili rellenos and cheesy broccoli and quinoa with sausage. I'd dug up delectable recipes while I was down the shore on vacation. Casseroles would be an appealing late-autumn option. I tried to concentrate, estimating a meat and vegetable order, but my mind kept looping back to Carlos and Chicago. I'd Googled Villariases in that area to no success. Ditto with Mark Johnson. No one fit his description. Of course, if Carlos was in the habit of altering his identity, who knew what other names he might have taken?

My pen ran out of ink and I rummaged in my bag for a replacement. I bypassed my wallet, keys, Kleenex, a power bar, and a bottle of aspirin. At the bottom of my bag was a ballpoint pen and an *Etonville Standard* review of *Dracula* from last week. I hadn't gotten around to reading the entire article. I skimmed it now. Generally glowing and congratulatory, it had to swell the collective ego of the Etonville Little Theatre. Muted praise for Walter's "novel decisions to update the gender of the Attendant and the age of the Maid." Less-than-enthusiastic mentions of Abby and Edna. However, Carlos received a rave for his portrayal of the vampire— no surprises there—he was a "natural, the role fit like a glove, as if he'd been born to play the part of the Transylvanian monster." Hmm…maybe Dracula "fit like a glove" because Carlos had played him before.

I pulled out my cell phone, tapped on the Internet, and paused. Then typed "Dracula productions in the Chicago area 2011-2015" and hit Enter. Up popped half a dozen links. There were three productions of the play in and around Chicago during that time period. Wow! One in the city proper, one in Glenview, and another in Naperville. I clicked on links for websites of each theater, perusing recent production histories and reviews with actor mentions, crossing my fingers that I'd find photos of the casts somewhere. The Chicago production had a ton of mixed reviews and a picture of Dracula that definitely was not Carlos. Ditto for the Glenview show. Although with better and more flattering notices. Then I checked Naperville. On the website, I found an archive with references to past productions. There was a profile shot of Dracula biting the neck of Lucy. It could have been Carlos…but maybe not. I turned to reviews, also mixed except for the character of Dracula. One critic claimed the role "fit like a glove." My heart slammed in my chest. I scrolled through reviews until I found one that included actors' names. One reviewer was very generous, giving everybody in the cast a positive notice. Dracula was played by Ethan Mercer. *Mercer.*

"Dodie!"

I flinched.

Henry stood above me, frowning. "We're short twenty pounds on the flounder. Again."

Barbara Mercer in Lennox. So, she was his mother. Also likely Mercer was Carlos's actual name.

"You hear me?" Henry asked.

"Yes. Twenty pounds of flounder," I mumbled, dazed.

"Short."

"Got it."

Henry sighed, stopped to get iced tea at the bar and have a word with Benny, and marched back into his kitchen cave. I watched Henry's progress, not really seeing him or absorbing the fact that Mr. Chicago had departed the restaurant. Some pieces of the Villarias puzzle were clearer now; others even more mystifying.

* * * *

Talk about a zombie. I'd gone about overseeing dining room preparation for the evening service in a fog, details bombarding me at every turn. Villarias, Johnson, Mercer…

And, of course, Daryl Wolf and Mr. Chicago. I was banking on Pauli coming through with results on that last one. Bill would have intel on Daryl Wolf by the end of this day. He should have texted or called by now to confirm his flight tonight. Why hadn't I heard anything from him?

My phone buzzed. Lola: *coming tonight?* I had already intended to stop in next door to offer support. However, now I knew Carlos's real name. I needed to think through my next move. I texted back: *wouldn't miss the brush-up!* I wasn't sure what I would do there…talk with Carlos? Confront him with what I knew? If his life was in danger, surely he and Bella would want to hit the road again after *Dracula* closed.

"Yoo-hoo! Dodie!"

I looked up from my cell. It was the Banger sisters, at a table in the middle of the dining room. Both of them wore their garlic necklaces. "Hi ladies. Something I can get you?" I said brightly.

They waved me over to their table, then bent their permed heads to speak to me as if in confidence. "We don't want to start any rumors…" said one.

Uh-oh.

"But we heard that you and…Chief Thompson…" said the other.

"Have called off your engagement." They gazed at me expectantly, eyes like saucers.

"What? Where did you hear that?" Now it was my turn to gawk. I knew the rumor mill worked overtime—Bill and I had been grist on more than one occasion. This was carrying things too far. "We're still engaged." I flashed my diamond, and the sisters shifted their focus from me to my ring. "You can spread that around. It won't be a rumor but the truth." I tried to smile pleasantly. It was more of a grimace.

Apparently satisfied, the sisters dug into their dinner of panko-crusted flounder and rosemary potatoes. I could swear when I wasn't looking they studied my every move like they were reading tea leaves. Which reminded me of Bella. Now there was a mystery. Assuming Carlos was the runner from Chicago, where did Bella fit in? While I had been busy trying to sort out Carlos's background, I'd ignored his wife's. What did I know about her? She read palms and tarot cards, had an herb garden, and was sociable enough. In other words, not very much.

I scanned the dining room. It was approaching seven and the evening rush was over, traffic into the restaurant a mere trickle. I was free to go because Benny would take over. I packed up my bag, grabbed my takeout container of coffee. "Night. See you in the morning."

"Hey," he said, "Have you heard what those batty Banger sisters are saying about you and Bill?"

I groaned. "Don't know who their source is."

"They don't need a source. They make things up out of thin air. Sometimes I think they're not playing with a full deck." He shook his head.

I laughed. My cell pinged. Bill: *got delayed here…taking flight first thing in the morning. can u talk now?* I texted that I could and left the Windjammer. On the sidewalk outside, I paused to inhale early November. The air was getting nippier by the night, the light breeze forcing me to flip up the collar on my leather jacket. I sat on the bench outside the theater. The lobby lights were on, the lobby itself empty. Probably the usual commotion in the theater that accompanied ELT brush-up rehearsals: Walter doing his best to run the pre-show warm-ups, Penny blasting her whistle to get everyone's attention, and the cast schmoozing and texting. Except for Carlos. He never schmoozed.

My cell rang. "Hey there, handsome," I joked. "Guess you're going to have to spend another night—"

"Dodie."

Bill's voice was grim, stopping me cold. "What's up?"

"This Daryl Wolf thing is taking a turn. Getting complicated."

My dread-o-meter shot up. "What's that mean?"

"I've already alerted Suki." He hesitated. "She told me about the note on your car door. Have you been investigating Daryl Wolf's death?" he asked abruptly.

"No," I said firmly. "Absolutely not." I hadn't done any digging into the murder victim.

"What's the note referring to?" He was exhausted and exasperated.

"Maybe a prank. I'll keep my eyes open."

He exhaled loudly. I envisioned him running a hand impatiently through the spikes of his brush cut. "According to the organized crime guys, the runner from Chicago? In the state witness protection program."

OMG! Carlos was in witness protection? Explains why he'd changed his name—

"…for testifying against a crime figure."

"What kind of evidence did he have?"

"Not completely clear. But the guy was an accountant, so he probably knew how the books were cooked and where the bodies were buried. No pun intended."

Carlos, the bookkeeper at Speedwell Auto Parts. I glanced at the entrance to the theater. He was onstage right now, pretending to be a bloodsucking villain, all the while he was one of the good guys, blowing the whistle on the mob.

"I don't get it. If he was in witness protection, why was he running loose?"

"That's complicated too. He was stashed in Colorado, but then he disappeared. The mob guys lost him until last summer, when they tracked him to North Jersey, which explains Daryl Wolf."

Last summer. When Barbara Mercer visited the "Johnsons" in Lennox for the last time. I swallowed hard. "The mob sent an assassin after Car... uh...the runner? That sounds like something out of *The Godfather.*"

"It gets worse. Today, one of the Chicago PD sources got some intel that the contract on the runner was picked up by another hitman."

"A second killer?"

"Yes. They don't have an ID, but they know there's a direct link to the crime boss."

I had to work to keep my voice steady, adrenaline coursing through my body. "I don't understand. If the runner already testified, why kill him? Revenge?"

"It's been known to happen. Code of honor and all that. But in this case, there's greater motivation to take out the guy."

"Yeah?" I whispered.

"Apparently, the testimony from the accountant focused on bookkeeping, money laundering, racketeering. All targeting associates of the boss. Now the Bureau of Organized Crime has figured out that there is something the runner has that implicates the boss directly." Bill paused. "Proof that he planned the murder of a politician."

"Like who?" I asked tentatively.

"An Illinois congressman who was pressing an investigation into the business ventures of said mob boss. This evidence would give the organized crime unit a direct link to a guy they've been trying to prosecute for decades. The runner apparently taped conversations, snapped photos of emails, got ahold of texts. Money laundering is one thing. Plotting to murder a high-profile politician is another."

Yikes.

"You've got to keep all of this to yourself." Bill paused. "Dodie?"

"If they know this hitman is here somewhere...near Etonville...what are they doing about it?" I sounded shriller than I intended.

"Calm down. These crime unit guys are pros too. They've sent their own man undercover to protect the runner. And find the evidence."

Both the mob boss *and* the Chicago police wanted to get their hands on Carlos's proof.

"They've asked the Etonville PD to help out. Which means me. Suki's on the case."

I got the hint: Stay out of the way and don't get involved. "Have you seen a photo of the...individual...in witness protection?"

"Not yet. But I have his name."

I held my breath.

"Ethan Mercer."

The nail in the coffin.

* * * *

I sat on the bench, stunned, for several minutes. It was good news, bad news for Carlos Villarias/Ethan Mercer. The bad news: a second hitman was either on his way or had already arrived in Etonville. Good news: the Bureau of Organized Crime from the Chicago Police Department had sent the cavalry in the form of an undercover cop who was here to protect Carlos. A bolt of investigative lightning struck. Mr. Chicago! Is that what the out-of-town stranger was doing here? Posing as a plumbing supplies salesman, eating at the Windjammer, taking Carlos to work, even coming to a performance of *Dracula*? His presence was beginning to make sense.

After warning me to be careful and stay away from trouble until he returned early tomorrow, Bill said good night and clicked off. Carlos had protection and Bill was on his way home; there was nothing for me to do but sit in the theater, watch the dress rehearsal, and chill, hoping that Carlos, and by extension, Bella, was safe.

I felt weary when I slung my bag over my shoulder and walked into the theater. I was late...seven forty-five. The rehearsal had probably already begun, unless, according to Penny, the ELT was operating on theater time, in which case I was early.

Romeo sauntered into the lobby, his face buried in his cell phone.

Why was he wandering in the house in costume? "Hey. Rehearsal not started yet?" I asked.

He gave me one of his typical bad-boy sneers. "The star's taking the night off," Romeo said with a touch of snark.

Oh no. Romeo continued to run his mouth about actors who weren't members of the Etonville Little Theatre corrupting the process with their egos. Did he hear himself? Romeo was the poster child for egotistical actors. I swept past him into the house.

It was a screwball scene. Walter onstage flapping his arms at JC, pointing to the trick bookcase, then the magical chair. One of the crew trying to control the flying bat, which swooped over the downstage area, narrowly missing Penny, who tooted a short blast on her whistle to get actors onstage. They meandered out of the green room, adjusting costumes, bewildered. Had the ELT ever rehearsed with the lead actor missing? Lola sat in the first row, tugging on a blond strand of hair. Even from behind, an aura of angst surrounded her.

I crept down the aisle, slipped into a seat next to her. "What's up?" I whispered.

Lola turned to me, dark circles under her eyes, frown lines splayed across her forehead. She was tired too. This show was taking a toll. "It's just too much. First the bookcase refuses to cooperate, then the crew can't get the flying bat under control. Walter is sulking because the Creston paper gave Carlos a great review but dinged his performance. And he doesn't like the way the trick chair is operating."

"Speaking of Carlos…?"

"He hasn't shown up yet. Penny has been calling and texting, but no response," she said with a grimace. "It's not like him to be late, or at least not to notify the stage manager."

We both looked up at Penny, who was writing furiously on her clipboard, ignored by the cast.

"Penny, get everyone in place for the warm-up," Walter demanded. "We're exploring the space."

Lola rolled her eyes, muttering, "Oh brother."

I recognized that exercise: the actors led one another, blindfolded, around the stage, trying to avoid set pieces while getting the lay of the land. It required trusting your partner and surrendering to the moment. Neither of which was on display in the theater tonight. Everyone was jumpy.

The stage manager inched her way to Walter. "Still missing Carlos."

As if this was news to him, Walter did a complete 360-degree pirouette, taking in the stage, Lola, and Romeo, who was taking his sweet time ambling through the house. "What do you mean, missing?"

"As in, he's not here," Penny said.

"How can he not be here? It's a brush-up rehearsal."

"I know. I tried—"

"No one is excused from a brush-up rehearsal," Walter announced.

"He's not answering his phone," Penny said.

"Then we have to find him. How can we rehearse *Dracula* without Dracula? After all, 'his performance was the highlight of an otherwise average production,'" he said petulantly.

"Quoting the review from the Creston paper," Lola murmured.

Geez.

I had an idea. "Lola, why don't you convince Walter to begin without Carlos? Maybe Penny could read his lines?"

We swung our heads toward the stage. Penny gave up on her whistle and lounged on the settee, tapping her cell phone and tossing blindfolds at actors. "Maybe one of the other actors who isn't in his scenes. Meanwhile, I'll take a quick trip to the Hanratty place to see what's keeping him."

Lola bounded to her feet and put a hand on my arm. "Thanks. I appreciate that. Please let me know when you find him, okay?"

If I find him. "Will do." I jerked my head in the direction of the stage, where blindfolded actors were bumping into furniture. "Good luck."

Lola crossed her fingers and headed for Walter.

I resisted the urge to check on the Windjammer. Benny was in charge and fully capable of keeping things running and monitoring Henry. I ran down the block, hopped into my MC, and turned the ignition key. Then I pointed my car toward the temporary home of the Villariases. I hoped I wasn't too late. But for what?

16

Traffic was light on the streets of Etonville as I drove down Main and turned left onto Amber. I passed the Municipal Building, wondering if Suki was in her office and if I should tell her what I was doing. To what end? Failing to appear for an ELT brush-up rehearsal was not against the law. The Chicago Police had the situation under control; all I needed to do was locate Carlos and convince him to get to the theater. Within minutes I was on the outskirts of town, guiding my MC through neighborhoods until I reached the road that ran past the Hanratty house. The moon provided the only light on the deserted lane.

I slowed as I approached the place. The Villariases' Subaru was in the driveway. Good. They were home. I rolled to a stop behind it. The place was as spooky as the night of the cast party—the weathered exterior walls, the rickety front porch steps, dim light from the first-floor parlor windows. None visible from the second or third floors. Did I really want to do this? To quote Edna, "It certainly looked haunted."

I counted to ten and left my car. The wind had picked up in the last hour or so and now whooshed about, tearing at my open jacket. I pulled it snugly about me. Once on the porch, I was alarmed to see the front door ajar. Not unlike the day Lola and I had visited with Bella. Didn't the Villariases believe in locks?

I peeked in. "Hello? Carlos? Bella?" Absolute silence. I tried the ancient-looking doorbell, all corroded around the edges. It tolled a mournful, two-ring chime. No response. Maybe Mr. Chicago had picked them up just as he had Carlos the other morning and taken them somewhere for safekeeping. Why hadn't Carlos notified Penny? Or Walter? This was most likely a waste of time. If Carlos had been available for rehearsal, he would have been there.

Before I left, I had to satisfy my curiosity. I glanced around the yard. Which was ridiculous: There was no one anywhere nearby to see me. I stepped into the foyer and, to make my presence known, called out again. "Carlos?" The parlor on my right was empty, a table lamp providing the only light from the first floor. I tiptoed down the hall to the back of the house and the kitchen. I waved my cell flashlight around the appliances. All was neat, nothing disturbed. On an old wooden kitchen table, Bella had arranged a dozen pots of herbs. Jars and vials were lined up neatly—the extracts and concoctions from her plants that would become lotions and salves and homeopathic remedies.

There was no sign of trauma or struggle.

I texted Lola: *at the Hanratty place...car here but no sign of Carlos or Bella.* She responded almost immediately: *thanks for trying...penny reading lines...ouch...coming back?* I agreed to rejoin the ELT and hold Lola's hand for the second act. I flicked off my flashlight, intending to beat it back down the hallway to the foyer and out of this old house. On my left, beneath the curving staircase that led to the second floor, there was a half-open door I hadn't noticed before. I grasped the handle. A set of steps led to a lower level; the basement, judging by the dank smell and clammy air. There was a light on somewhere down there. I stuck my head inside the door, inching halfway down the stairs.

"Carlos? Bella?" I called out. Being in the house alone was spooking me out. Lights on, nobody home. A whoosh of air behind me, then a thud against my back, thrusting me from behind. I felt myself falling. The last thing I remembered thinking: *I'll miss Act Two.*

* * * *

A blinding light shone directly into my eyes. "Take it easy. Let them examine you." It was Suki.

Paramedics took my vital signs and looked me over for damage.

"Where am I? What's going on?" I struggled to sit up and was slammed with a pounding head. I lay down again.

In the hazy illumination at the top of the stairs, I could see Lola and Carol on the periphery of the handful of technicians tending to me. "Thank God you're okay," Lola said.

"What happened?"

"You took a tumble down some stairs," Carol said.

"These old house are like death traps. Everything's rotten. Lucky you only fell a few steps," said an EMT as he put a bandage on my forehead.

"How are you feeling?" asked Suki, concerned.

"I'm fine," I asserted bravely. My head was killing me.

"Let's get her out of here." Hands lifted me onto a stretcher that was lugged up the staircase, through the hallway, and onto the front porch of the Hanratty house, where I was placed on a gurney. The cold air was a relief. Flashing blue and red lights whirled atop an Etonville PD cruiser, while an ambulance idled, ready to transport me to the hospital.

"I don't need to go to the—"

Suki motioned to the EMTs. "It's only a precaution. In case you have a concussion."

Lola and Carol followed the gurney. Lola grabbed my hand. "What happened?"

"We were so worried when you didn't return to the theater that we called the police," added Carol, slightly frantic.

"Good thing you did," I murmured. I was drowsy.

Lola looked devastated. "I'm sorry you came out here for nothing." Nothing?

"Carlos called an hour ago and apologized for missing rehearsal. Some family emergency," she said hastily, patting my hand as I was loaded into the ambulance.

"He's okay? Where was he?" He had no other family in the Etonville area, did he?

"Of course he's okay. Now you relax, and don't worry about anything. I'll come by the hospital in the morning." Lola waved goodbye.

The doors of the ambulance slammed shut, the colored lights of the various vehicles blurring as the ambulance lumbered away to St. Anthony's Hospital in Creston. I closed my eyes and saw myself flying through space. No matter what the paramedics said, I didn't fall because the house was a death trap and its structure rotten. Someone pushed me. I was lucky, all right. Lucky to be alive.

* * * *

I stood at the edge of a cliff looking down over waves crashing on a rocky shoreline. I couldn't breathe. Something hit me from behind and I fell forward, raucous laughter chasing me as I descended, headed straight for the jagged coast. Inches from the bottom, I sat up, gasping for air.

My body damp under the hospital sheet, I lay back against the pillow, my chest pounding. My subconscious working overtime. I'd spent a fitful night. Though I hadn't broken any bones, I was bruised on my shoulders and back and had scraped my knees. My head had apparently bounced off a step, leaving me with a monster of a headache but no concussion. I'd fallen four more steps, ending up on a landing as the stairs curved to the right. The landing prevented me from plummeting down the remaining flight of stairs. I was grateful for my hard head.

Pain meds made me drift off to sleep for a couple of hours, then I awoke again and slept intermittently until dawn, when sunlight crept into my hospital room. I was drained but wired. The events of last night only confirmed what Bill had shared. The stakes in the Carlos/mob boss game were high, and had risen after last night. Not only was Carlos probably in danger from the second hitman determined to prevent him from revealing evidence that would take down a Chicago crime figure. Someone was determined to prevent me from asking questions about Carlos's background. I was warned with a note, attacked in the Hanratty house, not to mention being locked in the coffin. What was left? I needed a caramel macchiato, clean clothes, and some answers. Not necessarily in that order.

I refused breakfast, texted Lola, and requested my walking papers. There was no reason to keep me now. Lola appeared at nine with a takeout container of caramel macchiato and a change of clothes. I kissed her! She helped me dress—slowly—to minimize contact with the contusions on my shoulders and back. Then I was pushed to the hospital entrance in a wheelchair. We settled into Lola's car. I didn't say a word as we eased away from the hospital, through the center of Creston, and onto the highway.

She peeked at my face. "You look fine except for the bandage on your forehead. You need to take the day off and lie around. Recover from your bruises. I'll call Henry if you'd like. Between Benny, Enrico, and Carmen, I'm sure the Windjammer will survive. Remember when the pipes burst and you had to—"

"Lola! Pump the brakes!" I said kindly. I knew she tended to rattle on when she was nervous. Right now I needed to focus. I stared out the car window.

"I feel so guilty. It's my fault you were at the Hanratty house. If I hadn't been so crazed about the rehearsal, you wouldn't have felt compelled to go out there to find Carlos."

"Not your fault. I wanted to see him. At rehearsal would have been better." I smiled. "So Penny read his lines?"

Lola relaxed her grip on the steering wheel, a slow grin spreading from ear to ear. "You should have heard her. Penny being Penny, she got into it a little too much. Hiding in the bookcase, playing in the trick chair, baring her teeth and threatening Lucy. Running after Renfield. Walter was into his own character, the rest of the cast gritting their teeth. Except for Edna, who's always a good sport." She took the turnoff into Etonville. "Hungry?"

I'd kill for a shower, but my stomach rumbled at full volume. I had to eat. Lola parked outside Coffee Heaven and I snapped on a ball cap and sunglasses. Maybe I could get in and get seated incognito.

"Dodie!" Jocelyn yelled when the jingle bells on the door announced our entrance. Every head in the place swiveled in our direction.

Lola headed for the last booth next to the back wall.

I tried to follow unobtrusively, my head down, my sore body hunched as I slipped between tables. No luck.

"We heard you were in a coma!" Nope.

"You didn't break both your legs?" Again, no.

"That place is haunted…" I was beginning to agree.

"Does this mean you're chasing a murderer?" *Yikes.*

"Now you all hush and get back to your breakfasts." Jocelyn put an arm around me. I winced. "Let Dodie have a little peace and quiet."

Etonville resumed eating, and I eased onto the bench. "Thanks for running interference."

Jocelyn tapped her order pad, glowering. "That old house should have been torn down years ago. And that Realtor never should have rented to Carlos and Bella." She lowered her voice and pointed her pencil in our faces. "I don't know who you're tailing, Dodie, and I don't believe in vampires. Not exactly anyway. But something is off with Carlos."

"Not that again," Lola said impatiently.

Jocelyn raised a hand as a stop sign. "I'm not talking about *Dracula* and stakes through the heart and all of that stuff."

She had our attention. "I saw him last night at the corner of Anderson and Main."

My little hairs stood at attention. I looked at Lola. "You did? What time? What was he doing?"

She raised her hand again to stifle my questions. "Seven, seven fifteen. Riding in the back seat of a dark car. His face was covered."

Whoa.

"He appeared disturbed." Jocelyn took our orders and stepped away.

Lola and I exchanged looks. "*She* must be disturbed. Not even a mention of Walter," Lola half-joked. "I suppose Carlos was on his way to the family emergency when Jocelyn spotted him."

I frowned.

Lola studied me. "What is it?"

"Do you remember what time Carlos called, and what he said to you?"

"He called at the end of Act Two. Before the blackout."

"So about nine thirty?"

"About. He didn't say much. Only that he was sorry to miss rehearsal because of a family emergency."

"That's it?"

"Yes. Then he hung up."

"Are you sure it was him?"

Lola looked thunderstruck. "I thought so. But the connection was fuzzy. In and out. I assumed he was out of town with the emergency."

"Why did he call you and not Penny?"

Lola's eyes grew wide. "I don't know. Do you think someone was impersonating Carlos? Why would someone do that?"

Why indeed? Jocelyn brought our meal, giving me one last eyeball and a warning. "Remember what I said."

My cell pinged. It was Bill: *have you seen the weather in Chicago? Bad...damn. Waiting for my flight to take off.*

He hadn't left yet? He was supposed to arrive in an hour. It was both positive and negative news. On the one hand, it gave me more time to get my investigative ducks in a row so that I could explain the Carlos case from beginning to end. On the other hand, the longer Bill was delayed, the more vulnerable I felt. Never mind. I had to suck it up. I Googled Chicago weather. The city was in the midst of a terrific rain- and windstorm. No wonder flights were delayed. "Between you and me, a rickety staircase was not the reason I fell," I mumbled to Lola.

She set her fork carefully on her plate. "You'd better tell me everything."

"Someone pushed me. Someone knew I was in the house. Someone tracked me there." I took a bite of my cinnamon roll. "For the record? I don't think that call was made by Carlos." Without betraying Bill's confidence and revealing the witness protection information, I told Lola that Carlos was in trouble, that he probably knew more about Daryl Wolf than he let on, and that there was a good reason he'd changed his name.

Lola called Carlos. No answer. She regarded me coolly. She understood there were things I couldn't share.

"What if Carlos doesn't show up again tonight?" I asked.

Lola had been through ELT traumas before. "We'll have to wait today and see what happens," she said calmly. "What can I do to help?"

"Thanks. First of all, I want to go home and clean up."

After assuring her that I was fine, despite the night's mishaps, and promising to take it easy, Lola dropped me off at my place, where my MC was safely parked in the driveway thanks to Carol.

"Stay put until Bill gets in, okay?"

I waved. I was afraid that ship had sailed permanently.

* * * *

Within the hour, I had texted Henry I was running late, soaked in an Epsom salts bath to soothe my aching body, and dressed for comfort in jeans and a green turtleneck sweater, wincing as I pulled the top over my head. While relaxing in the tub, I'd also organized my thoughts and my day. I was convinced now that Carlos, and perhaps Bella, had been snatched by the second hitman despite the presence of an undercover protector. The actor was in jeopardy. I imagined that the only thing keeping him alive, assuming he was still alive, was the evidence he held against the mob boss. And most likely it wasn't on his person; otherwise, there would be no need to impersonate Carlos. Someone was buying time.

Henry had told me, like Lola, to stay home; however, there was no way I could sit idle waiting for Bill. I still had to keep the Carlos investigation on the down low. I opted not to text Bill about my incident at the Hanratty house. It was likely Suki had already informed him, so no need to pile it on. No sense in making him worry more than he no doubt already was.

I breezed into the restaurant and casually walked to the bar. "Hey."

Benny did a double take. "What are you doing here? Henry ordered you to stay home."

"Just a little bump on the old noggin. Special inserts in the menus?" I asked, all business as usual.

"Wow. I don't know how you do it. You fall down a flight of stairs one day and you're back at work the next. What were you doing out there anyway?" He leaned in. "The gossip cops are saying it had something to do with the death in the cemetery."

I laughed. "Trust Etonville to stir the pot. I went looking for Carlos. He missed rehearsal."

"Uh-huh." Benny wasn't completely convinced.

"Anyway, my trip to the house was pointless. He had a family emergency. That's why he didn't show." Lola and I had agreed to maintain Carlos's alibi. At least for the present.

"Uh-huh."

Henry bolted into the dining room. "Benny! Where's today's inventory sheet—" He stared at me. His expression shifted from frustration to shock.

"The inventory sheets are on the clipboard, Cheney Brothers double-checked the weekend order, staff schedules are confirmed. And something smells good. Is that French onion soup?" I took Henry's elbow and steered him, mouth agape, back to the kitchen as the door opened and the welcome bells jingled.

I hid in the kitchen as long as possible, but there was a limit to how much stock organization and inventory I could do. Hanging around while Henry and Enrico whipped up today's sliders—the last of the specials, BLT avocado on a biscuit—was useless. I had to face the music.

I pushed open the swinging door into the dining room to a wave of chatter that abruptly ended as the occupants of the tables spied my entrance. Taking the bull by the horns, I decided to be proactive. "Hi, everyone. I'm alive, not in a coma. Didn't break anything." I grabbed a coffeepot. Did it work?

One by one, patrons gave me "okay" signs and signaled their relief. Despite their love of the rumor mill, the citizens of Etonville were willing to accept reality when it hit them in the face. Most of the time.

"So, Dodie, you don't think you had a near-death experience?" asked a customer.

Seriously? "Nope. Only a fall down some steps. All good now."

She scrutinized me skeptically. "We heard that the Hanratty house is alive. Things live in the walls."

Might have a point there. I moved on to another table.

By three o'clock, my head was thumping, my shoulders and back throbbing. I needed a break. I slumped into my booth with a bowl of onion soup and a couple of aspirin. Lola had texted to see how I was doing, Bill had texted to say that he was scheduled to leave at three central time, four my time, if the wind died down, and Pauli had texted to see if I wanted to talk. *You bet.* I was about to tap his name in my contacts when my cell rang. It was Bill.

"Hey," I said as brightly as I could. I was prepared to laugh off my "accident" and downplay my injuries in case Suki had notified him of last night's disaster.

"We're boarding in a few minutes," he said.

"Okay." I waited. Either Suki hadn't been in touch or Bill was playing his cards close to his well-muscled chest. A loudspeaker in the background announced the departure of a flight to Phoenix.

"Got a call from the medical examiner about Daryl Wolf. The initial results of the autopsy indicated a massive heart attack."

"Right. I remember."

"Well…I asked him to dig deeper…"

"The more specialized tests."

"Yes. Gas chromatography-mass spectrometry. The gold standard for forensic substance identification. Anyway, turns out there was a lethal amount of something known as aconite in his system."

"Aconite?"

"Derived from a potentially poisonous herb. If Daryl Wolf ingested something with aconite in it, he could have died in as little as an hour or so later. Maybe a half hour. Depending on the dose."

An herb. The only folks I knew in Etonville cultivating herbs were Henry, for the restaurant, and Bella Villarias. "Does this mean Daryl Wolf was…?"

"Murdered. Yeah."

My heart dropped into my stomach. Were we barking up the wrong tree? Was Bella somehow involved in Daryl Wolf's murder? I did find a piece of her jewelry in the cemetery….I felt confused and weak all over. I didn't believe that Carlos was a murderer, or that Bella was an accomplice, despite his having had a meeting with the Grim Reaper in the parking lot on Halloween night and her losing her necklace in the cemetery.

But what if *Dracula* was brought to a screeching halt because the lead actor became a prime suspect? Lola and the ELT would be devastated. No one was going to be able to take Carlos's place. *Dracula* would die a quick death. Stake or no stake.

"Dodie? Did you hear what I said?"

"The restaurant's noisy and—"

"I need you to do a little investigating for me," he said.

I was dumbstruck. "You're asking me to…?"

"That's right. It's a simple thing. Contact La Famiglia and find out who was in charge of catering the Halloween party. If the victim was there I'd like to know who cooked, who served…"

"To find out who might have laced the food with aconite."

"Yes. I'm looping Suki in on this, but I thought you might raise less suspicion. Can you concoct a reason to want this information? You're pretty good at inventing stories," he said wryly. "If you find anything sketchy with the La Famiglia staff, I'll follow up when I get back."

"Anything more on the second hitman or the runner?"

"Nothing at the moment. Everything calm out there?"

Well... Another announcement from the loudspeaker. This time for the Newark flight. "Carlos didn't show up for rehearsal last night, and today there's been no word from him. I'm getting a little concerned."

"The *Dracula* production is the least of my worries—"

"It's more than that. It's a long story, but I think I can cut to the chase. On Halloween night, Lola saw Carlos with a guy dressed like the Grim Reaper, and she was anxious to find out —"

"What did you say? Losing you."

A babble of announcements broadcasting departures and cities overrode his voice.

"I gotta go. Text me if you find out anything interesting. Love you," he said.

"I have some information that—"

The line went dead. *Sheesh.* I'd kept Carlos's problematic identity from Bill for too long. He would be in the air soon. I exhaled and typed a text: *looked into Carlos's background (long story) he's from Chicago (another long story) his name is Mercer (I can explain) think he's the runner. i'm worried (2nd hitman)??*

17

I waited for an explosion from the mobile telecommunication universe. Nothing. Bill must have turned off his cell phone instead of putting it in airplane mode. Maybe he needed to sleep. He'd sounded worn out when we talked these last few days. I was flattered that he'd asked me to help out. He hadn't done that before. In the early days, he grudgingly accepted my participation. More recently, he began to trust my instincts and share investigative information with me. This was taking my detection contribution to a new level. Before I attempted to contact La Famiglia, better known as conversing with the enemy, I wanted to research aconite.

I Googled the herb and clicked on websites. It had an ancient history as a poison and frequently showed up in fiction as the cause of death. I scrolled through a list of books, movies, and television series where perps used the herb as a murder weapon. Then I read more carefully. It was a plant native to Europe and Asia, its stalks covered with blue flowers shaped like the hood of a medieval monk. Aconite was also referred to as "monkshood." There were a number of varieties of the plant; all were toxic, though some people believed it had healing properties to cure a wide range of illnesses from colds to coronary disease. It was readily available at health food outlets and pharmacies, both online and in stores, as a powder, capsules, tablets, and liquid. It was the dosage and processing that determined aconite's toxicity. It could also be absorbed through skin or open wounds. The toxins of aconite were similar to that found in the venom of poisonous snakes.

This was some dangerous stuff. And easy to obtain... *life threatening... symptoms include difficulty breathing...irregular heartbeat...no known antidotes to aconite poisoning...fatal.*

Whoa. The killer wasn't fooling around. Then I read the last paragraph on the website. Aconite was also called "wolfsbane." I leaned back in the seat. Where had I heard that before?

I Googled the name. Up popped a picture and description of the aconite plant and a Wikipedia entry. I skimmed down the page. The fourth link was a reference to the 1931 classic movie *Dracula* starring Bela Lugosi. That was it! In the ELT production, Van Helsing held up a sprig of wolfsbane to ward off the presence of Dracula. It was supposedly as effective as garlic.

I felt a chill. Whoever had murdered Daryl Wolf had not only had a working knowledge of aconite as a deadly poison, but was familiar with the Dracula legend. First the stake and now wolfsbane…

It was four o'clock. I had an hour or so until the dinner rush. I could head over to La Famiglia and ask a few questions, keeping my expedition off-the-record. Henry was as sensitive as ever about his competition. I'd only eaten there once and he'd had a "conniption fit," as my great-aunt Maureen would have said.

I walked casually to the bar. "Benny, I need some fresh air. Think I'll go for a walk."

"Good idea. Clear your head. You need to take care of yourself."

Benny was sweet to be so concerned. I slipped on my lightweight coat and waltzed out the door. Once on the sidewalk, I hurried down the block to my car. La Famiglia was across town, a twenty-five-minute walk. I wanted to complete my mission and return to friendly territory by five. I gunned the engine, flew down Main Street, cut over Pinter Drive past the Shop N Go, and made a right turn. Left would have taken me to the cemetery.

As I pulled into the parking lot adjacent to the restaurant, my cell buzzed. Pauli: *talk?* He was a man of few words. I texted *okay* and my cell rang.

"Hey. What's up?"

Pauli cleared his throat, chewing something in my ear. "Like, I took the shot you sent—"

Mr. Chicago.

"—and dug into some databases."

"Any luck?"

"No record of any arrests. At least not in the federal police databases. They collect data from passports, drivers' licenses, airports."

"So he's not a criminal," I joked. "Great work as usual. I'm impressed."

"Piece of cake. Didya know about half the population in America is stored in facial recognition databases?" Pauli asked.

"You're kidding."

"Nope. Like, eighty percent of the photos are noncriminal too. Police use 'em to compare surveillance footage with databases of ID photos and mugshots."

"I had no clue. I simply figured you would know something about facial recognition."

Pauli warmed up to his topic. "It's a biometric ID system, like retina scanning and voice recognition," he said confidently.

The door to La Famiglia opened, and three women left the restaurant. Which reminded me, I had to get inside soon. "Pauli, thanks for this. If you find anything else in your digging…"

"So…do you wanna know his name and where he's from?" Pauli asked slyly.

"What? Of course!"

"John Doe from Las Vegas."

"What?"

"Like yeah. Funny, right?" Pauli cackled.

So Mr. Chicago was John Doe. What was that about? Who would name a child John if their last name was Doe? It had to be an alias. My cell pinged. "Pauli, I have to go. Text me later if there's anything else."

"No problem. Gotta bounce anyway."

Pauli clicked off, and I read my text. Lola: *any sign of carlos? might have to cancel tonight's show. how are u?* I texted back that I was fine, had not seen Carlos, and wished her luck. And now I wished myself luck. On the drive here, I'd formulated a plan of action. What did Bill say? Not arouse too much suspicion? I swiped on lipstick, ran a brush through my hair, straightened my coat. Good thing all of my bruises were hidden except for the one on my forehead. My bangs covered the bandage there.

I walked to the entrance calmly. I'd only been here twice before: once to pick up takeout garlic knots and once with Bill—our first almost-date that was a disaster. I opened the door. The rich aromas of Italian fare assaulted my nostrils. The restaurant was mostly empty, certainly less busy than it would be later. La Famiglia was just as I remembered it: brick walls decorated with watercolors of Italian country scenes, an open wine rack, a central oven and cooking area, and a parquet tile floor. The atmosphere oozed old-world gentility, placid and poised. I flashed on the often-frenzied ambience of the Windjammer, the dining room that featured a nautical-themed décor to replicate a nineteenth-century whaling vessel, complete with central beams, floor planking, and a figurehead of a woman's bust above the entrance. Never mind. I wouldn't trade its Etonville vibe.

I walked to the host/hostess station, where a thirtysomething woman in a stylish black suit typed into a computer. Checking reservations.

"Can I help you?" she asked in a light Italian accent, without looking up.

"Yes. I'd like to speak to your catering manager."

"What does this concern?"

Showtime. I smiled. "I'm interested in the staff who put together the food for the Halloween party."

"Oh. That." She sniffed dismissively.

The hostess provoked my defend-Etonville hackles. "It was a lovely event. And the buffet was terrific."

"So you needed…?"

"I'm Dodie O'Dell. Manager of the Windjammer." She regarded me with curiosity as though I was an alien creature. Compared to the management of La Famiglia, I guess I was. Then, completely throwing me off-guard, she broke into a huge smile, shook my hand, led me to a corner table, offered me something to drink, and disappeared into a back room to fetch Marcello.

What?

Marcello, whose Italian accent was thicker than the hostess's, with lustrous, wavy black hair, dreamy, deep brown eyes, and a sexy, sensuous mouth, was the sous chef, responsible for supervising catering for outside events. He seemed eager to connect with Etonville and its citizens. Truth be told, the clientele who frequented La Famiglia was a slightly different demographic than the Windjammer customers; they often came from surrounding towns as far away as the Pennsylvania border. The Windjammer was mostly homegrown.

I laid on the charm and informed Marcello that I was so impressed with his Halloween spread, we were thinking of attempting some of La Famiglia's catering menu. Nothing works like flattery. I had him eating out of my hand in minutes, giving me secret recipes, explaining the logic behind food choices for the catering, naming serving personnel when I complimented their professionalism. Yet nothing I learned seemed out of the ordinary as far as the Halloween party was concerned. I made a mental note of names, especially the three servers who'd worked the bar and buffet, gushed over Marcello's helpfulness, and regretfully declined to dine at the restaurant as his guest that evening. If I wasn't engaged with a diamond on my finger, I might have taken him up on his invitation. I said ciao, he kissed me on both cheeks and begged me to come back to taste the house specialties—sautéed scallops with a butternut squash caponata and shrimp fra diavolo. Marcello was half Latin lover and half Emeril Lagasse. Boom!

My bruises were catching up with me, and I felt the need to take a bona fide break. I texted Benny that I was running late but would be at the Windjammer by six, then cut across town to Fairfield and drove down Ames. A half hour nap would do the trick. I had barely closed my eyes, drifting off on the living room sofa under an old blanket, when my cell rang. I counted the rings…let it go. Bill would still be in the air. It couldn't be him. Whoever called could wait until later. Sinking into semiconsciousness, I snuggled deeper under the cover, my aching muscles getting a short reprieve. A burst of clanging from my phone woke me up again. Resigned, I threw the cover aside and swung my legs off the sofa. There was no escaping. I checked the caller ID. It was a number I didn't recognize. I tapped on the Answer icon as the ringing ended. There was no message on voicemail. Couldn't have been too important. A text came in from Benny: *did you get a call from Bella V? she wanted your number…hope you don't mind.*

They surfaced! was my first thought. My second was, no mention of Carlos. A knot formed in my midsection. I texted Lola, asking if Carlos had shown up. One way or the other, she had to decide soon, if she hadn't already. She returned my text: *no…deciding on Dracula in next half hour… Walter angry and frantic.*

For once, I sympathized with Walter. I didn't blame him for being angry because he wasn't privy to Carlos's backstory. He had no way of knowing that his lead actor's life might be in danger. What about Bella? The unidentifiable number could have been her. I had no idea what she could want with me. I called Benny.

"Hey. Did you get some rest?" Benny asked when he answered the phone.

"A little. So Bella wanted my number?"

"She came in here about an hour ago looking for you. I said you'd be back about six, but she didn't want to wait to talk to you. Did she get in touch?"

"Maybe. I missed a call that might have been her. No voicemail." I hesitated. "How did she seem?"

"Funny you ask. I remembered meeting her at the Halloween party. She was so…cool and calm, ya know?"

"Like she had the whole world under control when she read your palm. I know what you mean."

"Anyway, she came into the restaurant, a scarf around her head kind of hiding her face. And she was plenty nervous today. Looked like she hadn't slept in days." Benny whistled softly. "What's up with that?"

The knot in my stomach tightened. Something had happened to Carlos? I worked hard to keep my tone nonchalant. "Thanks, Benny. I'll see you shortly."

"Wait a minute. She said if she didn't reach you to let you know she'd wait outside the theater until eight."

The theater? Why would she go there? She must know *Dracula* could not go on without her husband. "Did she mention…Carlos?"

"Nada. Hey, Henry shifted the menu around tonight. He's serving meatloaf instead of the chicken noodle casserole."

"I'm on my way."

In my MC, I tapped on the unknown number in my Recents. After a greeting from Bella, the call rang through to voicemail. I left a brief message letting her know I would be in the restaurant for the rest of the evening if she wanted to reach me. Short and to the point. I zoomed down Main and wedged my car in a parking space directly in front of the theater between a pickup truck and an SUV. My petite MC was dwarfed by the oversize vehicles.

A small crowd had already gathered in the Windjammer for dinner, and I stopped to chat with a few tables. Letting everyone know I was alive… Benny jerked his head toward my back booth before I could make my way through the swinging doors into the kitchen.

"She came back right after we talked. Kind of desperate to see you. I figured tuck her out of the way."

Bella.

"Get her a cup of coffee?"

He shrugged. "I offered her something to drink. She refused."

I walked slowly, not wanting to arouse any more suspicion than had already been aroused. After all, half of Etonville knew I'd fallen down steps in the Hanratty house and that neither of its temporary occupants was at home at the time. Bella showing up now had to raise questions among the populace. More so once Lola posted the cancellation of tonight's performance. Somehow I had to get her out of here.

I approached Bella, startled to see her condition. A scarf was indeed wound around her head covering half her face and her hair. She looked up, her eyes rimmed in red with dark circles underneath, her face sallow, cheeks sunken. When was the last time I'd seen her? When Lola and I had come to grill Carlos and interrupted Bella's gardening session. She'd been curious about our visit, but still warm and engaging.

"Hi, Bella. Sorry I missed your call."

"No. I'm sorry to bother you." Her voice cracked; she raised a hand grasping a wad of Kleenex to her eyes.

"That's okay. What can I do for you?" I settled onto the seat, perched at the edge.

She paused. "I didn't know where else to go."

"It's about Carlos."

If Bella was disturbed by my statement she didn't show it. "Yes. He needs help. We…need help."

"Right." How much to admit to her? "You probably heard that I was at your house yesterday. And tumbled down the basement stairs."

Bella looked confused. "At our house?" she asked, momentarily distracted from the crisis at hand.

I explained how, when Carlos hadn't shown up at rehearsal, I offered to stop by their place to see where he was. The door being ajar, I entered, calling out for them, and saw a light in the basement. I went down to check it out, then fell on a stair and bounced down a couple more.

Bella gazed at me in amazement. "Were you hurt?"

"Bumps and bruises. I'll live." I regarded her warily. "Carlos called into the theater with a story about a family emergency. No emergency, right?"

She waved off my question. "Not that kind."

"Maybe we'd better talk." I motioned for her to stay put and walked to the bar. "Benny…I need that night off after all. My back is starting to kill me."

He glanced over at my booth, where the top of Bella's head was visible. Benny was good about not being too curious. "Sure. I'll take care of things."

I smiled my thanks. A text came in from Lola: *show canceled…might have to tie one on…you in?* I responded that I wouldn't be available until later, and I'd be in touch. No mention of Bella. She needed to be incognito for the moment. Which raised a good question: where to go with her? The Windjammer would be filling up soon, making it impossible to keep her presence hidden. No private nooks or crannies. Unless you counted the basement where Henry stored cases of wine and any produce that needed a cool environment. No, we had to get out of here through the back door.

Bella was nervously tapping her fingers on the table. "I need to get to the theater," she said.

"But there's no performance of *Dracula* this evening. Without Carlos—"

She nodded vehemently. "Of course. I still need to get there."

I waited only a fraction of a second before grabbing my bag. "Let's go." I led her to the back of the restaurant, exchanging brief signals with Benny as the rear door closed on us. Outside, we stepped onto a small cement porch that overlooked Henry's garden, where he harvested rosemary, thyme, sage, and basil, among other herbs. Which reminded me of Bella's garden and the wolfsbane/aconite. There would be time to confront the murder later. Maybe I could figure out a way of working the plant into our conversation—

"We have to hurry," Bella said abruptly. "Is that the back entrance to the theater?" She pointed to the loading dock next door, which held a half-full dumpster and two trash bins. It would be overflowing on strike night. Whenever that would be, given tonight's cancellation. She started down the porch steps.

"Wait a minute. What are we doing here?" I grasped at her coat. "Anyway, the theater is closed. No one's home."

Bella hesitated, partly because I had a gentle hold on her arm and partly because it appeared as if that possibility hadn't occurred to her. "Oh no."

I brushed some dirt off the step and sat down. "If we need to hurry, maybe you'd better tell me everything. And fast."

She glanced at the loading dock. Then sat down. "I hardly know where to begin."

I'd been there often enough, trying to explain myself to Bill. "Pick a spot and let it out," I said softly.

"I told Carlos doing this show was a mistake. Like some other decisions he made…"

"Leaving Colorado to come to New Jersey?"

Bella gasped. "You know?"

"About moving from Lennox to Etonville?"

Bella, stunned, bobbed her head. "I don't understand how you—?"

"Changing your names." This wasn't a question.

Bella surrendered. "Choosing 'Carlos Villarias' as an alias was another mistake. Anyone who knew anything about the history of *Dracula* could figure it out." She turned to face me straight on. "Anyone smart and perceptive."

I had to leapfrog over compliments and drill down fast. "Where is Carlos?" She wavered.

"Bella, if you want my help, you're going to have to trust me. You have no one else to turn to, right?" I reminded her.

"I don't know. They came to the house yesterday and grabbed us."

Almost twenty-four hours ago. That explained Bella's distressed appearance.

"We were blindfolded. We drove for about fifteen or twenty minutes and were taken into a building."

Someplace not too far from Etonville. "Do you know who the driver was? What he looked like?"

"There were two of them. Only one spoke. They wore dark clothes with ski masks over their heads." She broke down, crying.

"Why? What did they want?"

She wiped her face in the head scarf. "If you know about Colorado and Lennox and Villarias, you must know about the…"

"Witness protection program. The police in Chicago have been communicating with Etonville's police chief—"

Bella darted up. "They said no police or Carlos wouldn't live to see tomorrow morning," she cried.

"Okay. No police." For the moment. "Why did they let you go? What's with the theater?"

"Carlos turned over information on…men he was working for."

"I know. Organized crime guys."

"Yes. And we went into hiding. I didn't know that he kept a crucial piece of evidence as…insurance. I only found out about it a week ago. And now they've come to collect it. They are desperate to have it," she exclaimed.

"What is…*it*?"

"A flash drive."

Bill's words came rushing back: …*there's something the runner has that implicates the crime boss directly…proof that he planned the murder of a politician. OMG!* Carlos was sitting on that kind of evidence? No wonder they nabbed him. And were desperate to get their hands on the memory stick.

"They let me go…rather, they brought me back to Etonville and left me a few blocks away." Bella twisted her hands. "I'm supposed to get it. They'll call me and tell me where to meet."

This was sounding more and more like a B movie nightmare. Mafia bosses, kidnapping, ransom for evidence, drop-offs and pickups…and no contacting law enforcement. Except that it involved people I knew. "And if you don't have the flash drive…"

She let the implication hang in the air. "They'll call at eight o'clock."

It was six thirty. "So where is it?"

"Carlos said he hid it in the theater for safekeeping. In the scenery."

"On the set of *Dracula*?"

My thumbs bounced around the keyboard of my cell phone. First I texted Lola: *in trouble…need to get in theater on the qt…come to loading dock with key.* Next I texted Bill: *the crime boss evidence is in the theater…long story…come here when you land.*

I paused. I should let Suki know what we were up to but I had assured Bella the police wouldn't be dragged into the search. After we found the memory stick, all bets were off.

18

Within ten minutes, Lola's Lexus flew down the alley behind the theater and the Windjammer, came to a noisy stop, gravel flying sideways from beneath the tires of her car. She whipped into a space beside the dumpster and threw open the car door. Her feet hit the ground. "Dodie, what the—?" Shocked at the sight of Bella, Lola grasped the car door to anchor herself. "What's going on?" I'd caught her already dressed for the performance this evening: black tights, a long, royal-blue sweater that hugged her in all the right places, stiletto heels.

"We can explain everything later. Right now, we need to get onto the set of *Dracula*."

Lola wordlessly opened the loading dock door, flicked on a light in the scene shop, and led us through the green room onto the stage. In another minute, she'd popped on the stage lights. "Now what?" she asked.

Because the show had been canceled at the last minute, Penny had left the stage set for Act One for tomorrow night. "Lola, I can't go into detail now, but—"

Lola raised a hand to stop my explanation. "No need. What can I do?"

I squeezed her gratefully and turned to Bella, who stood, bewildered, in front of the French doors. "Where is it? What did Carlos tell you?" I said, coaxing some action out of her. She stood transfixed, or maybe disconcerted, at confronting the *Dracula* set—the desk and trick chair, sofa, and bookcase.

"I'm not sure now. He said 'Act One.' As if I'd know what that means."

"This is the setting for Act One," Lola confirmed.

What the heck kind of clue was that? Why not give Bella more information…unless he was wary of saying too much in front of his captors. Still, his life, and almost certainly Bella's, was at stake. "Bella, why didn't they come to search themselves? I don't get it. Why release you?"

Lola's eyes widened as she grasped the gist of the situation.

"Carlos insisted I go for it. And he told the men either it was me or they could shoot him."

Whoa. Something didn't feel right.

"He told them there was a copy of the evidence in a safe location that would be released to the Chicago press if anything happened to me. He didn't trust them. He barely trusts me," she said bitterly.

"Is that true? That Carlos made a copy and left it with someone?"

She tucked her arms around her waist, distraught and overwhelmed by the task ahead of us. "I don't know."

Despite his bravado, Carlos was playing fast and loose with their lives. More of a gambler than I imagined. "Was there anything else he said, something that might give us a hint?" I asked hopefully.

She shook her head vigorously. "Only Act One," she repeated.

We studied the set. There were potential hiding places everywhere. Doors, windows, furniture, even the trick chair and bookcase. And the thumb drive could be as small as an inch long. We had to begin somewhere. "I'll work stage left. Lola, you search stage right. Bella, why don't you head upstage to see if you can find anything around the doors and windows. Let's move. There's not much time."

"What are we looking for?" whispered Lola anxiously.

"A flash drive." My eyebrows lifted in a wordless signal: *life or death!*

We went to work. Running our hands around windows and doorframes, turning furniture upside down, even scouring obvious areas like the desk drawers, under lamps, around the bookcase. No luck.

After half an hour, we gathered downstage. My back ached. "That's it for the set," said Lola. "Maybe Carlos meant somewhere backstage? He moved back and forth from the doors and windows to the trick bookcase. And down the trap door."

Lola made a good point. "Okay, let's move offstage. I'll—"

The stage lights snapped off, leaving us in the dark. "Hey!" I shouted, and clasped Bella's arm.

"Don't move," Lola warned. "You might trip and fall. I'll see what's going on with the light board."

Dim light escaping through the green room door, which Lola had propped open, sent shadows skittering around the set pieces. Who had left us in the dark?

"Stage is off limits!" shouted a grouchy voice.

Penny.

"Turn the lights back on," Lola yelled in exasperation.

"Walter doesn't want civilians on set while the theater is dark."

Sheesh. It was dark all right.

"Penny, if you want to keep your position as stage manager, these lights will be on in two seconds," Lola said loudly and evenly. The stage lit up. "Thank you. Now you can leave." Lola was taking no prisoners.

Penny strode through the house and up the step unit leading to the stage. "I have to keep my eyes and ears on the ground. I'm the—"

"Production manager!" Lola and I yelled. We'd heard it often enough.

Penny crossed her arms and faced us. "What are you doing here?" She finally registered the fact that Bella was among us. "Thought you had a family emergency," she crowed. Penny loved to catch folks in the act of deception.

"We did. We do…" Bella gaped at Lola and me, begging for help.

Lola flipped her blond hair and assumed her diva face. "We are assisting Bella in a search."

"For what?" Penny pursued. "O'Dell, if you're involved, it's gotta be a disaster."

Sometimes Penny hit the nail on the proverbial head. "Carlos is with a sick relative and he sent Bella here to find a memory stick he lost because it has his calendar on it, and you know how disorganized life is without your calendar."

Penny threw up her hands. "Why didn't ya say so? Where'd he think he left it?"

Appealing to Penny's sense of organization had done the trick. We trooped backstage and proceeded to examine all spaces and anything that offered a hiding place—which was everywhere. The wings, the flies, around the coils of cable where, only last week, Gabriel had found the errant stake. No success.

"What about the trapdoor? Maybe it fell out of a pocket while he was descending?" I said.

Penny hopped to the trap, activated the device that lowered the platform, and rotated a flashlight through the opening. "Nothing down here," she muttered.

"It's small. Could it have fallen on the ground?" I asked, sensing Bella's growing anguish.

"I'd have seen it when I swept up."

"Swept up? Penny, you sweep the stage every night?"

"At least once. Sometimes more than once. Actors can be messy. Walter likes a clean stage floor."

"Maybe you swept up the flash drive."

Penny was off to sift through the trash barrel on the loading dock.

Lola sighed, and Bella dropped onto the sofa in despair. "I don't think we're going to find it. Time's running out."

It was seven thirty. We were stumped. "Don't give up, Bella. We'll think of something."

"Yes, of course," Lola chimed in, then looked at me as if to say *what are you talking about?*

"I'm afraid of what they'll do to Carlos..."

"Don't ask me how I know... the authorities in Chicago have sent help. Someone is keeping an eye on Carlos." I fervently hoped Bill's intel was correct and Mr. Chicago was on the scene.

Both Lola and Bella gazed at me, stupefied. "Are you sure?" asked Bella. "He never mentioned that to me."

"Yes, Dodie, are you sure?" echoed Lola.

"Positive." My fingers were crossed.

"In that case, maybe I should go to the police," Bella said carefully. "And tell them what I know."

"You have no idea where he is?"

Bella shook her head. "I was blindfolded going there and coming back here."

I debated. If we called Suki, it would take time to question Bella and call in state police reinforcements. They'd miss the eight o'clock deadline. And we still had no idea where the bad guys had stashed Carlos. Bill wasn't here. I needed to be proactive. We didn't have the flash drive, but maybe there was a chance we could locate Carlos and then loop Suki in.

Penny bounded back onto the stage. "Nada. Nothing in the trash barrel." She pushed her glasses up her nose, regarding us expectantly.

I hesitated. "Bella, I'm not sure how you'll feel about this..." I wasn't sure how *I* felt about it. But we were out of options.

Bella looked up.

"There was a program on NPR about...psychometry."

"What's psychometry?" asked Lola.

"Yeah, what's psych...whatever?" asked Penny.

I wasn't sure bringing Penny into the conversation was the best idea, but she was here and we had to move forward.

"It's similar to a psychic reading." Bella spoke slowly. "Instead of reading a person, you read an object."

"That's interesting," said Lola politely. "But what about Carlos?"

"He's gonna have to scramble if he doesn't find his calendar. He's probably lost the performance schedule, and—"

"Not now, Penny," Lola cautioned her.

"Whatever." She stood hands on hips, waiting for orders.

"Maybe you could try to do a reading with an object close to Carlos. Pick up the psychic energy it gives off. Get impressions. Like where he is." Did I actually believe Bella could do this? I hurried on. "If we know that, we could go to the police and get immediate results. Otherwise, it's like searching for a needle in a haystack. Even for cops."

Penny scrunched up her forehead. "O'Dell, I know his calendar is important. Going to the police? Isn't that a little over-the-top?"

"I think it's a good idea," Lola said, ignoring Penny. "What have you got to lose?"

Bella nodded. "I'll try."

Lola squeezed her hand. "You did a fantastic job reading palms and tarot cards."

"Do you have something of Carlos's on you?" I asked.

She dove into her purse, shoved her hands in pockets. Her face fell. "I don't."

"What about something he used here? In the theater?" I asked, acutely aware it was nearly eight o'clock.

Everyone looked around, as if something might pop out at us. Then Penny snapped her fingers. "His script. He left it in the dressing—"

We blew past Penny, Lola leading the way. She unlocked the door and switched on the light bulbs that encircled each mirror. The yellowish glow was warm, the mirrors reflecting our troubled faces. Only Penny's was neutral as she hung out in the doorway, skeptical even though she had no clue what we were up to.

Bella sat down and picked up the *Dracula* script, fanning the pages. Then she replaced it on the makeup counter, closed her eyes, and breathed deeply several times. She seemed to be centering herself as she rubbed her hands together for a minute, then moved her left hand in a circle over the script.

Penny barked a short laugh, interrupted by a stern look from Lola, who motioned to her to zip it—the shoe was on the other foot this time. Penny had no effect on Bella, who continued inhaling and exhaling, waving her hand in a circular motion. She stopped moving suddenly and carefully touched the play, running her left hand over the cover, then turning several pages and touching those.

"Carlos," she murmured gently, as if she was speaking directly to him.

The room was hushed, Lola and I hoping against hope that some impression would arise from the *Dracula* script. After all, Carlos had had an intimate relationship with the play for a number of years.

"I'm getting…"

We bent forward.

"I'm sensing that he's…" She broke off the thought.

We waited.

"I'm hearing loud, scraping sounds. Machinery."

That could be almost anywhere. "Any images of him?" I asked tentatively.

Bella slowly cocked her head to one side. "Cars."

"He's in traffic? Are they moving him somewhere?" My pulse quickened. Something had to give in a hurry if we were going to find him unharmed.

"Numbers."

"Like a license plate on a car?" I asked, excited. Now we were getting somewhere.

"No," she said firmly. "In a book."

She adjusted her head from side to side, then grew quiet. "Speed."

Scraping, machinery, cars, numbers in a book, speed. What did it add up to?

Bella's eyes flew open. "I had strong impressions. I simply don't know what they mean," she cried helplessly.

Lola patted her back sympathetically. Penny's hands twitched at her sides, missing her whistle and clipboard. I felt defeated, about to give up. Bella had to receive her call and announce that she hadn't been able to…

I felt a chill, a tingling that started at my neck and ran down my shoulders. Thumping in my chest. I repeated the words, this time out loud. "Scraping sounds, machinery, cars, numbers in a book, speed…"

They all stared at me.

"I think I know where they've hidden Carlos," I rasped. Could it be? *Speedwell Auto Parts in Bernridge.* Machinery, cars, numbers. Carlos was the bookkeeper. And Bella had almost "seen" one part of the company's name. I tapped numbers on my cell phone in a rush. "I'm calling Suki. Lola, would you take Bella to the station? I'll give her a heads-up that you're coming. She'll know what to do about Carlos."

"Thank you," Bella said, grasping my hands. "You may have saved our lives." She headed out the door with Lola, relief flooding her face. The first glimmer of hope since she'd appeared at the Windjammer this evening.

"Suki will take care of things." Along with Bill, who should be back home this hour.

I gave Suki a thumbnail description of the past couple of hours. If she was astounded at the revelations, she hid it well. Typical Suki. I felt better that she was on the case. The Etonville PD would have Carlos safe, the Bernridge Police raiding Speedwell Auto Parts, and the second hitman in custody before the night was over.

Penny had been observing the scene unfold silently. Now, she shifted positions and plopped into a makeup chair, stretching her legs onto the makeup counter. Walter would have a fit if he saw her. "Gotta hand it to you, O'Dell. You brought your A game."

"Thanks. I think." I slung my bag over my shoulder, pulling out my cell phone. I would text Bill that Lola and Bella were at the police station and—

"Carlos didn't lose his calendar, did he?" she asked.

I paused. "Nope."

"Hard to get anything past me." She tilted onto the two rear legs of the chair. "Walter will go ballistic when he finds out Carlos was playing hide-and-seek in Bernridge instead of at the brush-up rehearsal. Not very professional."

I shook my head. "Someone broke the mold when they made you, Penny."

She grinned and chuckled. "You got that right. I'm one of a kind."

Geez.

"I'm going to hang around the theater a while longer," I said. "No need for you to stay. I'll make sure the door is locked when I leave. And the lights off."

The front legs of Penny's chair landed with a thud. "O'Dell, you can't be in the theater alone without management." She pointed to herself. "*Moi.* And I have to leave. Got an appointment."

I had to think fast. "I'm on official police business. Bill...Chief Thompson should be here any minute."

Penny eyed me dubiously. "Nobody told me about it."

"This job is strictly on a need-to-know basis." Would that discourage her? "Penny, I need you to exit through the front door, park your car down the block, and keep an eye on anyone who tries to enter the building. Can you do that without being seen?"

"This has something to do with the guy in the graveyard, doesn't it?" she asked, excited.

"You didn't hear this from me...but..."

"Don't worry, O'Dell. I'm on it." She cleaned her glasses on her sweatshirt. "No one will get by me."

"What about your appointment?"

Penny smirked. "Dinner can wait."

"Be sure to text me if you see anyone."

"Got it." She left the dressing room.

The door to the stage opened and closed. Then silence.

The backstage was eerie. I flicked off the lights in the dressing room and walked onstage. As I stared into the house, the stage lights blinded me. I could hardly see the last row of seats. No word from Bill. I exited into the stage right wing, where I was confronted with a prop table, a rolling wardrobe rack, coils of electrical cable...and the coffin. When Bella had repeated Carlos's direction to examine the Act One scenery, the doors, windows, and furniture were the most logical places to search. And we'd found nothing. I was starting to wonder...Given Carlos's vague clue to the flash drive's whereabouts, maybe he didn't want that memory stick to be turned over to the hitman. Whatever evidence he had, Carlos, in his arrogant way, intended to keep it to safeguard his freedom. I figured he knew the criminal types he was dealing with and that his life—and Bella's—would be worth nothing once the flash drive was handed over. Despite his claim to have made a copy of the evidence. Though he'd told Bella to search the Act One scenery, it was possible he'd slipped the memory stick into the coffin.

The light was dim backstage. I flipped on my flashlight and lifted the creaky lid. I trembled involuntarily, remembering the last time I fooled with the box. I began a methodical examination of the interior. JC had covered the sides and bottom of the casket in black fabric to keep the stake-stabbing of the Dracula dummy as invisible as possible. I ran my hands around the rim of the box, feeling inside and outside the material. Nothing. Then I patted down the sides of the coffin, looking for even small bumps in the fabric where a tiny object could be hidden. Again, no luck. Maybe I was wrong.

Only the bottom was left to explore. JC had padded the surface with foam rubber to muffle sound. On top of it, every night he'd placed a small sandbox into which Romeo pounded the stake that ended Dracula's life. The foam rubber was tacked securely to the wooden box, leaving no room for objects to be slipped underneath. Being thorough, I ran my fingers over the entire foam surface. Frustrated at not finding anything again, I rocked back on my heels. Where was it?

I heard a faint thump, and my stomach twisted. I flicked off my flashlight and texted Penny: *see anyone come in yet?* My heart knocked against my rib cage. She answered: *nope.* That was bad news. Someone might have gotten by Penny and broken into the theater.

I closed the lid of the coffin and secured the latch. I stooped, duckwalking my way farther into the dark of the backstage area, scooting behind a tall pile of neatly folded curtains. I pulled them around me, willing myself into a tiny ball of humanity. The theater was silent. Could the thump have been my imagination? Minutes passed with no sign of an intruder. Then another thump from behind me, somewhere near the green room. No wonder Penny, sitting in her car out front, didn't see anything. Whoever it was probably broke in via the shop door that opened onto the loading dock. Less visibility through a back entrance.

My mind raced…in my panic to determine which way the visitor had entered, I hadn't stopped to consider exactly *who* the visitor might be. Could I have been wrong about Speedwell Auto Parts? Maybe Carlos wasn't being held there; maybe I'd sent Suki and the Bernridge cops on a wild-goose chase; maybe the hitman was still on the loose or in the theater now; maybe the government agent supposedly protecting Carlos had lost him; maybe—

A footstep scraped behind me. My pulse shot from zero to sixty. I burrowed deeper into my nest of curtains, squeezing my eyes shut. If I couldn't see them, they couldn't see me—

"Dodie?" a voice rasped.

"Arrgh!" I yelled, my arms flailing in self-defense.

Hands grasped me, pulling the curtains aside. "What are you doing in there?" asked Bill, squatting down to my eye level.

"You scared me half to death!" I continued to yell.

"Calm down. It's just me." He put an arm around my back. "Sorry. I wasn't sure if anyone was in the theater."

I took huge breaths.

"Suki called as my plane landed. I went straight to the station. Then came here."

"Did she fill you in on—"

"Yeah. Bella Villarias and the psychic thing. Speedwell Auto Parts. Bernridge PD, the whole enchilada." He brushed a loose strand of hair off my face. "You okay? And, more importantly, what are you doing *here*?"

"Why are *you* here?" I asked in return.

"You texted me, remember? When I didn't hear back, I thought I'd double-check to see what you were up to."

I was happy to see his grin appear, the left side of his mouth ticking upward.

"So Carlos is safe? They caught the hitman?"

Bill's face turned grim. "Things are in progress. Suki is handling the Etonville end. She'll keep me posted. Thanks to you, Carlos should be freed within the hour if all goes well."

Relief washed over me. But only momentarily. The flash drive was still missing.

"I didn't get the intel on how you knew about the Bernridge location. Suki wasn't clear on that."

Explaining how I knew about the site where Carlos was being held would require admitting to spying on him, which might lead to my snooping in Lennox, which could direct Bill to Pauli's deep search on the obits in the *Daily Herald*. Not to mention the warning note on my car and Mr. Chicago. All of it supposedly above my pay grade as a freelance Etonville sleuth.

"I'll get to that, but first I have to tell you about the flash drive."

One eyebrow shot up. "I know about—"

"That's why we were in the theater. The bad guys demanded Carlos's evidence, letting Bella go to retrieve it. Carlos told her to search the Act One set."

"Suki told me some of this."

"We couldn't find the flash drive. Lola escorted Bella to the police department and I was ready to let Suki take over."

Bill cocked his head as if to say *nice of you.*

"You know what I mean. I was about to leave the theater when I got a hunch. After I got locked in the coffin—"

He frowned. "You got locked in the coffin?"

"I'll get to that later. Anyway…I figured the memory stick might be hidden somewhere inside or outside the coffin."

"Was it?" he asked, on the alert.

"No. At least not that I could find. I was trying to decide where to look next when I heard you come in. Not knowing it was you, I scrambled into this pile of curtains. Penny's on the lookout on Main Street, though that's a mixed blessing."

"Penny?"

"I had to get her out of the theater so I could dig around. Did you come through the lobby?"

Bill pulled me to my feet. "No. I picked up a master key Lola left at the station so I could enter from the loading dock in case…"

He didn't need to complete the thought: in case I was in trouble and he needed to make a stealth entrance. "I thought I heard a noise from the front of the theater," I said, as much to myself as to Bill.

"Noise? What kind of noise?" His hand crept under his all-weather police jacket, feeling for his service revolver.

"A...thump. Like someone opened a door. Or closed it."

"Stay here. I'll check the house and lobby."

"Okay, but—"

He put a hand on my shoulder, gently nudging me downward to a sitting position. "I'll be right back," he murmured.

He disappeared into the black of the backstage area. As per his instructions, I stayed where I was. Seconds ticked by. I texted Penny again: *any sign of anyone?* She responded: *o'dell...duh...nothing gets by me.*

If only.

Then a text came in. Lola: *where are you? went home...nothing to do till Carlos surfaces...call me.*

Later. After Carlos was safe, the flash drive in Bill's hands, the bad guys in custody.

Another noise from the direction of the lobby. "Bill?" I called out softly. Guess he hadn't found anything.

A ruffling sound from onstage as someone brushed the side curtains that ran parallel to the main drape.

A head emerged in the dim light.

"Gabriel?" I said, surprised. Renfield. "I thought you were Bill."

"Sorry to disappoint you."

"No show tonight. Too bad."

"Yes. Too bad," he repeated, stepping closer, one hand jammed inside his coat pocket.

I waited. What did he want? "Did you see Bill? He went to the lobby."

"I saw him."

The hell with hanging around backstage as per Bill's orders. Gabriel's behavior was unsettling. "Well...hope the ELT has better luck tomorrow. See you." I turned to go.

Gabriel shifted in the shadows to face me, his other hand, and a suspicious bulge, in his other coat pocket. "Can't let you do that just yet."

I froze, my neck hairs screaming a warning. Too late.

He withdrew his hand and aimed a gun at me, his eyes dark and wild. "Where is it?"

19

"Where's Bill?" My mind scrambled to make sense of the moment. Gabriel? Connected to organized crime and the mob boss? The madman in *Dracula*?

"Never mind about him. I want the flash drive." He clutched my upper arm. "Where is it?" he repeated roughly. "I know you all were searching for it."

"W–we didn't find it," I stammered. I had to get a grip. "Anyway, I'm not talking until I see Bill," I said with fake confidence. I took a calculated risk—possibly making him angry. On the other hand, if he thought I knew the whereabouts of the memory stick, I was valuable.

Gabriel dragged me from the pile of curtains onto the stage, threading our way around the scenery, the gun wobbling in his hand. Too much nervous energy, or else the actor wasn't used to managing a weapon. Gabriel managed intimidation well. I had to stall for time. Surely Bill would notice I was incommunicado and come after me.

"Doesn't Carlos have it?" I asked.

He shoved his gun into my ribs. "You know he left it somewhere on the stage."

Gabriel scanned the set quickly, his eyes swinging wildly from the doors and windows to the fireplace and bookcase. "Gotta be here somewhere." He prodded my torso until I was standing stage center. "Find it." He waggled his gun in the direction of the upstage doors.

"But we already—"

"Move."

"Not until I see Bill," I said firmly.

In a flash, Gabriel twisted my arm behind my back, yanking it upward. I yelped in pain. He meant business, his strength surprising for such a slight person. "Now," he sneered.

He released me with a shove. I fell to the ground and crawled out of his reach, heading toward the upstage wall of the set. Was Bill injured? Or worse? My hands began to shake.

He flicked a glance at the French doors. "Over there. Move."

I obediently shuffled to the open doors and examined the hinges and latches. I knew I wouldn't find the thumb drive hidden there; but all the same, as long as I kept searching, I created time to formulate a plan. I sneaked a peek at Gabriel, who had returned to the center of the *Dracula* set, eyes darting wildly. He swiped at a film of sweat on his forehead, then rubbed his hand on his trousers. "Hurry up. I don't have all day."

"Should I look at the windows?" I asked helpfully.

He nodded. "Do it."

I hurried to the wall stage left and ran my hands around the frames. "There's nothing here."

"The bookcase," he said urgently.

What was making him so panicky? I should have been the one jumping out of my skin.

The fake bookcase hid the trick door. I had seen it operated half a dozen times and knew that if I got close enough, I could activate the offstage mechanism that opened and closed the sliding door. But then what? If I slipped through, I'd be trapped in the offstage escape. Gabriel could easily intercept me. I had to think of something else.

I pretended to be engaged with the frame of the bookcase, running my fingers around the edges.

"The trick door." Gabriel ran a hand through his hair, tension streaming off him, and charged at me. "Get out of the way." Keeping one eye, and his gun, on me, he triggered the sliding door through which Dracula disappeared and reappeared, jiggling the latch. Nothing.

"I told you—"

"Shut up!" he shouted and ran to center stage.

Gabriel was going to have a coronary. I peeked into the hiding space behind the bookcase door, weighing whether I could run for it, when I saw a panel of buttons and levers on the theater wall. My heart bounced around in my chest. I knew what it was: the operating mechanism for the hydraulic trapdoor that JC had installed over the summer. I'd seen him activate it during an early rehearsal and I'd witnessed the effect it had created on stage when the vampire dematerialized in thin air. Technically, through the stage floor. The trapdoor was right beside the desk. It was a desperate long shot, but I was out of options, ready to "throw a Hail Mary" as Bill would have said.

I eased halfway into the space behind the trick door, pretending to focus on the frame and hinges. Then, as if I had a sudden inspiration, I pointed across the stage. "We might have missed the desk. Behind the drawers or along the base underneath."

Gabriel's head shot up. "Do it," he demanded.

I needed to keep both Gabriel and the trapdoor operating device in sight. "What about the back of the bookcase flat? Should I finish here? Maybe the flash drive is stuck in the rails or stiles—"

Without waiting for me, a frantic Gabriel leaped to the corner of the desk and paused. I said a silent prayer to the snoop gods that he had placed himself in the correct spot, ran behind the bookcase flat, and jammed my hand against the button that operated the trapdoor. I heard a thud and the kind of swearing that my great-aunt Maureen would have said was "unladylike" as the trap descended rapidly with an astounded Gabriel clinging to the sides of the dropping platform. JC had constructed the device to fall swiftly and quickly to create the desired effect. Of course, Carlos had the benefit of being prepared and knowing how many seconds he'd have on the falling floorboards. There was scaffolding beneath the stage for safety, and Carlos could hang on until the elevator had hit the understage floor. A crew member had to reverse the process from down below and bring the platform back to stage level once Carlos had hopped off.

But Gabriel? I didn't intend to hang around to see if the actor could work his way back to the stage. I sprinted through the house and burst into the lobby "Bill!" I screamed.

Muffled thumps originated from the interior of the box office. Usually it was kept locked, but I could see the handle had been jimmied. I yanked it open. *OMG!* Bill sat hunched over on the floor, his mouth covered, his hands and feet securely wrapped in duct tape. I ripped the tape off his mouth. "Bill...?"

He exhaled, coughed, and panted. "The kid got a jump on me."

"Are you hurt?" I wrenched open drawers under the ticket counter to find something... a screwdriver! I ripped at the tape binding his hands.

"Got clocked good. He was on me before I could react."

"You should go to the hospital."

"Where is he?" Bill asked grimly, ignoring my advice. "He took my gun."

"Hopefully, under the stage."

Bill cut through the tape on his ankles. "How'd he get there? And how'd you get away from him?"

"He stepped on the trapdoor. I sent him below. He's after the flash drive."

Bill yanked off the last of the duct tape and shot me a look of admiration. "Got to hand it to you… thanks for coming to my rescue."

I shrugged. "I've owed you." I had to admit I enjoyed having the tables turned for once. Saving Bill instead of waiting for him to save me.

He grabbed the screwdriver. "Have your cell?"

"Yeah."

"Call Suki and fill her in. She might be in Bernridge." He ran into the lobby.

"Be careful."

"Now you get out of here. Go next door to the Windjammer and call Suki."

"What if you need help? Backup won't be here in time and—"

"Go!" he ordered.

Gabriel wouldn't get a drop on Bill a second time, gun or no gun. Still, I couldn't leave him alone. There was a possibility that Gabriel would extricate himself from the hydraulic machinery under the stage. If so, he might try to make a getaway through the scene shop…or the lobby. Which put me squarely in his path.

I dialed the Etonville police station, left a message via Edna—who spouted codes and exclamations—for Suki as Bill instructed, and hunkered down in a corner of the lobby behind a stack of folded banquet tables used for intermission concessions. I removed the canister of pepper spray from my key ring, my trigger finger gently massaging the release button, and waited. The silence was killing me. Seconds ticked by, then minutes. At ten, I was ready to charge into the theater regardless of Bill's warning and tackle Gabriel myself.

I was spared the decision. The thud of footsteps traveling up an aisle inside the theater was followed by the madman himself, bursting through the lobby doors, slamming them into the walls. Gabriel limped across the tile floor, waving Bill's service revolver, making his way to the exit. *Not if I could help it*. "Gabriel!" I shrieked.

He spun around, disoriented, his face contorted in pain.

I closed my eyes, one arm over my face to avoid blowback, and sent a jet of pepper spray his way. He howled and collapsed onto the floor as Bill rushed into the lobby, screwdriver held high. *Yowza*.

* * * *

"I told you to go next door," Bill said.

"Someone had to have your back." I handed wet paper towels to Gabriel, who sat propped up against the door of the box office, huffing indignantly and wiping his face.

"I need a doctor," Gabriel cried.

"The emergency techs will be here in a minute. Your eyes will clear up. She mostly missed you."

My aim had been less than accurate. Good for Gabriel. Bad for me if Bill hadn't burst onto the scene.

Bill holstered his gun. "They'll look after your foot too."

Unprepared for the descent—one foot on the stage and one on the trapdoor—the actor had fallen and twisted his ankle when the elevator platform descended, depositing him on the understage cement floor. Without a crew member to guide him off the platform, he had to negotiate the trapdoor machinery alone before limping his way to the lobby. Rapidly. Where he'd unfortunately run into my self-defense pepper spray. Outside, a police cruiser and an ambulance came to a stop; must be Ralph, who loved to do lights flashing and sirens wailing. I wondered how things had gone down in Bernridge.

"Why did you murder the hitman?" I asked hastily. I had to know, and time was running out.

Gabriel looked aghast. "What are you talking about? I didn't murder anybody."

"Dodie!" Bill gave me the look that said *keep your mouth shut*.

I couldn't help myself. "The aconite? You poisoned him!"

"Aconite?" Gabriel looked truly mystified.

"Was it in a spiked drink you gave him at the Halloween party?" I spat out.

"Spiked drink? I don't know anything about that. All right, so I trailed you and left the note on your car—"

"That was you?" I sputtered. Then it hit me. "The coffin too?"

"I was trying to scare you. To get you to…"

"What?" I pressed Gabriel.

Bill's volume ratcheted up. "Dodie, this is official police business. You *cannot* interrogate a suspect in a murder investigation."

"To get you to stop asking questions. Digging your nose into…" Gabriel hung his head. "I only wanted the flash drive."

"You're the one who pushed me down the steps?" I said triumphantly.

"No! That wasn't me!"

"What steps?" Bill was totally lost.

"You and the bad guys planned to dump Carlos and probably Bella and skip out?"

"Dodie! That's it—"

Gabriel broke in vehemently. "You're wrong. I was trying to save Bella by finding the flash drive. To protect her."

"Save her? Really?" The kid was naïve if he thought Bill—or me, for that matter—would buy this garbage.

"Yes."

"Why save her once you got your hands on the evidence?" I asked.

"Why *wouldn't* I save her?" He hung his head, partly in shame, partly in defeat. "She's my mother."

Bill's eyes widened; my jaw dropped. *OMG.*

"You'd do the same if it was your mother!"

He was right.

"Carlos told me yesterday he'd hidden the flash drive in the theater for safekeeping."

Ralph banged through the lobby doors, gun drawn, followed closely by the EMTs. "Hey, Chief. Edna said it's a 245"

20

"I can't believe what we didn't know about Gabriel." Lola sipped her chardonnay. "Now that I know he's related to Carlos, I can see the resemblance."

I couldn't. As far as I was concerned, Gabriel was adopted.

Penny stirred her martini. "You know what they say. Blood isn't as thick as water."

Lola and I gawked at her. Penny was feeling important. According to her, she saw Gabriel enter the theater and was about to text me when the police force arrived. Never mind that those two events were at least forty-five minutes apart. We'd been sitting at the bar of the Windjammer for the past hour. *Dracula* was off; Bill was at the station; Gabriel was in custody. I hadn't heard anything about Carlos and Bella and the second hitman or the person sent to keep an eye on Carlos.

"Sorry the show never went on tonight," I said. And wouldn't with Renfield in the county jail, awaiting arraignment on assault charges. Coldcocking a cop and swiping his gun was a huge mistake.

Lola flipped her ponytail. "Wasn't meant to be. I would have loved to see another weekend of *Dracula*. And its box office." She drained her glass. "Can't complain. We've already done better than any other show's opening weekend last season."

Penny popped an olive into her mouth. "*Dracula* was a bad omen from the start. Missing props, light cues off. Not to mention having a vampire walking around town."

"Penny, Carlos is an actor. Not an actual vampire," Lola said patiently.

"Whatever."

I had to smile. A week ago, Lola herself was lamenting the presence of the paranormal on the Etonville stage. I gestured to Benny to refill Lola's glass. I was sticking to seltzer, preparing for a long night ahead of me. I intended to wait up for Bill and get a progress report on the events at Speedwell Auto Parts. And the status of the flash drive. Lost in all the current excitement was the identity of the first hitman's murderer. I was betting that Gabriel knew more than he was admitting. As Bella's son, he would have been at the old Hanratty place on many occasions and was probably familiar with the aconite herb, though he had played dumb earlier. I trusted Bill and the county prosecutor would get to the bottom of Gabriel's story. And tie up loose ends. I hated loose ends.

"Another?" Benny asked.

"Nah," Penny said. "Got an early morning."

"At the post office?" I asked.

"Before that. Creston."

"What's up?" Lola asked.

"…exercise…gym," she mumbled.

"Are you still on the Mediterranean diet?" I asked. I'd seen Penny gobble up sliders this week. Clearly a departure from seafood and vegetables.

"O'Dell, some things in life aren't worth the trouble."

Amen to that.

"I'm off the diet. I'm into exercise at the Y."

"That's fantastic, Penny." Which reminded me, I needed to get back into my own workout program before I seriously considered a wedding dress. "Aerobics? Weight lifting?"

"Nah. Got a personal trainer," she snickered.

Lola and I exchanged looks.

"I'm kickboxing. Spinning. Resistor training."

"Resistance training?" Lola asked.

"Whatever. He's cute."

I waved off Penny's attempt to pay for her drink, and she heaved herself off the stool. "Walter's gonna need some hand-holding when he finds out about Gabriel. And the show closing."

Lola sighed. "I'll be on it first thing in the morning."

About the same time the whole Carlos-Bella-Gabriel scenario would hit the Etonville gossip machine.

"Later, O'Dell." Penny gave us a half salute and sauntered out the door.

Lola checked her watch. Ten forty-five. Felt like midnight to me. She pushed away her unfinished wine. "I need some sleep. Keep me posted?"

She hugged me goodbye, pulled the collar of her coat up around her ears, and ventured into the night.

The dining room had emptied, the three remaining patrons at the bar paying their bill and gathering their belongings. Henry had closed the kitchen and Enrico and Gillian had departed half an hour ago. "Go home. I'll close up," I told Benny. He'd been picking up a lot of my hours lately.

"Thanks. Gotta take the princess to the doctor in the morning if her cold isn't gone." He tossed a bar rag into the sink. Benny looked worried and tired—he was a good dad.

"Hey, come in late tomorrow. I'll cover for you."

He nodded and left. The Windjammer was suddenly quiet. My cell buzzed. I jumped. A text from Bill: *you up? at work? call me.* I tapped Bill's number.

"Hi," I said in a rush when he answered. "What's going on? What happened in Bernridge?"

"Carlos and Bella are safe. We debriefed them. The owners of Speedwell Auto Parts are in custody. Along with Gabriel Quincey. The Villariases are retaining a lawyer for him. Suki's in Bernridge, wrapping things up."

"And the Chicago hitman?"

"They're being pretty tight-lipped about him and their connection to him."

"Sounds like a good day's work."

"Thanks to you. That parlor trick Bella did got you thinking, which in turn led to Bernridge. You never did tell me how you knew about Speedwell—"

"Anybody confess to the murder?" There would be time later to confess to my unofficial detection.

"Not yet. Somebody will cave. Wouldn't be surprised if we have a case of 'no honor among thieves.'"

"Meaning?"

"According to a conversation Carlos claimed he overheard at the auto shop, the Speedwell people were going at it pretty badly. Seems there was some disagreement about how to handle him. And the flash drive."

"It's still in the theater."

"I know. Carlos is stalling for the moment. Wants to reclaim it before he says anything else. Can't blame him. His state witness protection experience was hellish. Living like a caged animal. Not like in the movies, according to Carlos. I guess the isolation and lack of financial support and being dumped in Colorado with no family or friends or identity got to them."

Which prompted the move to New Jersey, where their son lived.

"Then the mob discovered their whereabouts," Bill added.

"The flash drive is evidence in the murder case, right?"

"Possibly. It gave Carlos protection against the mob. And the state of Illinois cut him loose. He already testified for them. Sure, they're gonna want that flash drive, but it's Carlos's property. His insurance."

"And Gabriel? What did he plan to do with the flash drive?"

"He claims he wanted to bargain for his parents' lives."

That sounded sketchy to me. "What about the aconite? I got the names of waiters from La Famiglia. You'll want to question them. See if anyone spiked the hitman's punch."

"Assuming he was at the Halloween party."

"He was there. Photographic proof. Besides, I saw a Grim Reaper drinking a cup of the punch."

"This whole thing is tricky. Hope to know more in a few hours."

He sounded exhausted. Between Chicago, traveling, and getting bonked on his noggin, Bill had had a rough few days. "How's your head?"

"I'll live."

"Any chance you'll get home soon?" I asked softly.

"Soon." He lowered his voice. "Keep the bed warm."

"I'll be waiting up," I said in my sexy voice and clicked off.

I mopped the floor, wiped down the bar, and flicked off the lights. Time to head home.

Outside the Windjammer, I paused. The night was dark, the moon hidden behind a cloud cover. Didn't bode well for tomorrow's weather. A brisk wind swirled a few dead leaves hither and yon on the sidewalk. I buttoned my coat. I should have marched to my car, settled into its front seat, and barreled to Bill's place. I could make a mug of hot tea, burrow into the comforter, and wait—impatiently—for him to arrive.

Something was niggling at the back of my mind. And rattling my radar. Bill was right—the pieces of this puzzle were complicated.

Carlos had the flash drive as insurance…supposedly, the Chicago mob wanted it badly enough to kill for it…before the hitman could execute the contract on Carlos, he died via aconite and a heart attack…the mob sent a second guy who must have hooked up with Speedwell Auto Parts and kidnapped the Villariases to get the flash drive…meanwhile Carlos's son assaulted a police officer trying to find the flash drive on his own. Was he really trying to protect his parents, or did he have another motive… After all, he'd admitted to chasing me through town, leaving a threatening note on my windshield, and locking me in the coffin.

My head hurt from sorting through the facts of the case. I walked past the theater and stopped. I turned back. Illumination from the exit lights and an emergency light in the lobby threw shadows onto the sidewalk outside the entrance. There was also a line of light visible in the lobby from the bottom of the doors that led into the house. *Someone was in the theater.* Had to be Carlos. My money was on a break-in. He wouldn't want witnesses to his hiding place. The evidence was too hot and dangerous.

My curiosity battled my desire for creature comforts. Still, I intended to keep a safe distance. I hopped in my MC and pulled onto Main Street. Around the corner, I scooted down the alley that ran behind the ELT and the Windjammer. A Subaru was parked at the theater's loading dock. *The Villariases' automobile.* I pulled into a slot adjacent to the Windjammer's dumpster and slumped down in my seat. Carlos must have broken in the back door, stealth being of the utmost importance.

I felt safe enough in my MC, doors locked, cell phone charged. I could make a quick getaway if I needed to. With the engine off and no heat, the air inside my car had become decidedly nippy. I wrapped my arms around my midsection, tucked my nose inside my coat collar, and waited. It was eleven thirty.

My eyelids drooped, the day's ordeals catching up with me. My cell pinged. It was Pauli: *hey... kept searching databases. john doe has Illinois govt. id.* So my hunch about Mr. Chicago alias John Doe was correct. He probably worked for the Illinois state organized crime unit and was sent to Etonville to guard Carlos. I thanked my technical authority and dropped my cell onto the seat next to me.

Another five minutes passed. I leaned into the headrest and surrendered to exhaustion. My eyes closed. I had barely drifted off when a slam jerked me awake. Over the rim of the steering wheel, I saw shapes form on the dock. I sat up, alert and cautious. Then voices floated through the air. There were two people. Carlos and Bella. That made sense. They stood together, appearing to wait for something. Or someone.

The door to the scene shop opened again, and another figure emerged. *Whoa.* Walter! What was he doing there? My confusion level skyrocketed. Walter had every right to be in the theater. In fact, his presence explained how Carlos had gained entry. But who in their right mind would involve the anxiety-ridden, Xanax-popping director in something this sensitive? Had Carlos explained the witness protection program and mob boss evidence to Walter? Carlos was a shrewd man, deceptive when he needed to be, ingratiating when the moment called for it. Walter's ego was susceptible to fawning. Aiding Carlos and Bella in a crucial, survival caper would be right up his alley. The three conferred, then they climbed into the car, Carlos behind the wheel, and slowly crunched gravel as they drove down the alley. I waited a minute, then tailed them, headlights off. In front of Coffee Heaven, Carlos stopped, Walter alighted, and the Villariases drove off. The taillights of the Subaru receded into the night as Walter unlocked his Jeep and got in. He hadn't had time to shut the door before I whipped into a space next to him.

"Walter!" I called out.

He peered through the driver's side window. "Who is it?" he asked, suspicious, slamming the door shut.

I knocked on the window. "Dodie."

He flicked on the overhead lights, his face stubbly with a day-old beard, his hair askew as if he'd literally been yanking on it. He had a muffler wound around his neck. "What do you want?"

I rejected vinegar and applied a little sugar. "I'd like to talk to you. For a minute," I said sweetly.

He glared at me.

"Please?"

"Why?"

I jumped into the fray. "It's about Carlos and the flash drive."

Obviously curious, Walter lowered the car window. "What flash drive?"

I was skating on thin ice. "The one he hid on the *Dracula* set," I said firmly.

Walter scratched his head.

"That's what he was doing in the theater, right? You let him in to find it, didn't you?"

Walter harrumphed. "It's very late and I'm tired. Bad enough that we had to cancel a show tonight. Of course, emergencies can't be helped…"

Carlos was still dishing out that line of BS?

"…but getting out of bed…"

That explained his look.

"…to open the theater so an actor can retrieve his script…" Walter complained.

Aha. "Did he find his script?"

"I assume so. I was in the office when Carlos went backstage because Bella needed to Xerox some papers."

And, alone, he took the opportunity to pick up the flash drive. Mission accomplished. "That was nice of you. Coming down here to open up."

Walter looked skeptical. "I suppose."

"You feel okay?" I asked.

He sniffed. "I'm getting a cold." He tightened the scarf. "Anyway, why are you asking all these questions?"

I scrambled for an answer. "Part of the murder investigation." Would he buy it?

"Playing detective again. Maybe you ought to forget about the *restaurant* business. You spend more time snooping into *people's* business—" He sneezed.

Walter had a good point. "Try a hot toddy. My great-aunt Maureen swore by them. She usually came down with a cold every month. By the way, did Carlos say where he was going?"

"Home, if he had any sense. Which is where I intend to—"

"Did he say 'home?'" I asked suddenly.

"Actually, he got a call from his sick friend. He had to go back there. If it's any of your business," Walter said sarcastically. "And what's this about a flash drive?" He sneezed again.

"I was wrong. About the flash drive."

Walter was shocked. "Never heard you admit that."

"Yep. First time for everything." I smiled. "Thanks. Have a good night."

Walter pressed the ignition button. "At least the show can go on tomorrow."

Obviously, word of Gabriel Quincey's detention for assault hadn't reached his ears yet. I played along. "Good."

"I don't blame them for leaving town when the show closes. Etonville is full of nutty people."

Takes one to know one. "They're leaving town?"

"Packing up, he said."

21

Was Carlos revealing his next move? To Walter? With the flash drive in hand, he and Bella could disappear again, without Gabriel, whose future was now in question. Only a few of us were aware, at the moment, that *Dracula* would not reopen this weekend.

Walter's Jeep backed out of his parking space and crawled down the street.

Across Main, the lights of the Municipal Building were burning brightly. Should I stop in the police station to see if Bill was finished for the day? He no doubt had a stack of paperwork to wade through. There was still a murder to solve… Or should I head home and, as he suggested, keep the bed warm? I yawned and opted for home.

As I headed down Main Street, a text came in from Pauli: *digging on john doe…apb for him.* Wait…what? Mr. Chicago worked for the Illinois organized crime unit, right? He had no criminal record, right? Why the all-points bulletin? I answered his text: *when issued?* My cell rang. I pulled over to the curb.

"Hi Pauli. You're up late."

"Yeah. Talking with Janice."

"So the APB?"

"Yeah. Issued yesterday."

Did Bill know anything about this? "Why?"

"Dunno. Doing deep search into Chicago organized—"

"—crime unit. Good work, Pauli." Good but confusing work. "So we need to keep this between us." I could almost hear him grinning.

"Natch. Gotta bounce."

We clicked off. What did this latest piece of Pauli's intel mean? Someone who was hired by law enforcement to protect an informant was wanted for some unlawful act. Mr. Chicago had been Carlos's personal babysitter. Something had gone south? The nape of my neck prickled with misgivings, details about the case pushing one another out of the way like kids trying to claim first in line at a candy counter. I wracked my brain to remember tidbits about Mr. Chicago. He showed up immediately after the murder... said he was a plumbing parts salesman...apparently knew Carlos. Bill had said Chicago sent someone to keep an eye on Carlos. I assumed it was him. *What if he wasn't Carlos's guardian angel but the opposite?* There was no mention of a John Doe tonight at the Speedwell raid.

I swung my MC in a wide U-turn. Carlos had the flash drive and was heading home. To pack. I texted Bill: *carlos in danger from his protector... on way to his house to warn him...send help.* I jammed my foot on the accelerator and zipped to the outskirts of Etonville, exceeding the speed limit. At midnight, the streets were empty, its citizens tucked in for the night. A tiny nudge from the recesses of my mind advised me that I should wait to hear back from Bill. Yet the relief on Bella's face tonight when we figured out where Carlos was being held, her final words that I might have "saved their lives," pushed me onward. I had to let him know that Mr. Chicago was no friend.

Within five minutes, I was barreling down the road that led to the Hanratty homestead. I slowed as I approached the house. My heart thumped loudly in my ears. Even in the dark, I could see two automobiles in the circular driveway. The Villariases' Subaru and the dark sedan that had dropped Carlos off at Speedwell Auto Parts in Bernridge. *Mr. Chicago's car.* I switched off my lights and coasted to the side of the road, twenty yards from the house.

My hands shook. I texted Bill again: *sos...carlos in trouble...Hanratty place. get here.* Bill had said Suki was in Bernridge earlier, wrapping up the raid. In case she'd returned, I left a voicemail message for her too. Then stuffed my keys and phone in my pockets, softly opened and closed the car door, and stole down the street, staying in the shadows that lined the road. I paused as I neared the front yard. From my vantage point, the house still looked haunted: exterior dilapidated, dim light escaping from the downstairs parlor windows. With the curtains pulled, it was impossible to see who was in the front room of the house.

I slipped to the perimeter of the property to avoid detection from anyone glancing out a window. The bare trees and a weathered, wooden bench were my only protection. I crept past the side of the house, the windows here also blocked by drapes, and found myself in the backyard. This was new territory. I looked around. The remains of Bella's garden occupied most of the space, along with some outdated lawn furniture. The dark of the yard provided some safety, so I inched toward the small patch of cement that served as a back porch. Light shone from the kitchen windows. Maybe I could get close enough to see if Carlos and Bella—

A blast of white light turned the night into day and caught me smack in its center. Too late, I realized the Villariases had installed motion-activated security lighting. I dropped to my hands and knees, my fingernails digging into damp mud, the knees of my pants already wet. *Put it in reverse!* I told myself, backing up. Straight into a pair of legs.

"Nice of you to join us." A hand grasped my arm and forced me to my feet. Mr. Chicago.

I was right. He was no protector, and the Villariases were in deep trouble. "I know about you," I said as he dragged me into the kitchen.

"You do? What do you know?"

The room was brightly lit, the kitchen a mess. Cupboard doors open, packaged food piled on the counters. Carlos sat at the wooden table, the pots of herbs and vials I'd seen the last time I was in the house replaced with pots and pans. Someone had been rummaging around. "Carlos! You're in danger!" I twisted to see Mr. Chicago's face, struggling in his arms. "He's not here to protect you. He's going to kill you and take the flash drive!"

"Dodie, why don't you sit down?" Carlos said in his deep, rich, soothing baritone.

What was the matter with the man? How could he sit there so calmly when his life was at risk? "Did you hear me?" I shrieked.

"Simmer down." Mr. Chicago thrust me into a chair and clamped a hand on my shoulder to keep me seated.

A far cry from the genial plumbing parts salesman who ate sliders at the Windjammer. For that matter, Carlos's attire was unusually rough and ready: work boots and a quilted vest over a hooded sweater. So unlike the previously dapper gentleman routine. I glanced around the kitchen again. Dirty dishes were stacked in the sink, a greasy skillet on the stove. When I'd been in the kitchen looking for Carlos yesterday, the place had been spotless. Now the messiness cried out for a good cleaning. A horrifying foreboding inched up my spine.

"Where's Bella?" I asked. The tension in my chest like a fist that kept squeezing more and more tightly.

"Never mind about Bella," Mr. Chicago growled.

"She's fine." Again, the smooth-talking Carlos.

As if I was rotating a kaleidoscope from my childhood, the pieces of the Carlos-Mr. Chicago relationship changed position, and a new pattern emerged. How could I have been so blind? *Carlos wasn't in any danger from his "protector"...because the two of them were somehow working together.* The flash drive? The murder? Where did that leave Bella? I had gotten pretty good at talking my way into and out of things in the past, but this time? Carlos studied my expression and smiled slowly.

"You finally sorted it out." He laughed warmly. "Ah yes. I knew you would. Especially after I heard about your detection skills. I warned them all you were very bright. Bella, Gabriel, even John here. No one took you as seriously as I did." He drummed his fingers on the surface of the table. "Maybe it's my theatrical background. Pretense and all. I can spot a counterfeit persona a mile away."

Despite the jeopardy confronting me, I couldn't help myself. "Counterfeit? What're you talking about?"

"You're a phony, Dodie O'Dell. You pretend to be a small-town restaurant manager when all the time you are a shrewd detective."

I was astounded. Despite my investigative capers during the past four years, no one had ever declared that I was a better detective than a manager. I didn't know whether to be flattered or insulted. I opted for the latter. "You're kind of a counterfeit yourself, aren't you? Not much of an actor. Dracula is all you can play. I've seen the playbills from Chicago. You're probably a better accountant than you are an actor."

For a split second, his nostrils flared, the only visible sign that I might have gotten to him.

"I know about the witness protection program. And the aconite." I was swinging for the fences. Spilling everything I knew, hoping for a response that gave me insight into Bella's whereabouts. At a minimum, I could stall for time. Bill or Suki had to get my SOS soon. "I even know what's on the flash drive."

"Told you," Carlos sang out, laughing, delighted that he had been right about me and that everyone else had been much too slow to appreciate my expertise.

A clatter of footsteps interrupted his laughter and Bella appeared at the door of the kitchen. "What is *she* doing here?" she asked, low and intense.

I gawked at Carlos's wife, dressed in jeans and a down vest, her hair tied back in a tight bun. She carried a piece of luggage. "Bella? Are you all right?"

She was frantic. "Why couldn't you have stayed out of this?" she said to me, hanging her head. "Now you're in as much danger as…" She sent a fleeting look to Mr. Chicago.

"Bella dear, trust me. Everything is going to be fine."

"Trust you?" Her voice climbed an octave. "You? Who said we only needed to make him sick long enough for us to get away. To be free—"

"Daryl suffered from heart disease."

"You didn't tell me that," she screeched.

"You assured me the aconite would leave no trace in his body," Carlos said tightly. "If he hadn't died, Daryl would have found us. No matter where we went."

Whoa. "The two of you...murdered the hitman?" I gasped. *Daryl.* He and Carlos were on a first-name basis. Of course. The mob's accountant *might* be familiar with the boss's associates.

"Shut up," Mr. Chicago growled.

Bella, exploding, eyes blazing, ignored him. "It was stupid to insist on meeting him in the cemetery. But oh no, you had to play the big-shot actor, running around in a costume because it fit your sense of theater. Demanding that Daryl dress up as that ridiculous Grim Reaper."

"That's what we called him in Chicago," Carlos interjected.

"'I know Daryl,' you said. 'We can negotiate our way through this.' And then, when we couldn't *'negotiate'*—"

"You were tired of running."

"We should have left town after he overdosed. You said 'no, it would look suspicious.' *And* you had to finish the production!"

This was not the graceful, unruffled woman who read palms and dealt tarot.

"You wanted to be near Gabriel," he reminded her.

Bella's outrage disintegrated, leaving her deflated. She shrunk into herself. "You should have told me about *him*," she said bitterly, jerking her head at Mr. Chicago.

"Knock it off. I'm getting tired of you two," the mob guy snarled.

And then it hit me. *The mob sent a guy and the crime unit sent a guy. Problem was, they turned out to be the same guy.* "Whoa," I said aloud.

As if all three had forgotten about me, they swiveled their heads in unison.

Mr. Chicago dragged me to my feet, yanking my arms behind my back and securing them with a length of rope. He pulled and pushed me toward the hallway that led from the kitchen to the front rooms of the house. I was not going to go easily. Wherever he was taking me. I kicked him in the shins. He howled and slammed me against the wall, one hand squeezing my neck. Bella screamed. He might have completed the job had Carlos not intervened.

"There's no point in violence," the actor said, shoving my attacker aside. "We're not going to hurt you, Dodie. We need to tuck you out of the way until we can make our exit stage right. You're a bit too curious for our safety."

I coughed, gasping for breath. Was he crazy? "No violence? After you poisoned Daryl Wolf? Seems pretty violent to me."

A buzzing from my back pocket interrupted the exchange. Mr. Chicago reached inside and withdrew my cell phone. He got a glimpse of the text. "Who's Bill?"

Oh no.

Carlos smiled smoothly. "Etonville's esteemed police chief. And our Dodie's love interest."

Would this guy never stop? His debonair act was getting tiresome.

"He knows I'm here," I said with a touch of desperation.

Mr. Chicago extended the phone to Carlos. "He thinks you're in danger. Keys."

It wasn't a request. I dug them out of my pocket.

"Get rid of her car. It's down the road. And when the cop shows up, you better put on the acting job of a lifetime."

"Careful. We don't want anything permanent to happen to her," Carlos said.

"Dodie…I'm so sorry…" Bella thrust herself in my direction, as if to rescue me.

Mr. Chicago slapped her arm away. "Get going," he said.

Carlos guided a distraught Bella out of the kitchen and into the foyer. "Stay up there until I call you." She hesitated, then ran up the stairs.

Mr. Chicago shoved me forward, opening the door that led to the basement. I knew this staircase.

"So you're the one who shoved me down the stairs?" I said shakily, twisting my hands in the rope. Even if I freed myself from the restraint, what could I do? Running would get me nowhere with my captor holding on to me more viciously than before and Carlos up top, waiting for Bill. I had no cell phone.

The basement smelled of dampness and mildew, the air clammy. My eyes adjusted to the dark—I could only make out hulking shapes that gave me the creeps. On the bottom step, Mr. Chicago paused and flicked on his cell phone flashlight. The shapes materialized as old furniture stacked in a corner: a table, some chairs, a shabby sofa. On the opposite wall was a tall wardrobe, with two doors that opened outward. He forced me toward the wardrobe, flinging me to the ground. I looked sideways. I could swear something moved on the bottom of the closet. Spiders? My heart plummeted. Who would find me in here? I was on my own.

"You won't get away with this. The whole Etonville police department will be on your trail."

"By the time somebody looks in here, we'll be long gone and you'll be managing the big restaurant in the sky." He stuffed a gag into my mouth, wrapped a cord around my ankles, and removed a syringe from his pocket. Totally ignoring Carlos's request that I not be "permanently" damaged. "You're too smart for your own good."

He removed the cap of the syringe, tapped the needle a few times, and lowered the syringe to my arm. "You know something about what this baby can do."

Aconite. One shot. Depending on the strength of the poison, I could be gone in minutes. My mind raced, my heart in my throat.

He hesitated. Upstairs, we heard someone moving down the hallway. Then two voices. Both male. One brusque and crisp, the other deep and slow. Bill and Carlos. What line of bull was the actor handing the police chief?

"Mmm!" I made as much noise as I could, shaking my shoulders from side to side, lifting my legs and punching the floor with them. Mr. Chicago dropped the syringe, throwing himself on top of me, covering my head and torso. Sweat and stale cologne assaulted my nose. The gag already made it difficult to breathe; his weight made it nearly impossible. I pushed at his body with every bit of strength I had. It was no use. He was just too heavy.

The footsteps sounded again. More this time. Bill and Carlos moving around the first floor of the house. I squirmed until I managed to raise my knees a few inches. Mr. Chicago reached for the syringe, which had rolled a couple of feet from the wardrobe, keeping his other arm squarely planted across my chest. I closed my eyes to concentrate, counted to three, then kicked my legs upward as swiftly as possible. *Bingo!* He groaned, grabbed himself, the syringe forgotten for the moment, and, muttering curses, toppled over onto his side. Unfortunately for him, it was to my right side; to my left was the back pocket where I'd stashed the pepper spray.

My hands secured behind my back, I rocked to my left, stretching my right arm nearly out of its socket to reach into my pocket. Upstairs, there was silence. Downstairs, Mr. Chicago was recovering from my attack and turning his attention back to me. My fingertips touched the canister and I eased it out of my pocket, feeling for the release button. He sat up, once more grasping the syringe. It was now or never.

I yanked my arms to the right, pulled my legs into a fetal position, and aimed the canister upward as far as I could stretch, shutting my eyes good and tight, praying the stream would get closer to his face than my own. I depressed the lever and squirted. Some of the spray found its mark: He yowled in pain and fell backward. My own eyes were stinging; I dared not open them yet. I jerked and thrust my legs, hammering Mr. Chicago, who rubbed his eyes, scrambling for me. I rolled over, onto the cold cement floor, scooting away from the wardrobe. He was blinded for the moment, but I didn't trust that the effects of the pepper spray would last forever.

Even in the dark, with my eyes closed, I knew that the staircase to the first floor was to my right. Like a fish out of water flapping its tail, I bounced across the basement floor to the steps. I was gambling that no sounds from upstairs meant Carlos was out of the house. I reached the first step, hopped up, pulled my legs after me, started for the second step.

A hand clamped my foot. "You'll pay for this," Mr. Chicago snarled.

In my hurry to climb the stairs, I hadn't heard him behind me. I pumped my legs, slashing them from side to side. He hung on. I had no choice. I whipped the canister around my side again and sprayed. He screamed, tumbling backward. I scrambled up the steps, kicked the basement door, and hopped to the kitchen sink. Once my head was under the faucet, I risked opening my eyes a bit. The burning had lessened. I fumbled along the counter next to the sink. I'd seen a set of kitchen knives in a rack there. Squinting, I lifted my arms to counter level, knocked over the rack, and pulled out a paring knife. Wedging it between my wrists, I sawed gently until the rope snapped. I tore the gag from my mouth, letting sharp, deep breaths fill my lungs. In another minute, I had the cord off my ankles. Downstairs, I could hear thumping. Mr. Chicago was on his way to this floor. I ran to the front door.

"Once again, we underestimated you."

I froze. The deep baritone had an impatient edge to it. "Carlos," I said, spinning around to face him. He'd come in the back door and now held a gun trained on me. "You don't want to do this. Killing a hitman from the Chicago mob is one thing. It might have been a mistake or self-defense. Killing me could get you life in prison," I said in a rush. I'd placed the pepper spray in my front pocket. Though how I could distract Carlos long enough to retrieve it and hit the button was beyond me. Yet, I knew, when in doubt, keep 'em talking.

He gestured with the gun in the direction of the basement.

"What about Gabriel? Your son! He's going to jail and he was only trying to help!"

"My son. Ah yes. Bella's son, actually. No love lost between us."

That explained a few things. "He wanted the flash drive to... what? Protect Bella? Your landlady in Lennox said your son visited often. I never thought it was Gabriel. Did you move here to be closer to Bernridge? That must have been Bella's idea."

Carlos stared at me, then burst out laughing. "You've missed your calling entirely. You're better at this than the Chicago OCU."

"Guess the witness protection program didn't work out?"

"Back downstairs." He prodded me with the muzzle of the weapon. "I'm afraid you've left me little choice this time. We can't afford to have you snitching on us."

My heart pounded, my pulse in the danger zone. Where was my backup? Bill? Suki? I dragged my heels down the hall, only a few more steps to go until we reached the door to the basement. "I thought Mr. Chicago was here to protect you. Turns out he was an accomplice," I said, my back to Carlos.

"That's what happens when one goes rogue." He shoved me toward the door.

"He'd been a member of the Chicago organized crime unit, right? I guess it was more lucrative to defect to the mob."

Carlos ignored me, sticking his weapon in my back again.

"Tell me something," I said, easing my hand into my pants pocket. "Who got you the position at Speedwell Auto Parts? Was it him?" I peeked over my shoulder.

His silence was my answer.

"You think he can negotiate with the mob for you? You'd better hang on to that flash drive. Because the minute he has it, you're dead."

Carlos looked startled for a second, long enough for me to grip the pepper spray, swing the basement door open, and get behind it. Before he could get off a shot, Mr. Chicago staggered up the stairs like a blind, drunken sailor, waving his gun wildly. I jumped from behind the door, aimed the canister at Carlos, and yelled his name. As he turned to face me, a thunder of footsteps bounded down the hall behind me. Bill was shouting for Carlos to drop his gun, while Suki and another officer smashed through the front door.

I collapsed to the floor.

* * * *

"Thanks," I said to the EMT who rinsed my eyes as I sat at the kitchen table. "Much better." In the yard of the old Hanratty house, once again the blue and red lights of police cruisers flashed and an ambulance was parked in the driveway.

Down the hallway that led to the front door, I could see Suki bundling Carlos and Bella out of the house, while another EMT worked on Mr. Chicago. Bill conferred with a plainclothes cop from the county prosecutor's office, then shook hands and motioned to Ralph to keep the crowd that had gathered outside under control. Ralph's specialty. Then he looked up and joined me in the kitchen.

"I know what you're going to say." I ran a dish towel through my wet hair.

"You do?" Bill asked.

"I should have kept my nose out of the murder case. And out of Carlos's identity, and Lennox, and the Chicago newspaper, and digging into John Doe, and—"

Bill gawked. "You did all that?"

"—and Speedwell Auto Parts…go ahead and say it."

The left side of his mouth ticked upward. "I was going to say I thought you'd done enough pepper spray for one day."

"That too. I might have gotten carried away."

Bill turned serious. "Good thing. But if Suki and I hadn't shown up when we did, you'd have done all right. And Carlos would be getting his eyes rinsed out too."

We both glanced at Mr. Chicago being taken away in handcuffs. "Maybe."

Bill tucked a loose strand of my hair behind an ear. "I think you can take care of yourself."

"I think so too," I said. Then I smiled. "It was nice hearing you bust through the back door."

"I assumed Carlos was lying when he said you'd been there and gone."

"It took you long enough to get here. I had to fight off Mr. Chicago, cut the wrist rope and ankle cord, keep Carlos talking…"

"And I had to get all my backup in place. After all, you weren't answering your phone."

"True."

"Which was when I knew something was wrong." He pulled me to my feet and into a warm embrace. His body felt strong and safe.

"We rescued your car. Suki is having it delivered to my place."

"Thanks."

"I'll have Ralph take you home. Let you get out of those wet clothes. I'll only be a little while."

In dunking my head to douse my eyes, I'd also doused myself from the waist up. "I could use a date with a hot toddy and a warm comforter."

His mesmerizing blue eyes twinkled, his muscles tight under his uniform jacket. "And me."

Yahoo!

22

Outside the Windjammer, the wind whipped down Main Street, scattering leaves, sending wisps of smoke from fireplace chimneys twirling in the late afternoon air. The sun was setting, though it was only four thirty. Inside the restaurant, the temperature was comfortable, the atmosphere cozy. A Thanksgiving tradition in progress: some twenty-five of Etonville's finest citizens enjoying a turkey feast planned by Henry, aided by a crew consisting of his wife, Enrico, Bill, and Carol and her husband. Benny and Carmen, with help from Lola's daughter, Pauli, and Janice, had set a long banquet table that stretched from one end of the Windjammer to the other. Glassware sparkled and silverware glistened. The white linen crisp and starched, the candles flickering. Benny served drinks.

"You can top mine off," Lola said, sitting at the bar, extending her wineglass to Benny as he made the rounds with bottles of red and white wine. Folks mingled around the dining room, chattering happily, waiting for the spread to emerge from the kitchen.

Benny obliged. "Here ya go." He smiled and headed across the room to see to his wife and daughter. Vernon entertained the princess with the only magic trick he knew: making a coin disappear behind his ear. Benny's daughter giggled and clapped her hands.

I plopped onto a stool beside Lola. I'd been up early, helping to prep the kitchen. I was ready for a break. "Whew. It takes a village," I said and sipped my seltzer, gazing at the crowd in the dining room. I smoothed my green silk blouse.

Lola flipped her blond hair over one high-end, designer-dress shoulder clad in burgundy knit. "I must say, something is smelling delicious."

I agreed.

"This is a lovely tradition. I don't have to cook." She wrinkled her nose. Kitchen capers were not Lola's strength. "Speaking of cooking…we need to consider catering when we investigate more wedding venues."

"Aye, aye, Captain." I raised my hand and saluted her playfully, light from the candles glinting off the facets of my engagement ring.

Lola studied my face. "You went through a lot this last month. Falling down steps, fighting off Gabriel, escaping from the wardrobe and John Doe…" She shivered, putting an arm around my back.

"Not to mention pepper spraying everyone who got near me."

"That too," Lola said. We shared a laugh.

"I'm glad to be celebrating Thanksgiving in one piece."

Lola was silent for a moment. "Maybe this tradition will change after you're married."

"Why would it change? We all need to eat, and Bill loves to cook," I said.

Change *was* coming, my life about to be altered permanently. I'd been obsessed with identity these last weeks, my own and the people around me. Carlos and Bella had adopted different identities—from Mercer to Johnson to Villarias in the witness protection program—to escape the Chicago mob. John Doe had switched his identity as an agent for the Chicago OCU to a hitman for the same Chicago mob, for money, to obtain the flash drive. He'd tried to convince an overconfident Carlos that together they could outsmart the mob and use the flash drive as financial leverage, that Carlos would be able to buy his and Bella's freedom by surrendering the evidence. When Carlos still hesitated to turn it over to him, kidnapping was the last resort, and the Speedwell folks were simply pawns in John Doe's plan.

If the actor hadn't felt so invincible, he might have realized he couldn't trust Mr. Chicago either. Once the former government agent turned mob enforcer had the evidence in his hands, he had no intention of keeping the Villariases alive. Even Gabriel had surrendered his identity as Bella's son to keep their secret safe.

What did I have to fear? Bella's reading of my palm was both right and wrong. I was "making a momentous decision," but my life wouldn't be "surrendered" to anyone else. Becoming Bill's wife would only be one aspect of my identity. I could maintain my individuality as a restaurant manager, BFF, Etonville Little Theatre supporter. *Your palm doesn't control your fate. You do.*

"Hey, O'Dell."

Penny had donned a brown sweater and stretchy black tights for the occasion. "Hi, Penny. You look nice. All that personal training is paying off."

She sipped a martini, then popped an olive into her mouth. "You know what they say."

I couldn't imagine.

"What doesn't kill you makes you live longer."

I stifled a grin. "Working out was tough?"

"O'Dell, let's put it this way. You can't fool around with your health. It's better to be safe *and* sorry."

"Got it."

"Things in Etonville will be a little less dodgy with you-know-who behind bars."

"Carlos."

Penny leaned in conspiratorially. "I knew something was off with him from the beginning. That vampire stuff."

"He's an actor. Was an actor. The 'vampire stuff' was part of the act."

"That's what they all say until…" She mimed a knife crossing her throat. "…there's a dead body." She looked at me meaningfully.

Penny had a point. Carlos had perfected the "vampire routine" on and off the stage, freaking out Etonville in the process. The coroner even found two "bite marks"—well hidden in Daryl Wolf's armpit—where the aconite was delivered by syringe after Carlos knocked him out with the stake.

"Speaking of dead bodies…heard you're thinking of moving out of town after your wedding," she said casually.

"Moving? Where'd you hear that?" The Etonville rumor mill.

Penny nudged her glasses. "Was hoping that Etonville could settle down."

Her euphemism for "no more murders."

"Later, O'Dell." She held up her martini glass. "Only two hundred calories."

I motioned to Benny to bring me the whole bottle of wine.

I scanned the room; everyone looked to be enjoying themselves. Aromas leaking out of the kitchen indicated dinner was imminent. I stared. "Unbelievable," I muttered to myself. In a corner, Walter and Jocelyn were deep in conversation. She was animatedly explaining something, and he was listening intently. What in the world could they be talking about?

"Surprising." Lola laughed at my side. "And we thought Jocelyn was barking up a nonexistent tree."

"Especially after Bella read Walter's tarot cards and told him he would be taking advantage of a new love interest."

"Speaking of Bella…too bad about how she ended up," Lola said.

"According to Bill, her part in the murder plot was negligible. She hadn't intended that Daryl Wolf die. Might get off with involuntary manslaughter.

Now that the police have the flash drive and her testimony against John Doe, the Chicago organized crime unit has the potential to take down a bunch of mob guys."

"And Carlos?"

"He's trading his evening dress for an orange jumpsuit. His acting career is on hold for the time being."

"Did Bill find out where Carlos stashed the memory stick?" Lola asked.

I shook my head. "He claimed he never intended that Bella find the evidence. He thought sending her to the theater would keep her safe until John Doe, or the police, came to his rescue. The Bernridge police got there first. He did *not* trust anyone. Including his wife. He never did say where the flash drive was hidden."

"And all the while, John Doe was hanging around, waiting for Carlos to hand it over. Where was he during the kidnapping?" Lola asked.

"Turns out he never believed the flash drive was in the theater. Too obvious, he thought. While we were searching the set, he was ransacking the Hanratty place."

"So glad *Dracula* is over," Lola said with relief.

Lola and I clinked glasses, toasting the end of the paranormal in Etonville.

The swinging doors into the kitchen opened with a flourish, accompanied by oohs and aahs from the assembled guests. Bill, Enrico, Henry's wife, Carol, and her husband began a slow procession of sides to the table: stuffing, vegetables, salads, several kinds of potatoes, and pasta. The last was at Carol's insistence—her family was Jersey Italian. No holiday meal was complete without a macaroni dish. I moved around the room playing the role of hostess, making sure everyone had a full glass of something.

"I'd say we have a Code 7," Edna announced enthusiastically and took a seat next to the Banger sisters.

"Edna and her codes. I *never* know what she's talking about." Mildred took a sip of wine and tittered. Thanksgiving was one of the few times all year the choir director allowed herself to imbibe.

"Got something to do with the grub coming." Vernon sat next to his wife.

"Meal break," Edna beamed.

"Copy that," I said.

"Dodie, we're so glad you're able to join us for Thanksgiving," said a Banger sister.

"Especially after you sprained your ankles, broke a wrist, and got an eye infection from that pepper thing," said the other.

Yikes! "But I didn't..." I was about to protest and deny when I inspected their lovely, smiling faces. I gave up. "I heal fast."

The sisters, Mildred, and Edna nodded. Vernon harrumphed.

Henry emerged from the kitchen, decked out in his white chef's apron and hat, holding the turkey aloft like a sacrifice to the gods. The room erupted into spontaneous applause.

With everyone seated, Mildred said grace.

Then I raised my glass. "I'd like to make a toast."

The restaurant fell silent, expectant faces turned to me, standing at one end of the table. "We have a lot to be thankful for this year." Heads nodded, and there was some vocal agreement. "Besides this beautiful meal…"

Henry beamed.

"…there are wonderful friends, a lovely community." I felt a lump in my throat. "I see a lot of love around this table tonight."

Jocelyn winked and covered Walter's hand with hers; Pauli slid his eyes at Janice, who blushed; Lola nodded; Mildred lowered her head to Vernon's shoulder. The Banger sisters glowed.

"To us!" I said.

"Hear, hear!" echoed Edna.

"Let's eat," announced Vernon.

From the other end of the table, Bill mouthed *I love you.*

* * * *

The remnants of the pumpkin and mince pies lay on dessert plates, coffee cups nearly empty. The candles had burned down, the room toasty and snug. The guests were full, relaxed, and heading toward drowsy.

Bill motioned to me. I waited a second, then slipped away from the table and followed him into the kitchen. "Where are you?" I asked.

"In here." The pantry, whose shelves were lined with canned goods, jars of condiments and spices.

"What are you…?"

He held a square object wrapped in a brown bag. "Thought we needed a little privacy for this."

"What is it?"

"Something I've been meaning to give you."

"Pretty fancy wrapping," I joked.

"I was in a hurry…anyway, I have the feeling you've been worried about your… changing status after we get married."

How did he know that?

"Am I right?" he asked kindly.

"Well…"

"Thought so."

"Bill, I don't want to lose who I am. I don't want to change."

"I know that, and I don't want you to change—"

I continued in a rush. "I mean…maybe I should be thinking of doing more, doing something else with my life—"

"I agree, and—"

"Not that I'm not thrilled to be getting married. And I love the restaurant. But—" I stopped. "What did you say?"

"I said I agree. About you doing more with your life."

"Right," I said slowly. There had to be a catch.

"So I got you this." He grinned and handed me the package.

I tore at the brown paper. It was a book. *Private Detection 101.* "Wha…?"

"Consider it a prewedding gift. You'll need it when you enroll in the certification course. For private investigation."

I teared up. "I don't know what to say. I'm speechless."

Bill kissed me sweetly. "That would be a first."

"I mean, even Carlos said I was killing time here at the Windjammer when I was actually a detective at heart, but I love this place," I said.

"First of all, you don't need to leave the Windjammer to take an online course. Second, *really*? You're listening to a soon-to-be-convicted murderer?"

"Thank you." I flung my arms around his shoulders and laid a big one on his mouth.

He finally came up for air. "Should we get back to our guests?" he murmured.

"In a minute. Right now, I'm having my own Thanksgiving." I covered his face with smooches, saving his lips for last. "I love you!"

Private Investigator Dodie O'Dell…*OMG!*

Acknowledgments

This book, like the others in the Dodie O'Dell Mystery Series, is the result of help from a number of people. I owe them a debt of gratitude.

Thanks to all who entered the *Killing Time* character name contest, especially the winners: Tim Capalbo, Glen Holley, Katherine Wortman, and Andrea Karwandy. You'll find your creative entries in the pages of this book.

Once again, I am grateful for the support I received at Kensington to make this mystery series a reality, especially from John Scognamiglio and Rebecca Cremonese.

I appreciate Dru Ann Love, Lori Caswell and the Great Escapes Tour bloggers, Roberta Isleib from Mystery Lovers Kitchen, and Brooke Showalter for their help in promoting my mystery series. Finally, thanks to my friends, family, and readers who supported my Dodie O'Dell journey. I have appreciated your sense of humor, inspiring feedback, enthusiasm, and the odd cup of tea (or something stronger) when needed. You know who you are!

Finally, my thanks to Elaine Insinnia, my first and last reader, who consistently and generously provided story ideas and encouragement as I wrote and rewrote. I couldn't have done it without you....

About the Author

Suzanne Trauth is a novelist, playwright, screenwriter, and a former university theater professor. She is a member of Mystery Writers of America, Sisters in Crime, the Dramatists Guild, and the League of Professional Theatre Women. When she is not writing, Suzanne coaches actors and serves as a celebrant performing wedding ceremonies. She lives in Woodland Park, New Jersey.

www.suzannetrauth.com

Printed in the United States
by Baker & Taylor Publisher Services